ANCESTOR

BY MATT SHEEAN
AND MALACHI WARD

PUBLISHED BY IMAGE COMICS

ANCESTOR, BY MATT SHEEAN AND MALACHI WARD.

PART ONE OF FOUR: *THE SERVICE.*

8:45 P.M.

PETER, DISRUPTIONS IN SEROTONIN AND NOREPINEPHINE INDICATE THAT YOU'RE FEELING ANXIOUS.

IN THE PAST SONGS LIKE "LAURA" BY JULIE LONDON, OR "WHAT A DIFFERENCE A DAY MAKES" BY DINAH WASHINGTON HAVE HELPED ALLEVIATE ANXIETY.

WOULD YOU LIKE TO HEAR ONE OF THOSE SONGS NOW?

"WHAT A DIFFERENCE."

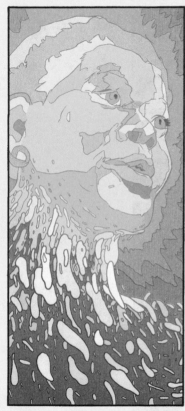

WHAT A DIFFERENCE A DAY MADE,

TWENTY-FOUR LITTLE HOURS

BROUGHT THE SUN AND THE FLOWERS

Mmmmm WHERE THERE USED TO BE RAIN...

MY YESTERDAY WAS BLUE, DEAR

TODAY I'M PART OF YOU, DEAR—

...TODAY I'M PART OF YOU, DEAR...

MY LONELY NIGHTS ARE THROUGH DEAR, SINCE YOU SAID YOU WERE MINE—

THIS ISN'T WORKING.

RUN ANXIETY RELIEF PROGRAM.

WELCOME TO DYSK'S AGGRETORY ANXIETY DISORDER RELIEF PROGRAM. BROUGHT TO YOU BY ELENALE.

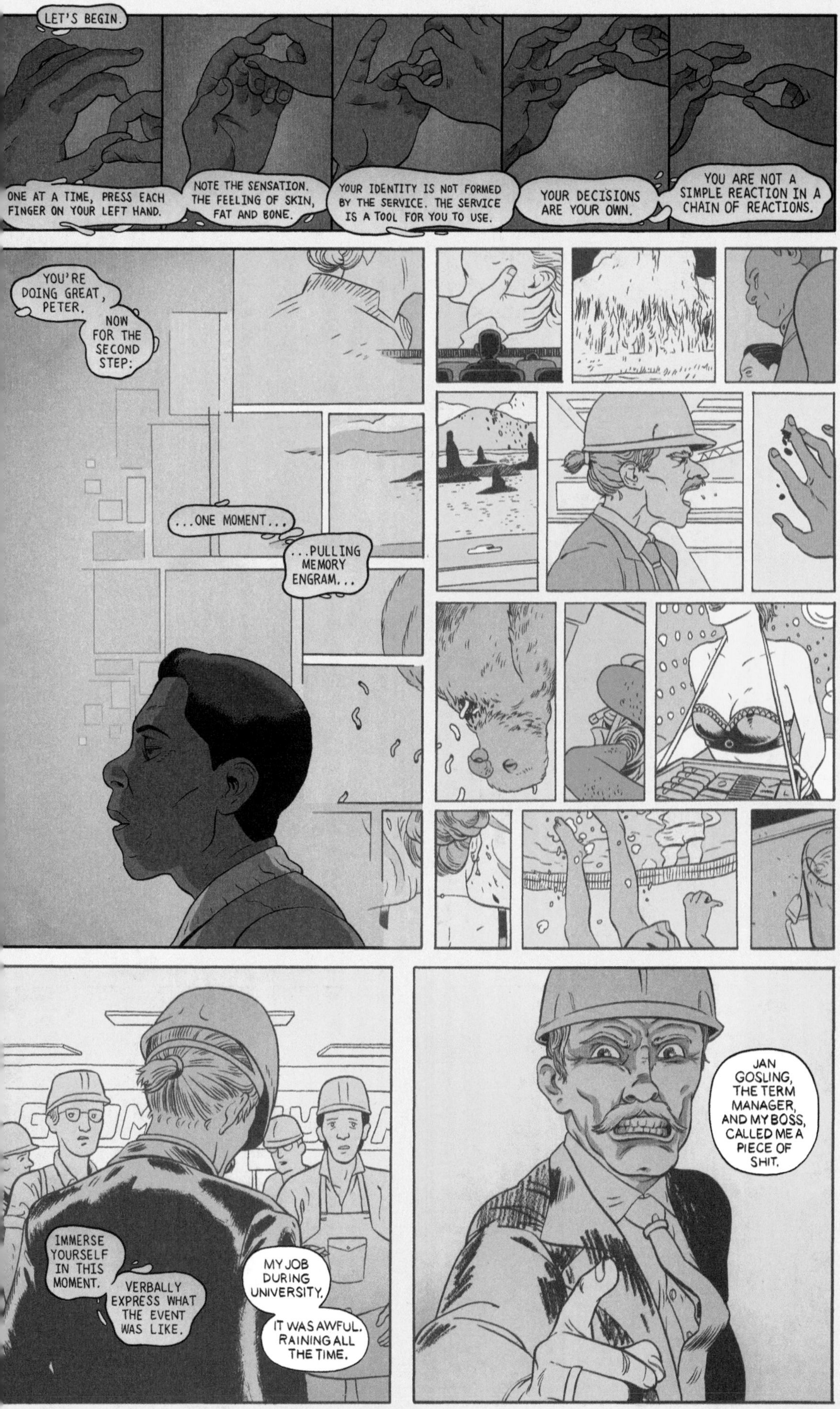
LET'S BEGIN.
ONE AT A TIME, PRESS EACH FINGER ON YOUR LEFT HAND.
NOTE THE SENSATION. THE FEELING OF SKIN, FAT AND BONE.
YOUR IDENTITY IS NOT FORMED BY THE SERVICE. THE SERVICE IS A TOOL FOR YOU TO USE.
YOUR DECISIONS ARE YOUR OWN.
YOU ARE NOT A SIMPLE REACTION IN A CHAIN OF REACTIONS.
YOU'RE DOING GREAT, PETER.
NOW FOR THE SECOND STEP:
...ONE MOMENT...
...PULLING MEMORY ENGRAM...
IMMERSE YOURSELF IN THIS MOMENT.
VERBALLY EXPRESS WHAT THE EVENT WAS LIKE.
MY JOB DURING UNIVERSITY.
IT WAS AWFUL. RAINING ALL THE TIME.
JAN GOSLING, THE TERM MANAGER, AND MY BOSS, CALLED ME A PIECE OF SHIT.

I HAD ONLY BEEN THERE A WEEK, BUT I QUIT ON THE SPOT.

LATER, AT HOME, I CHANGED INTO DRY CLOTHES.

MY ROOM WAS WARM, I HAD CLEANED UP RECENTLY.

I DON'T KNOW... I FELT RELIEVED.

JUST LISTENING TO THE RAIN ON THE WINDOW.

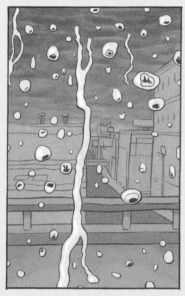

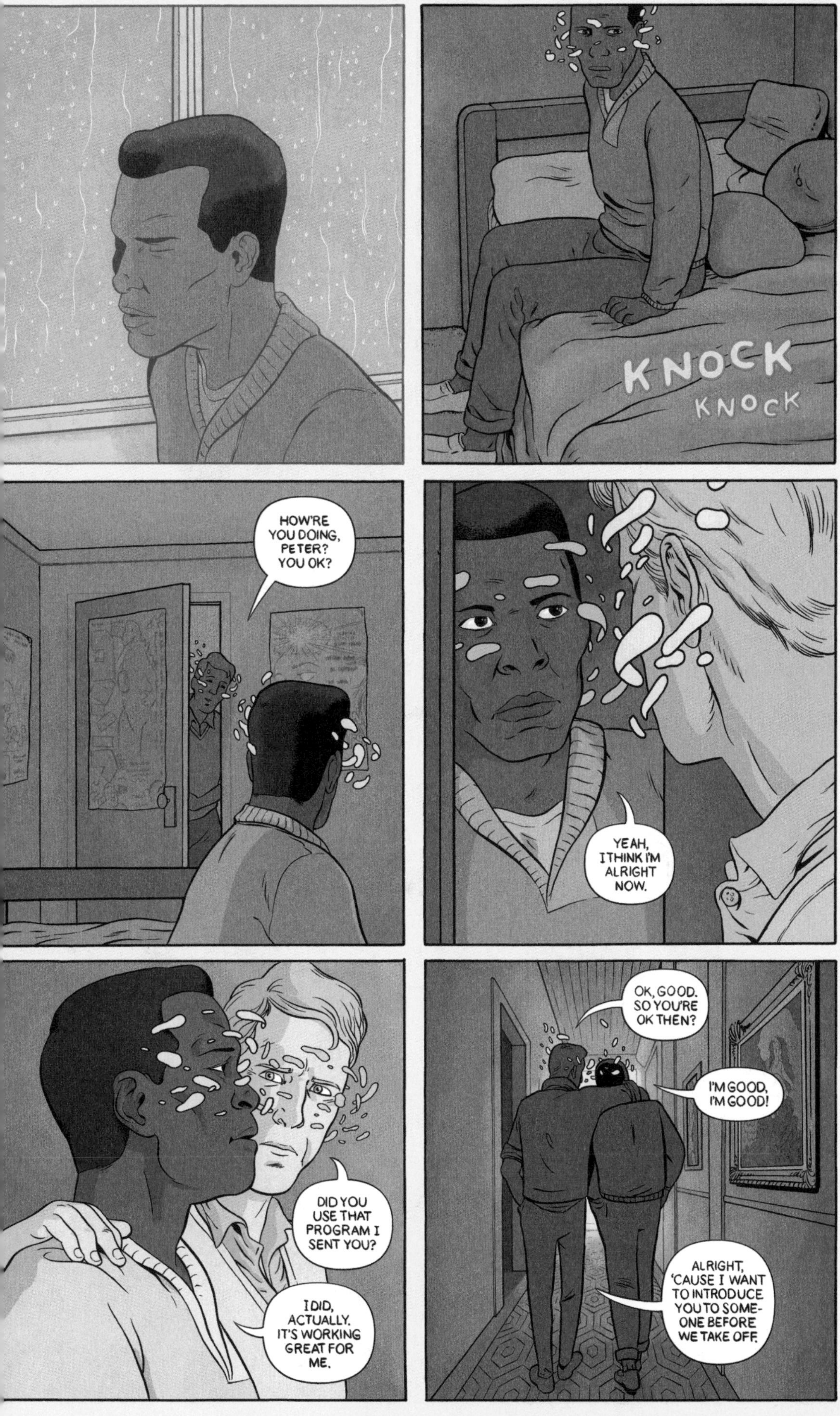
KNOCK
KNOCK
HOW'RE YOU DOING, PETER? YOU OK?
YEAH, I THINK I'M ALRIGHT NOW.
DID YOU USE THAT PROGRAM I SENT YOU?
I DID, ACTUALLY. IT'S WORKING GREAT FOR ME.
OK, GOOD. SO YOU'RE OK THEN?
I'M GOOD, I'M GOOD!
ALRIGHT, 'CAUSE I WANT TO INTRODUCE YOU TO SOME-ONE BEFORE WE TAKE OFF.

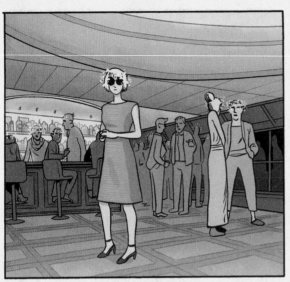

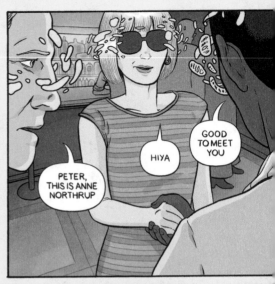

PETER, THIS IS ANNE NORTHRUP
HIYA
GOOD TO MEET YOU
ANNE'S FAVORITE
SHOWS
MOVIES
SHARE YOUR FAVS WITH ANNE
SMILE
TRIP 2061
SHARE MEMORY?
NEW SERVICE UPDATE
SMALL TALK TIPS
THE FILMS of POWELL & PRESSBURGER
WATCH NOW
SHOP!
DOLCE GABBANA $210
SPONSORED
WHERE ANNE'S BEEN
ANNE'S DNA PROFILE
WHAT MEMORIES OF YOURS ARE PUBLIC? CHECK NOW
SEND ANNE A GI
SPONSORED
'S MEMORIES
PERIENCE ONE NOW
ANNE K. NOR
SAVE IMAGE
H: 5'4"
SEP. 1, 2029
PLACE OF BIRTH: PA
FIND OLD
"MY ART IS A WAY TO EXPLORE THE ...
MORE OF ANNE'S QUOTES
RISD
ANNE'S BROTH
Life of the PARTY INC. HIRE NOW...
MAKE ANNE A DRINK
DINAH WASHINGTON
LISTEN AGAIN
Bar Tndr
YOUR FORT IS UNDER ATTACK!
OPEN BATTL NOW
LIKE GAMES?
NEW EPISODE
AVORITE FOODS

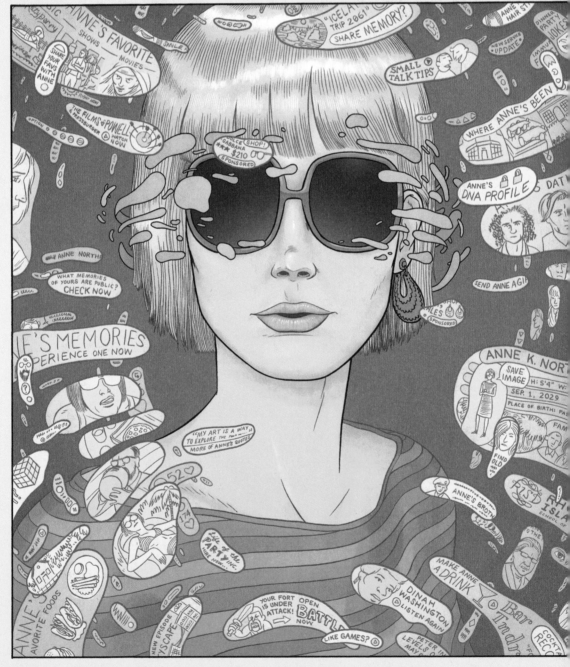

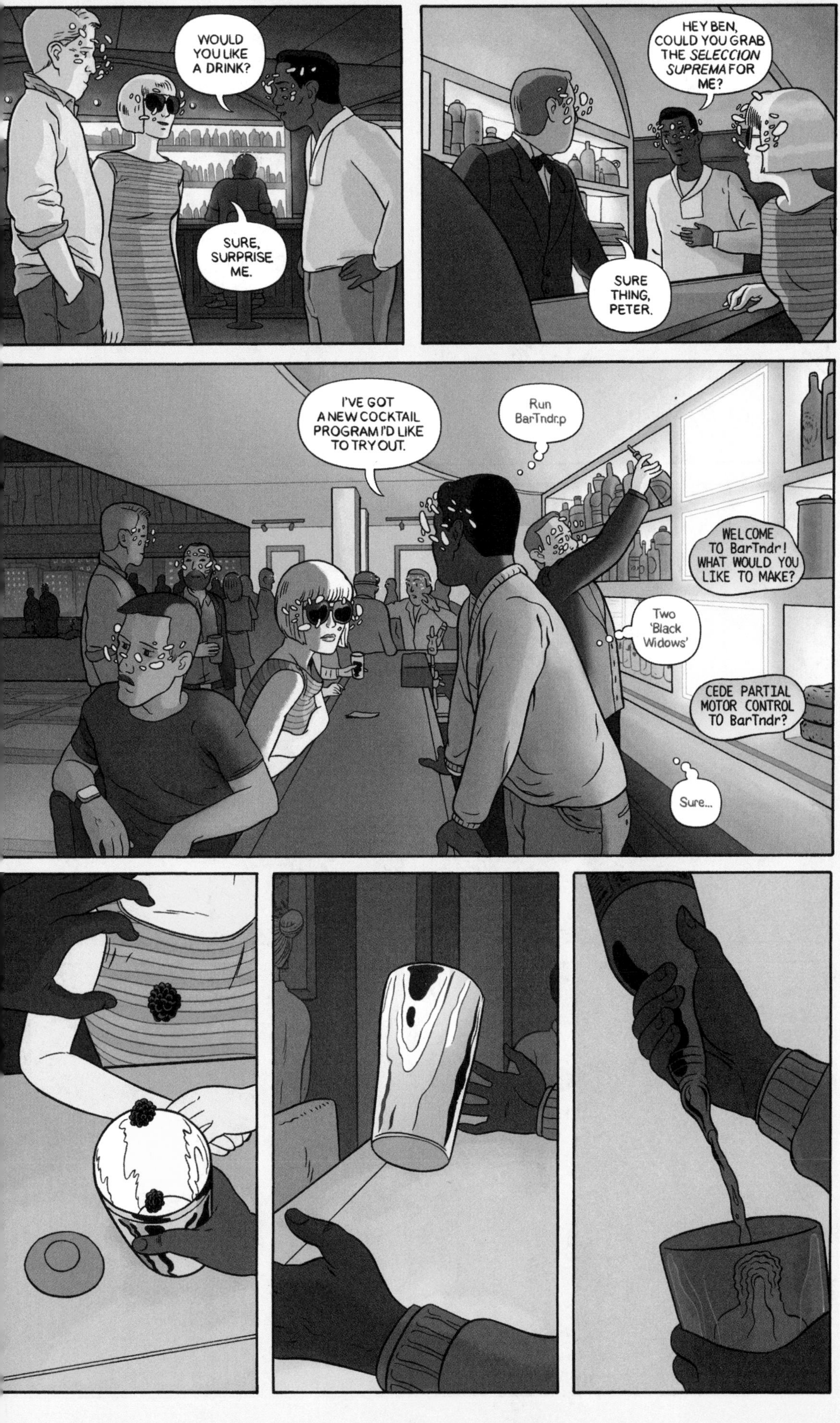
WOULD YOU LIKE A DRINK?
SURE, SURPRISE ME.
HEY BEN, COULD YOU GRAB THE *SELECCION SUPREMA* FOR ME?
SURE THING, PETER.
I'VE GOT A NEW COCKTAIL PROGRAM I'D LIKE TO TRY OUT.
Run BarTndr.p
WELCOME TO BarTndr! WHAT WOULD YOU LIKE TO MAKE?
Two 'Black Widows'
CEDE PARTIAL MOTOR CONTROL TO BarTndr?
Sure...

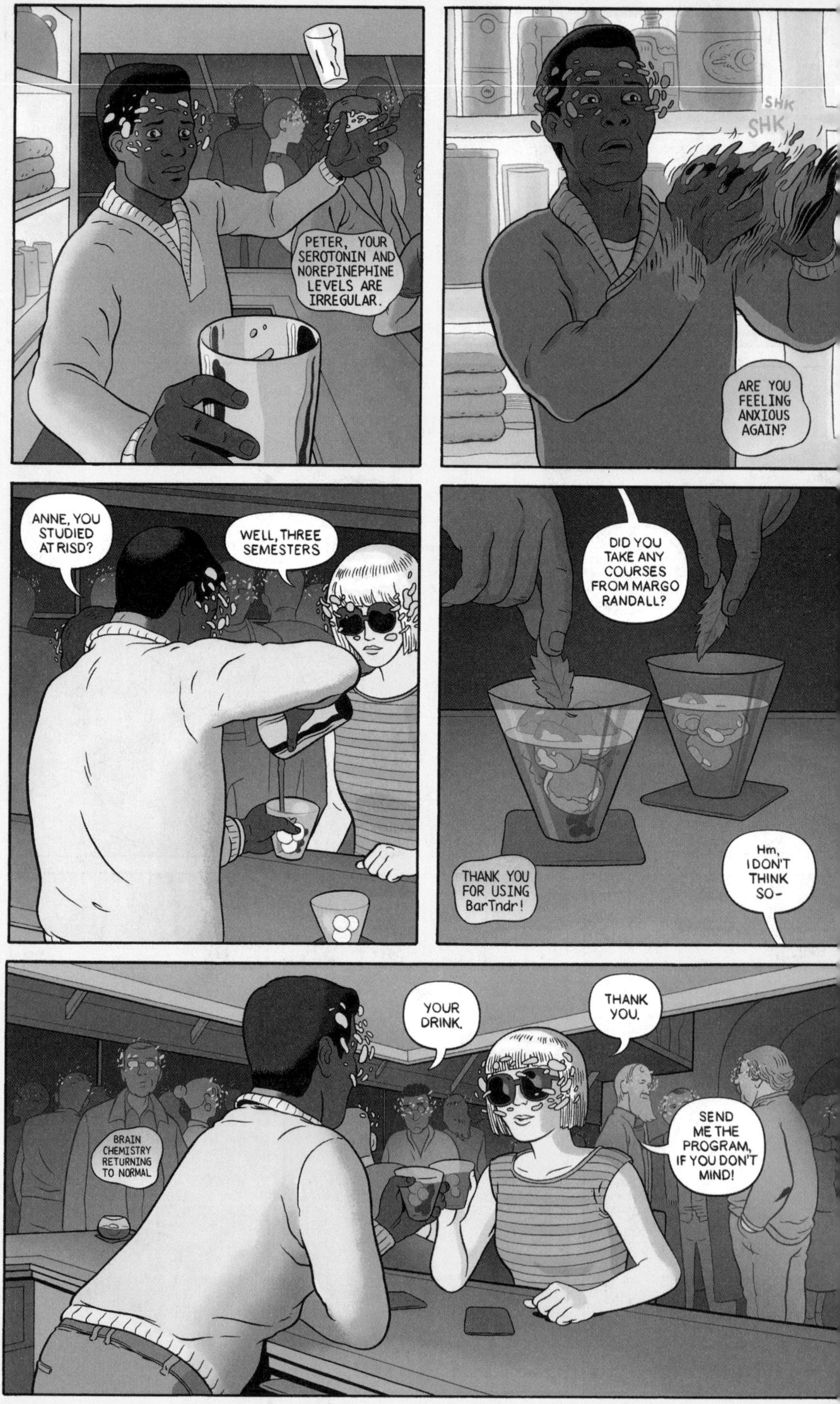
PETER, YOUR SERATONIN AND NOREPINEPHINE LEVELS ARE IRREGULAR.
SHK
SHK
ARE YOU FEELING ANXIOUS AGAIN?
ANNE, YOU STUDIED AT RISD?
WELL, THREE SEMESTERS
DID YOU TAKE ANY COURSES FROM MARGO RANDALL?
THANK YOU FOR USING BarTndr!
Hm, I DON'T THINK SO-
YOUR DRINK.
THANK YOU.
BRAIN CHEMISTRY RETURNING TO NORMAL
SEND ME THE PROGRAM, IF YOU DON'T MIND!

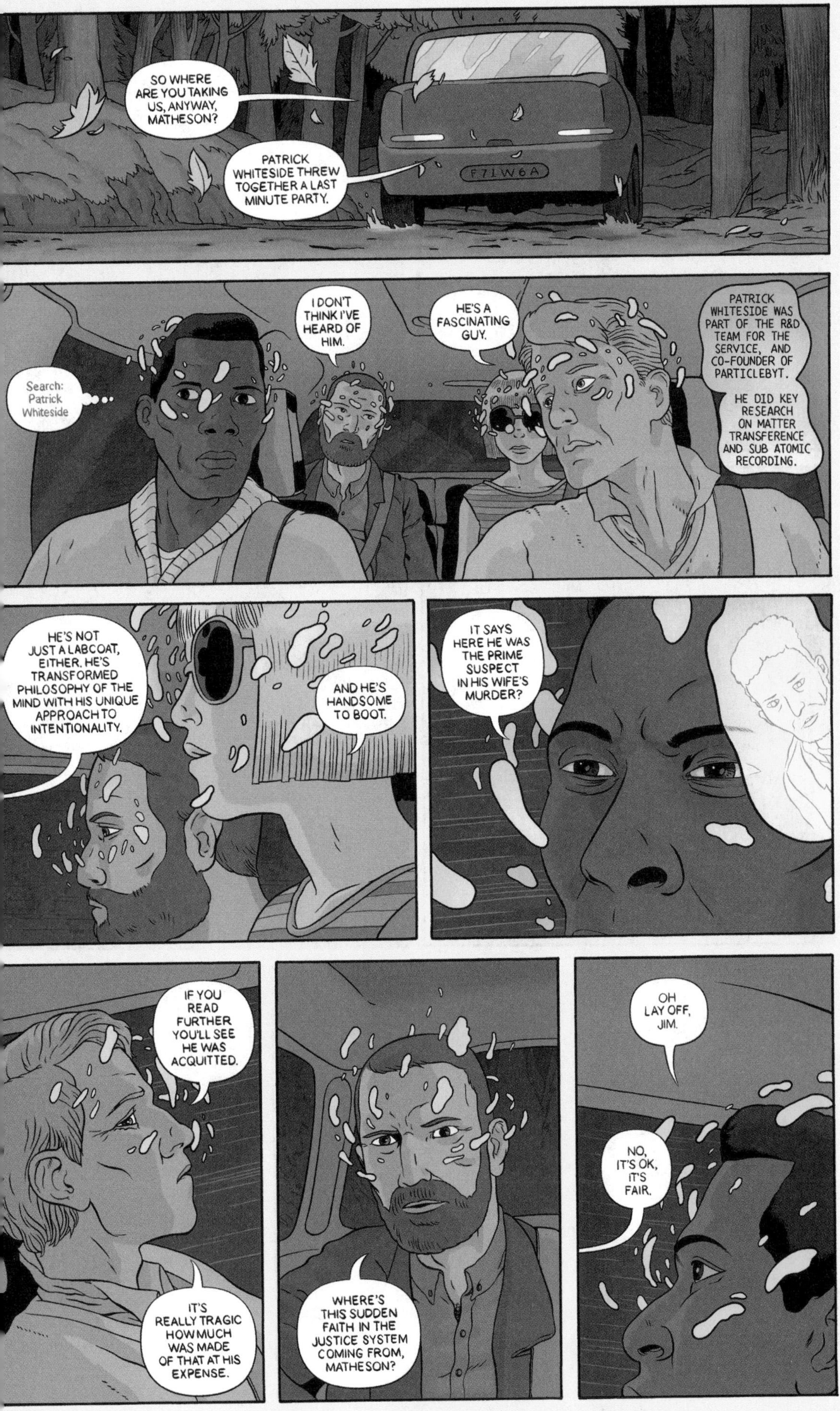
SO WHERE ARE YOU TAKING US, ANYWAY, MATHESON?
PATRICK WHITESIDE THREW TOGETHER A LAST MINUTE PARTY.
F71W6A
Search: Patrick Whiteside
I DON'T THINK I'VE HEARD OF HIM.
HE'S A FASCINATING GUY.
PATRICK WHITESIDE WAS PART OF THE R&D TEAM FOR THE SERVICE, AND CO-FOUNDER OF PARTICLEBYT.
HE DID KEY RESEARCH ON MATTER TRANSFERENCE AND SUB ATOMIC RECORDING.
HE'S NOT JUST A LABCOAT, EITHER. HE'S TRANSFORMED PHILOSOPHY OF THE MIND WITH HIS UNIQUE APPROACH TO INTENTIONALITY.
AND HE'S HANDSOME TO BOOT.
IT SAYS HERE HE WAS THE PRIME SUSPECT IN HIS WIFE'S MURDER?
IF YOU READ FURTHER YOU'LL SEE HE WAS ACQUITTED.
IT'S REALLY TRAGIC HOW MUCH WAS MADE OF THAT AT HIS EXPENSE.
WHERE'S THIS SUDDEN FAITH IN THE JUSTICE SYSTEM COMING FROM, MATHESON?
OH LAY OFF, JIM.
NO, IT'S OK, IT'S FAIR.

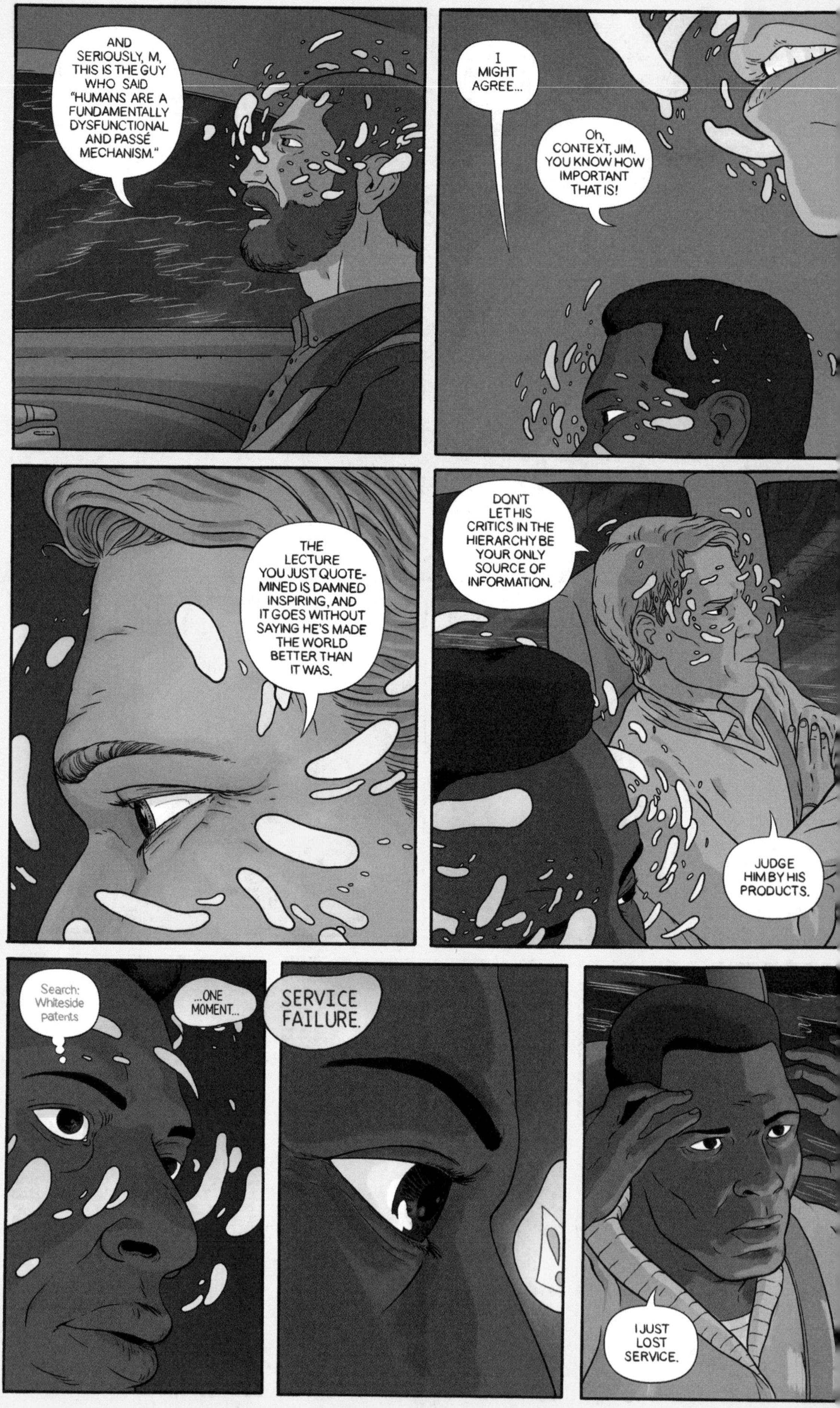
AND SERIOUSLY, M, THIS IS THE GUY WHO SAID "HUMANS ARE A FUNDAMENTALLY DYSFUNCTIONAL AND PASSÉ MECHANISM."
I MIGHT AGREE...
Oh, CONTEXT, JIM. YOU KNOW HOW IMPORTANT THAT IS!
THE LECTURE YOU JUST QUOTE-MINED IS DAMNED INSPIRING, AND IT GOES WITHOUT SAYING HE'S MADE THE WORLD BETTER THAN IT WAS.
DON'T LET HIS CRITICS IN THE HIERARCHY BE YOUR ONLY SOURCE OF INFORMATION.
JUDGE HIM BY HIS PRODUCTS.
Search: Whiteside patents
...ONE MOMENT...
SERVICE FAILURE.
I JUST LOST SERVICE.

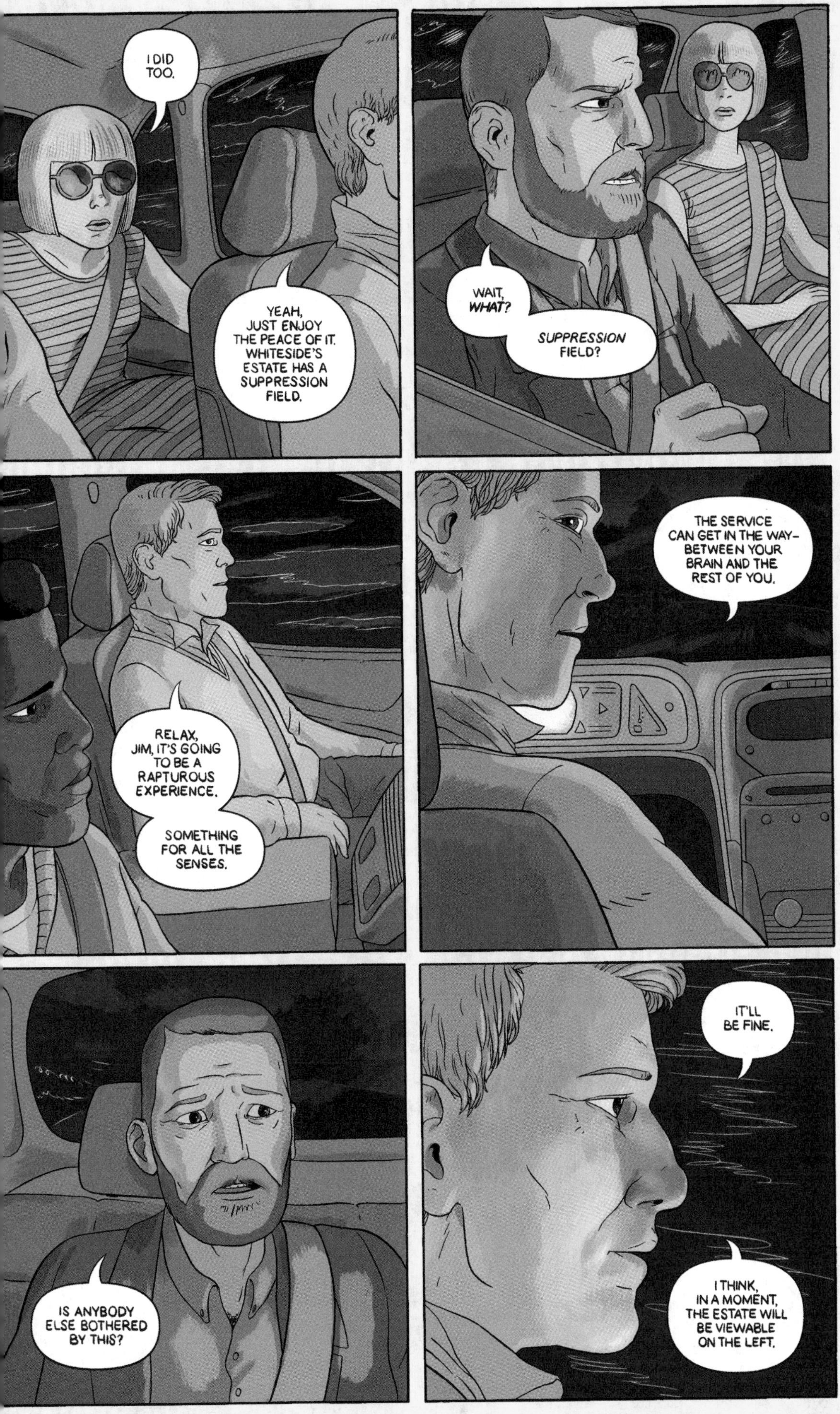
I DID TOO.
YEAH, JUST ENJOY THE PEACE OF IT. WHITESIDE'S ESTATE HAS A SUPPRESSION FIELD.
WAIT, *WHAT?*
SUPPRESSION FIELD?
RELAX, JIM, IT'S GOING TO BE A RAPTUROUS EXPERIENCE.
SOMETHING FOR ALL THE SENSES.
THE SERVICE CAN GET IN THE WAY- BETWEEN YOUR BRAIN AND THE REST OF YOU.
IS ANYBODY ELSE BOTHERED BY THIS?
IT'LL BE FINE.
I THINK, IN A MOMENT, THE ESTATE WILL BE VIEWABLE ON THE LEFT.

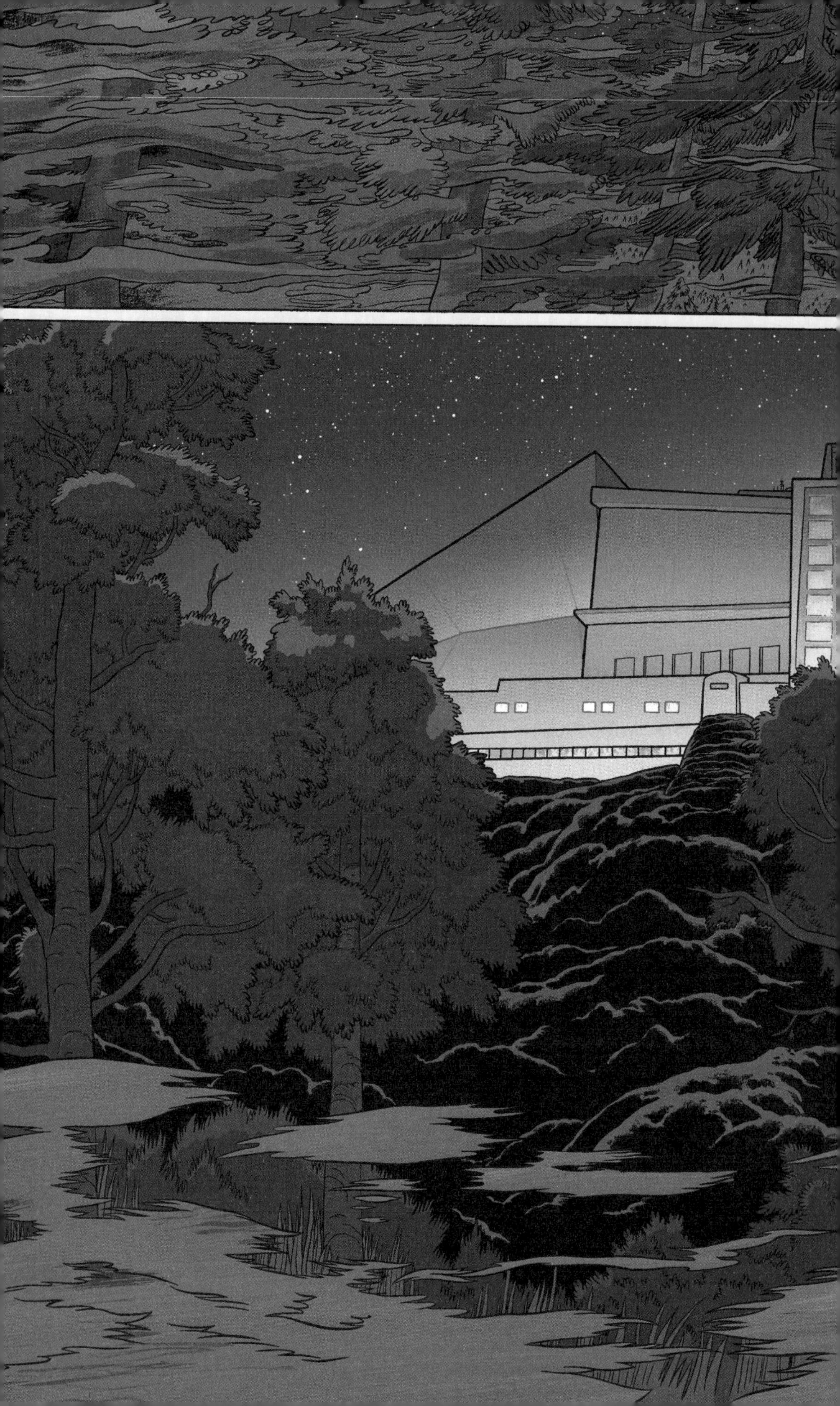

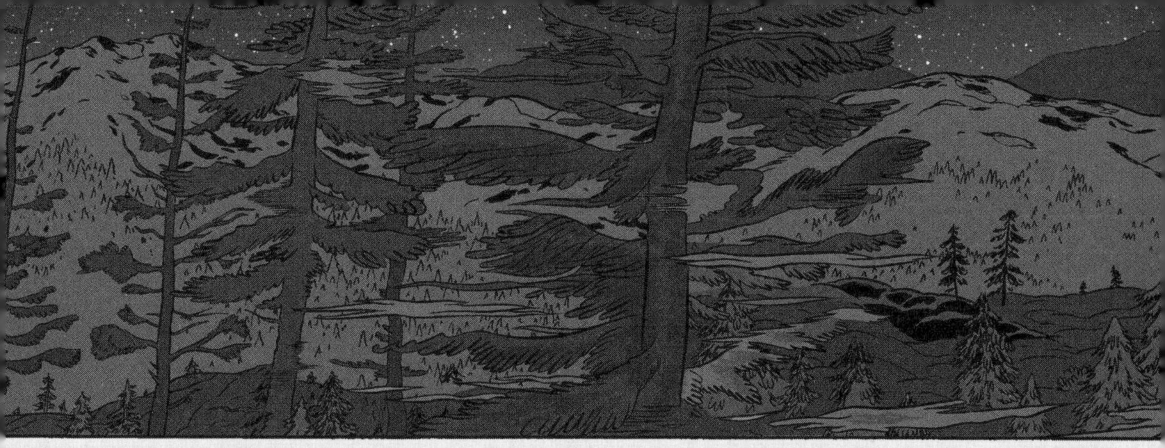
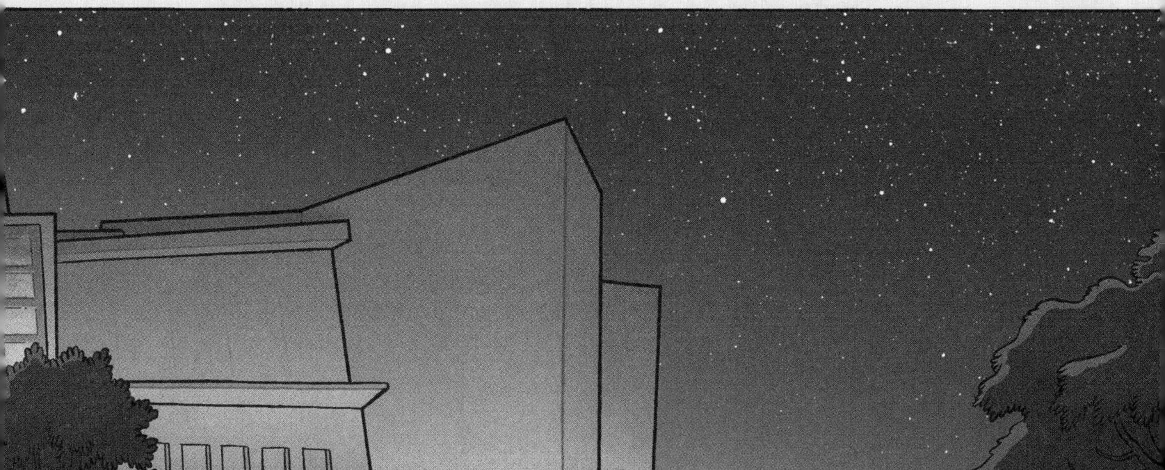
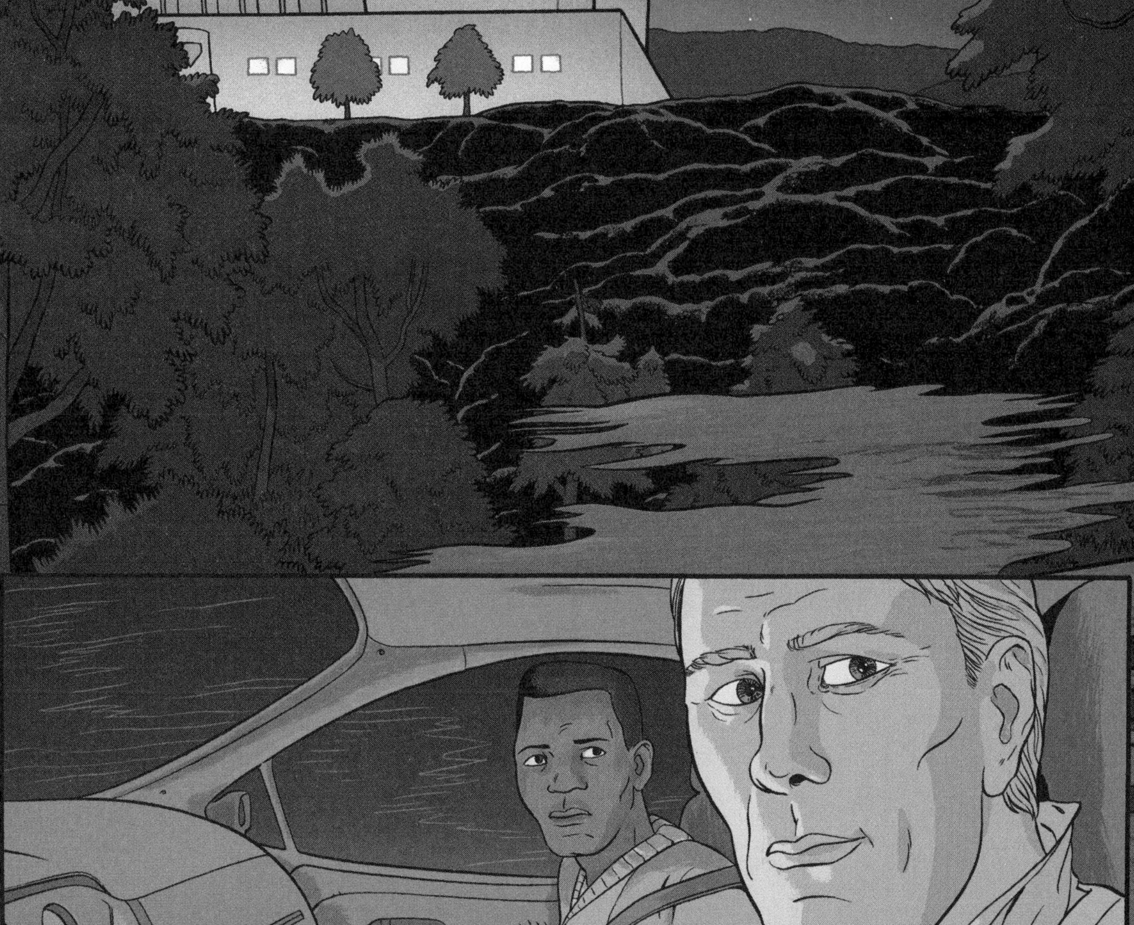

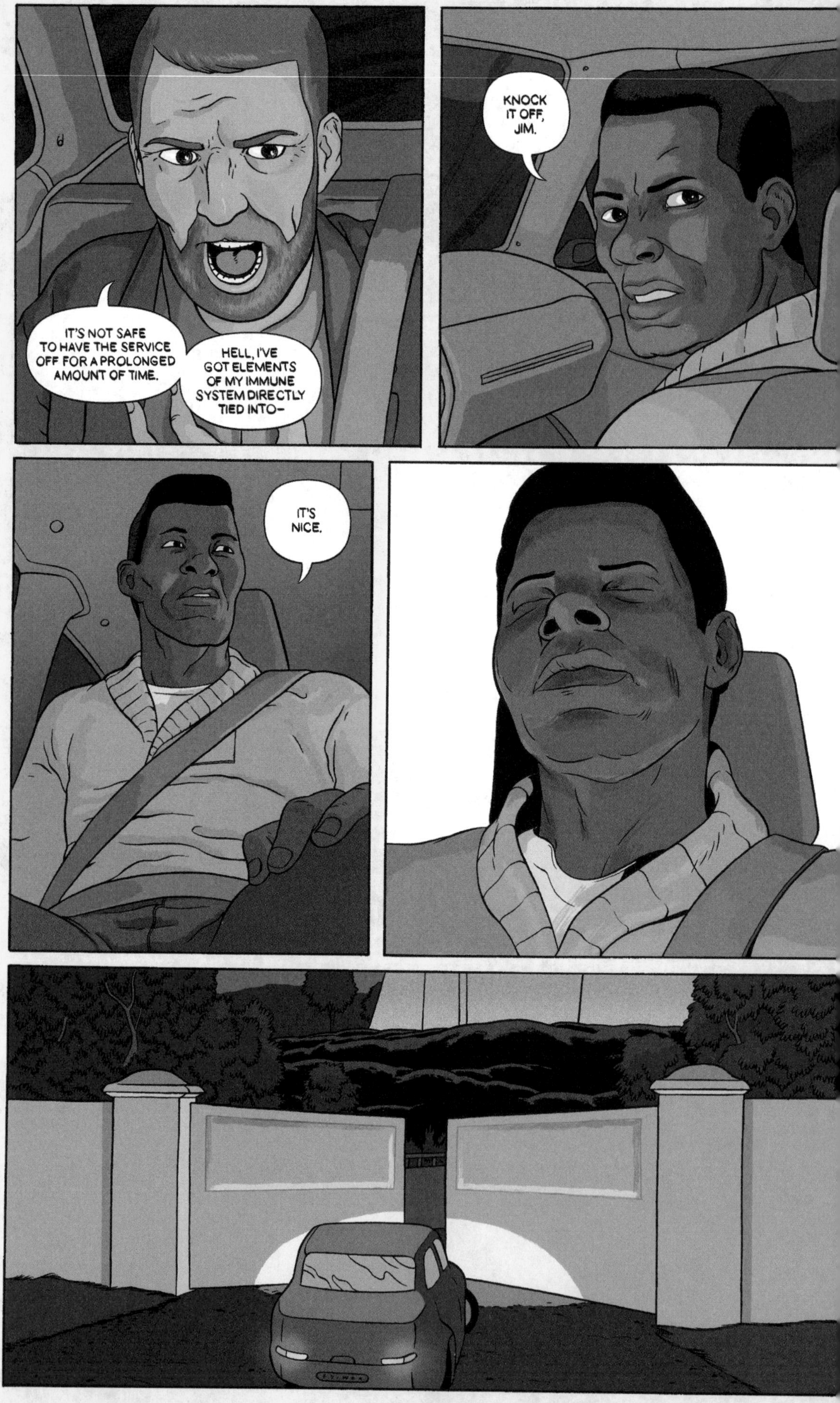
IT'S NOT SAFE TO HAVE THE SERVICE OFF FOR A PROLONGED AMOUNT OF TIME.
HELL, I'VE GOT ELEMENTS OF MY IMMUNE SYSTEM DIRECTLY TIED INTO–
KNOCK IT OFF, JIM.
IT'S NICE.

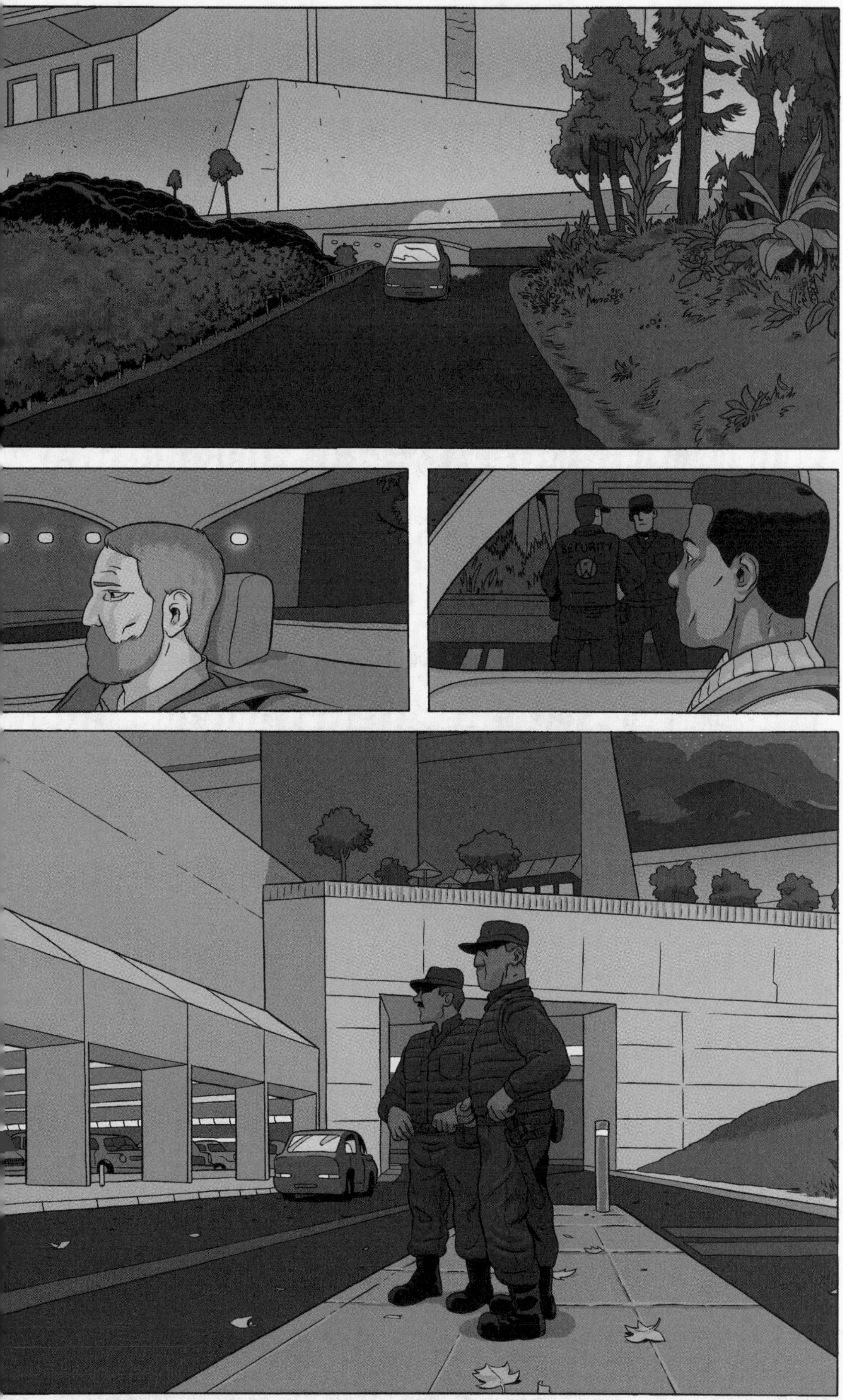
SECURITY

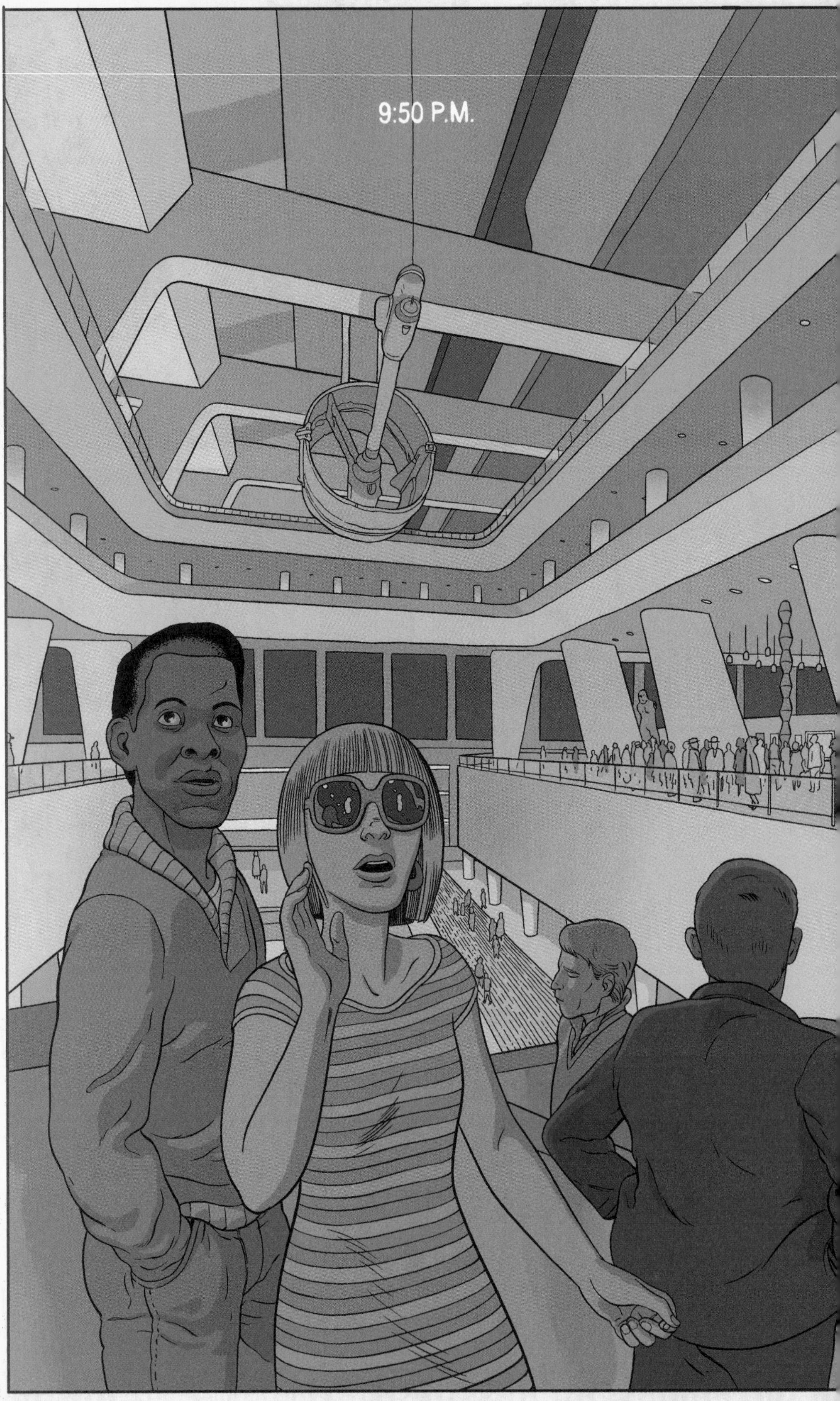
9:50 P.M.

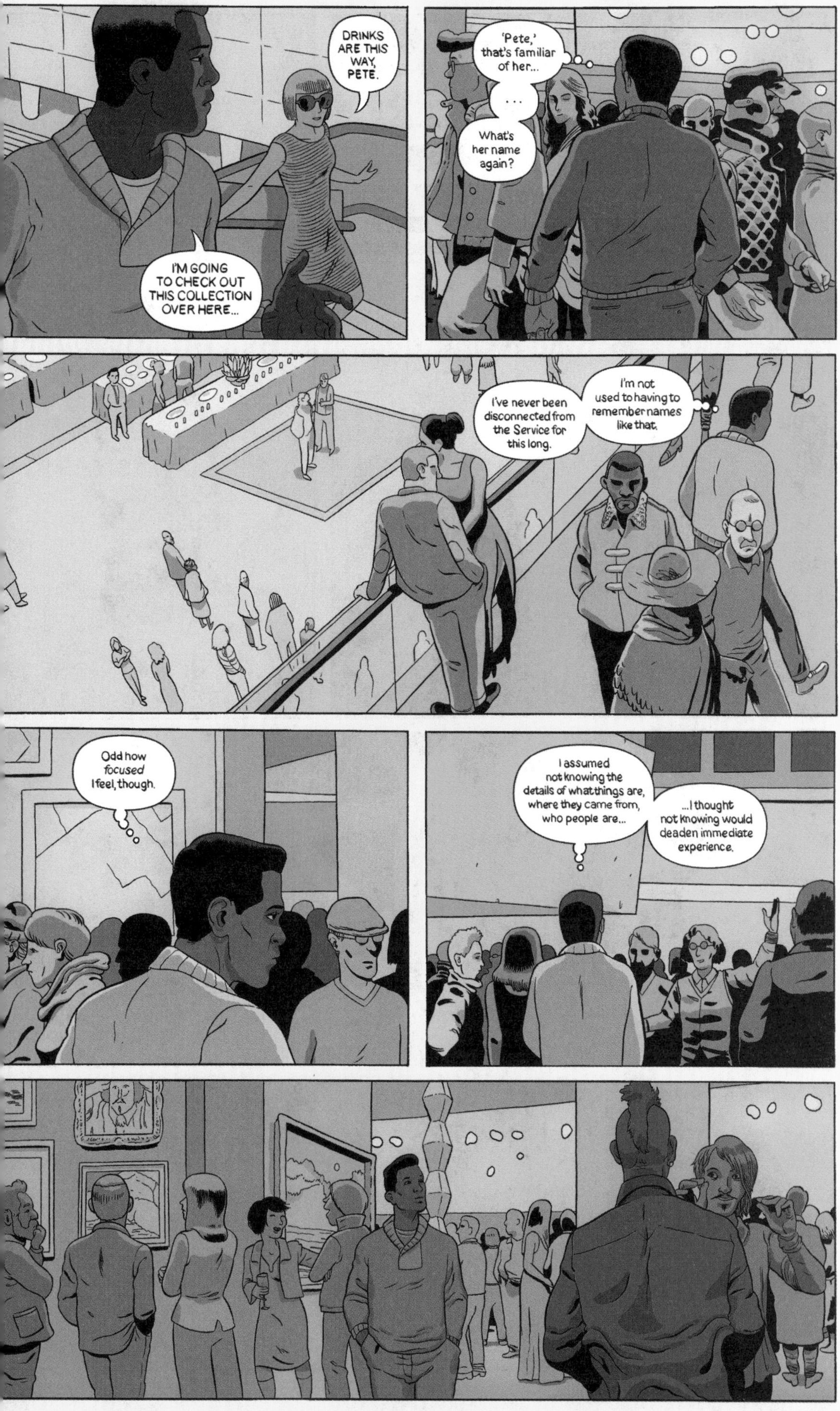
DRINKS ARE THIS WAY, PETE.
I'M GOING TO CHECK OUT THIS COLLECTION OVER HERE...
'Pete,' that's familiar of her...
. . .
What's her name again?
I've never been disconnected from the Service for this long.
I'm not used to having to remember names like that.
Odd how *focused* I feel, though.
I assumed not knowing the details of what things are, where they came from, who people are...
...I thought not knowing would deaden immediate experience.

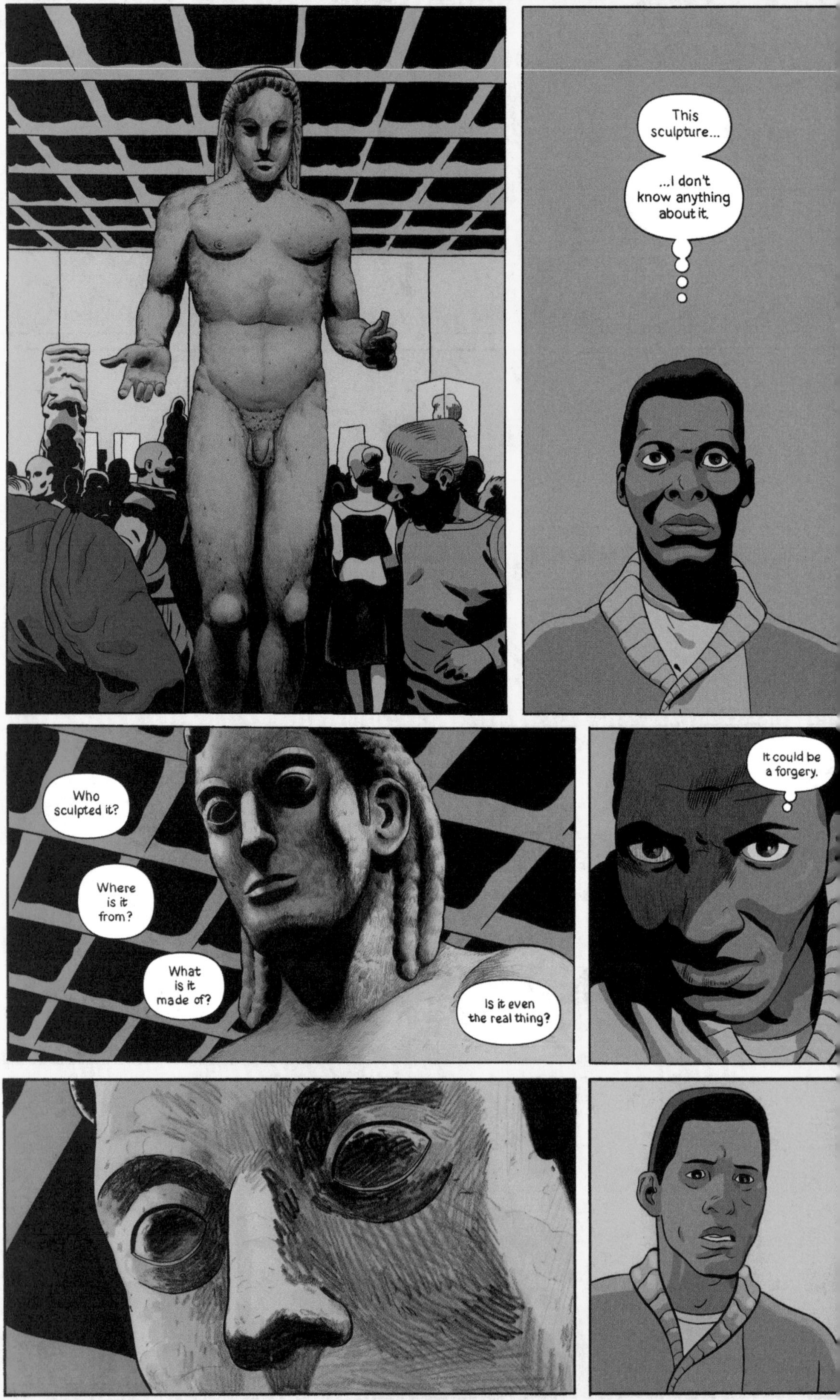
This sculpture...
...I don't know anything about it.
Who sculpted it?
Where is it from?
What is it made of?
Is it even the real thing?
It could be a forgery.

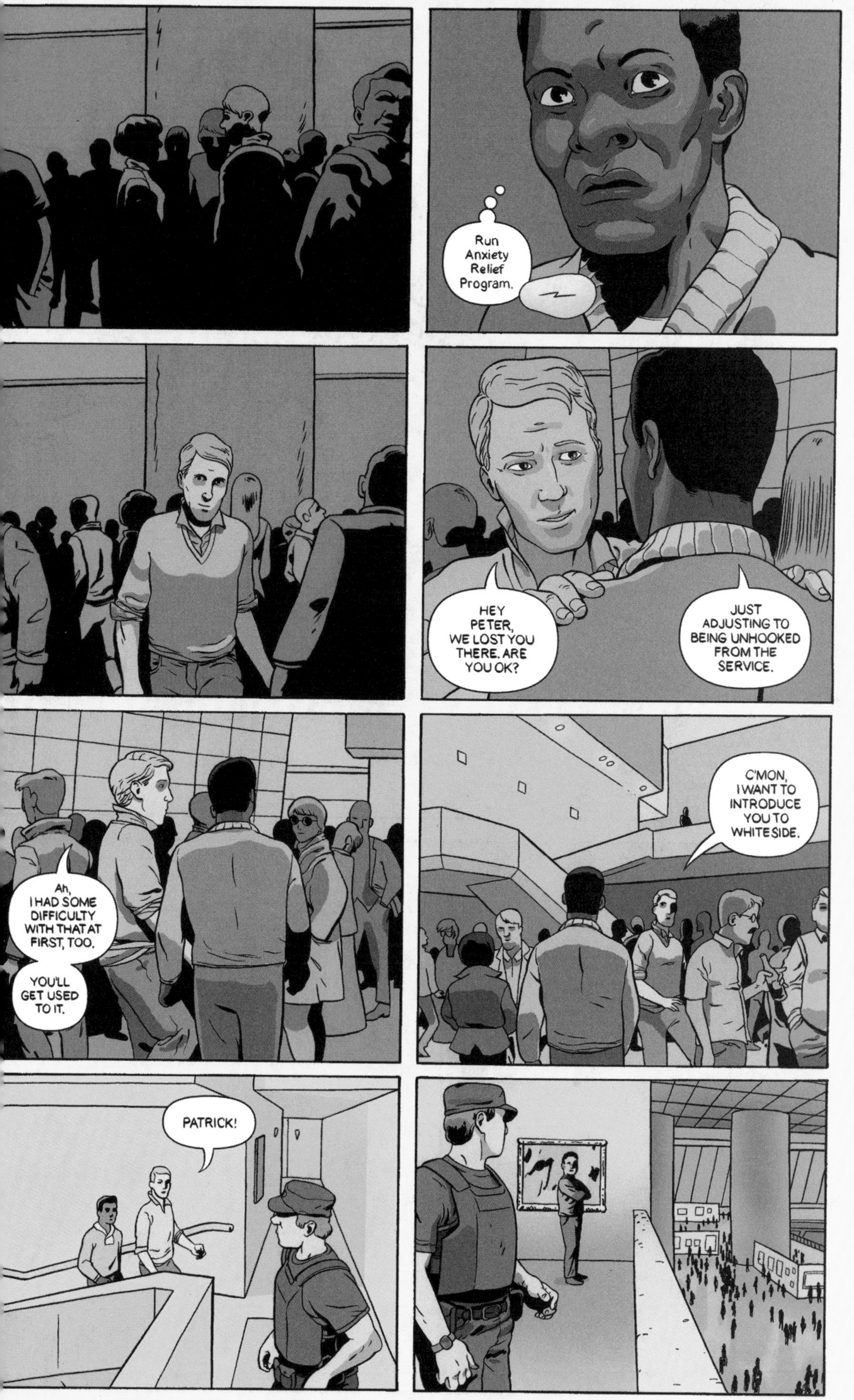
Run Anxiety Relief Program.
HEY PETER, WE LOST YOU THERE. ARE YOU OK?
JUST ADJUSTING TO BEING UNHOOKED FROM THE SERVICE.
Ah, I HAD SOME DIFFICULTY WITH THAT AT FIRST, TOO.
YOU'LL GET USED TO IT.
C'MON, I WANT TO INTRODUCE YOU TO WHITESIDE.
PATRICK!

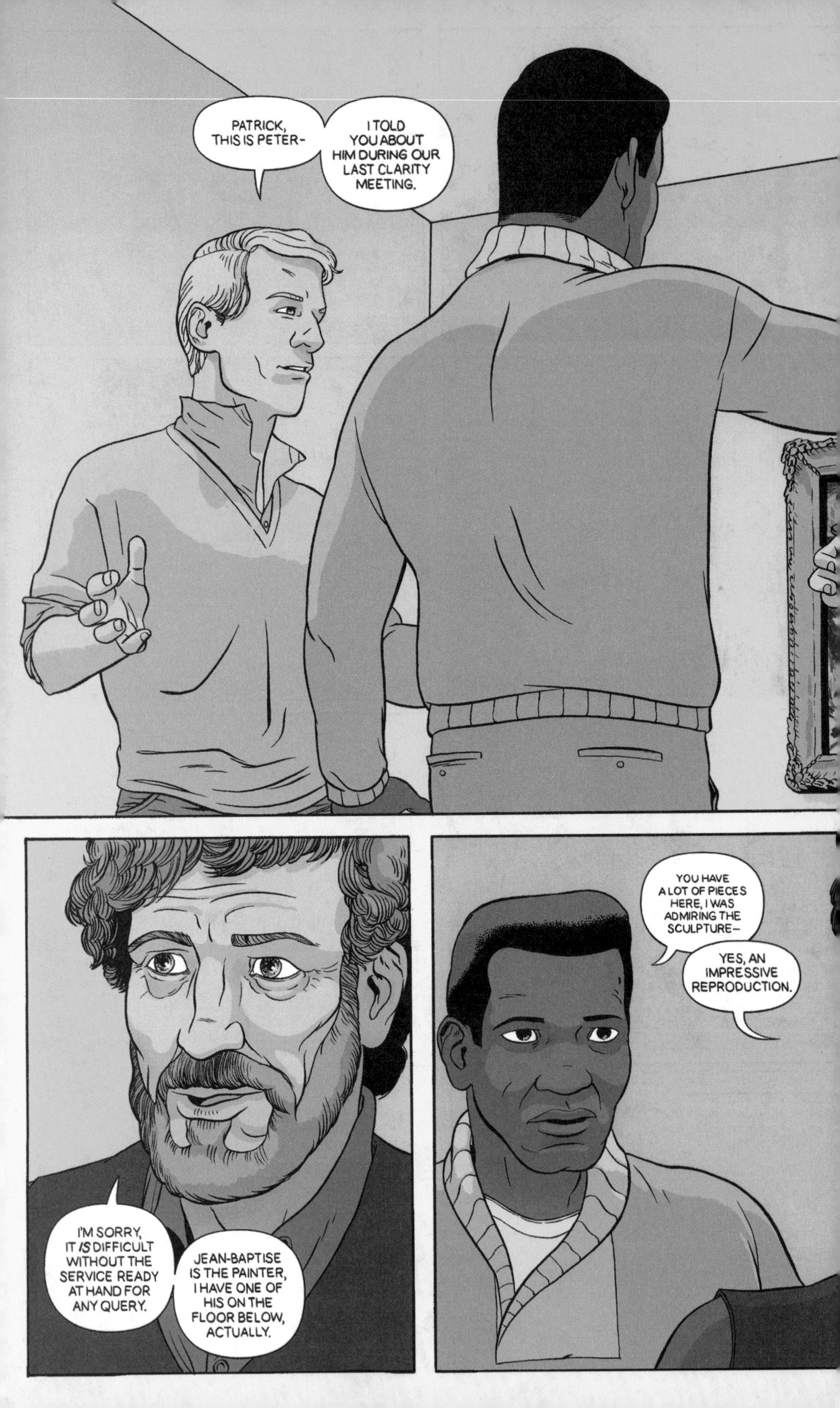
PATRICK, THIS IS PETER-
I TOLD YOU ABOUT HIM DURING OUR LAST CLARITY MEETING.
I'M SORRY, IT IS DIFFICULT WITHOUT THE SERVICE READY AT HAND FOR ANY QUERY.
JEAN-BAPTISE IS THE PAINTER, I HAVE ONE OF HIS ON THE FLOOR BELOW, ACTUALLY.
YOU HAVE A LOT OF PIECES HERE, I WAS ADMIRING THE SCULPTURE-
YES, AN IMPRESSIVE REPRODUCTION.

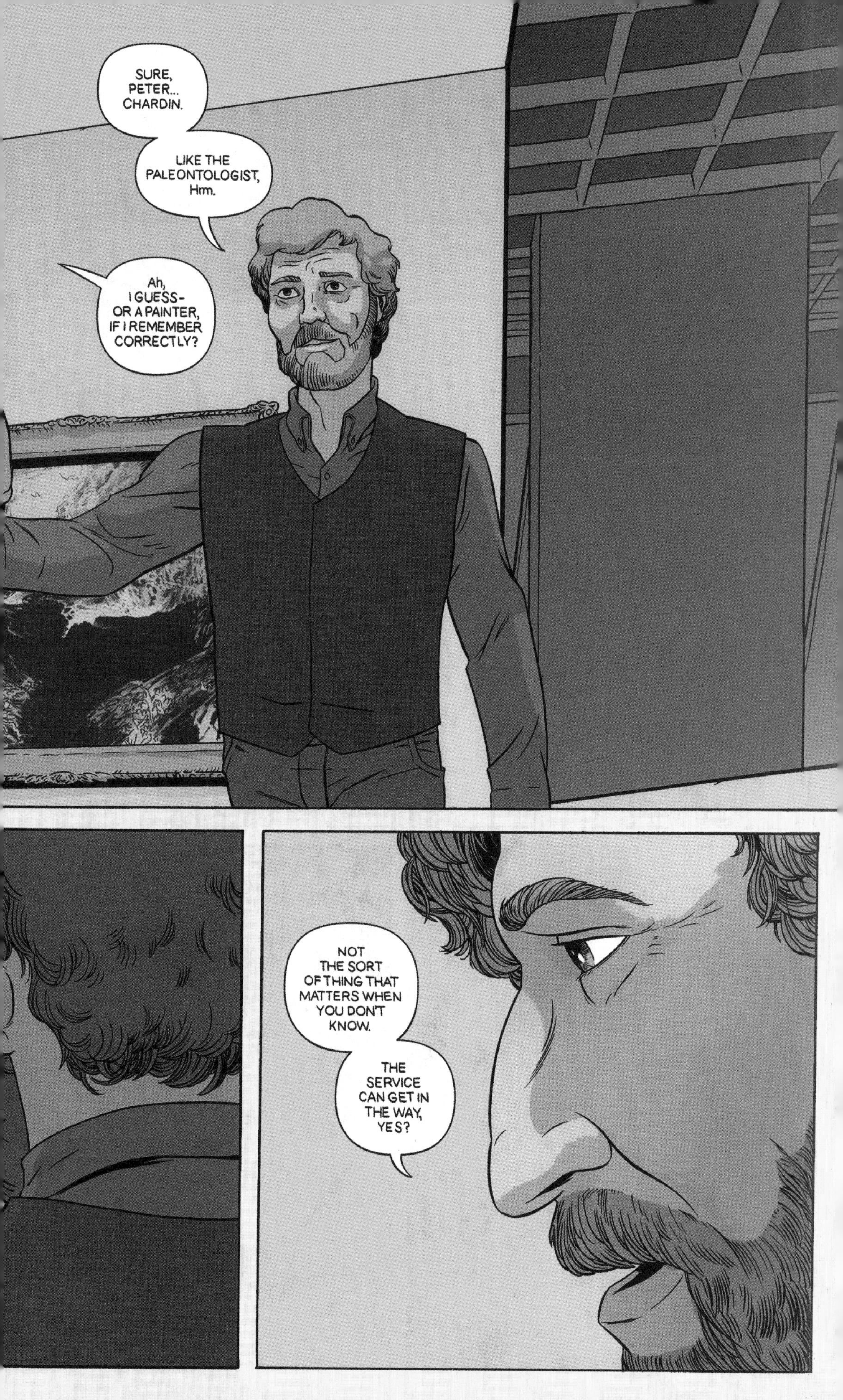
SURE, PETER... CHARDIN.
LIKE THE PALEONTOLOGIST, Hm.
Ah, I GUESS- OR A PAINTER, IF I REMEMBER CORRECTLY?
NOT THE SORT OF THING THAT MATTERS WHEN YOU DON'T KNOW.
THE SERVICE CAN GET IN THE WAY, YES?

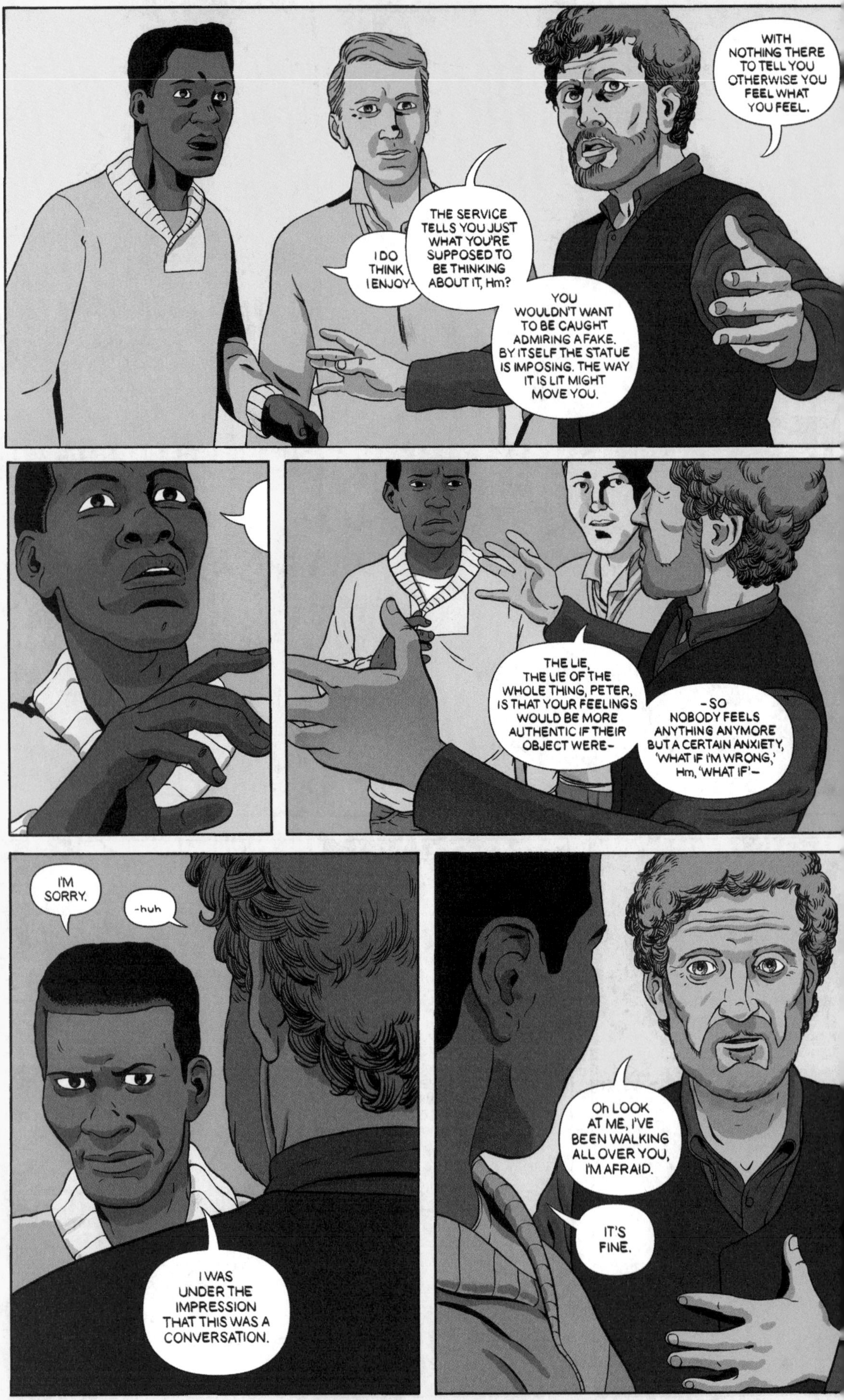
WITH NOTHING THERE TO TELL YOU OTHERWISE YOU FEEL WHAT YOU FEEL.
THE SERVICE TELLS YOU JUST WHAT YOU'RE SUPPOSED TO BE THINKING ABOUT IT, Hm?
I DO THINK I ENJOY-
YOU WOULDN'T WANT TO BE CAUGHT ADMIRING A FAKE. BY ITSELF THE STATUE IS IMPOSING. THE WAY IT IS LIT MIGHT MOVE YOU.
THE LIE, THE LIE OF THE WHOLE THING, PETER, IS THAT YOUR FEELINGS WOULD BE MORE AUTHENTIC IF THEIR OBJECT WERE-
-SO NOBODY FEELS ANYTHING ANYMORE BUT A CERTAIN ANXIETY, 'WHAT IF I'M WRONG,' Hm, 'WHAT IF'-
I'M SORRY.
-huh
I WAS UNDER THE IMPRESSION THAT THIS WAS A CONVERSATION.
Oh LOOK AT ME, I'VE BEEN WALKING ALL OVER YOU, I'M AFRAID.
IT'S FINE.

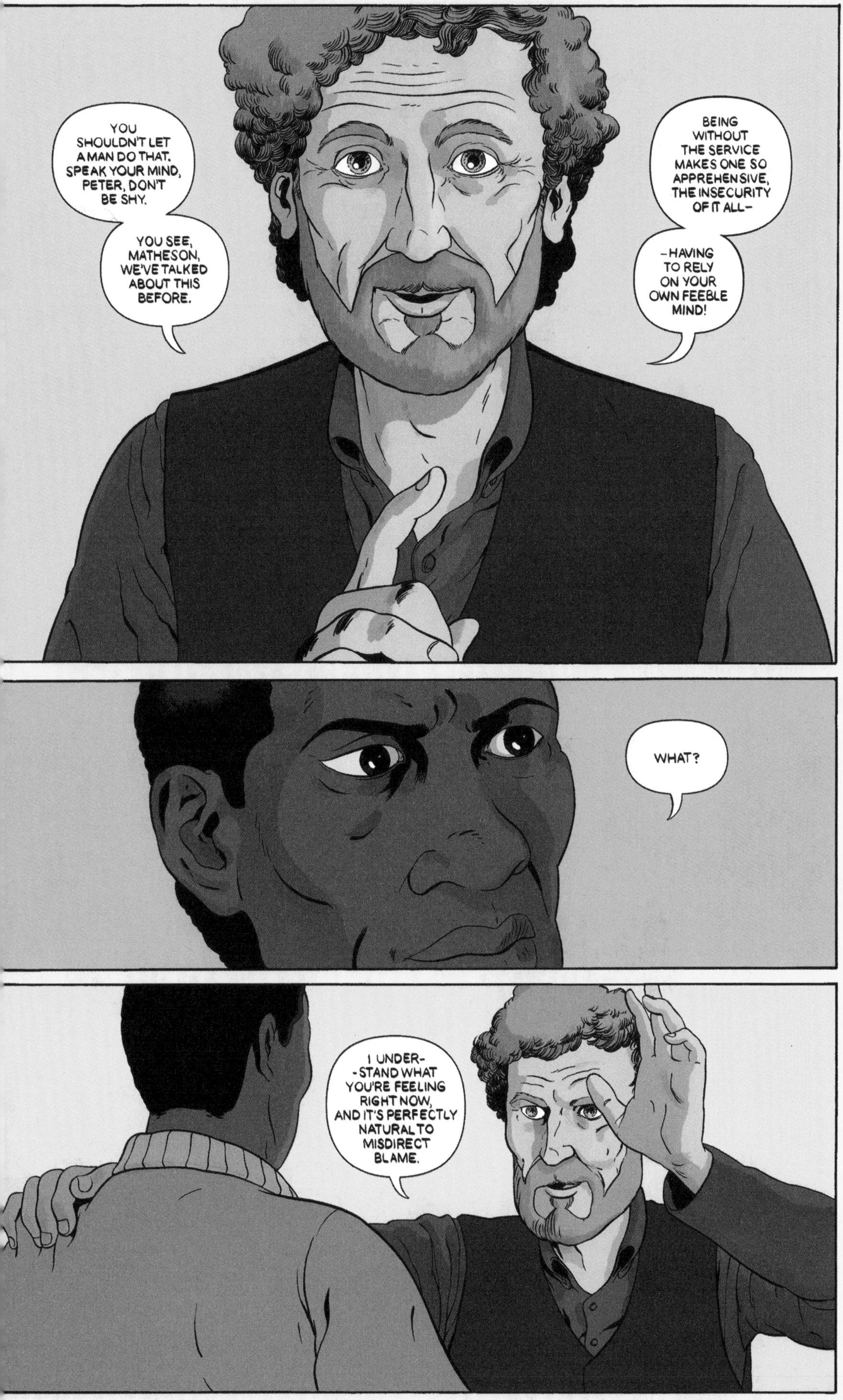
YOU SHOULDN'T LET A MAN DO THAT. SPEAK YOUR MIND, PETER, DON'T BE SHY.
YOU SEE, MATHESON, WE'VE TALKED ABOUT THIS BEFORE.
BEING WITHOUT THE SERVICE MAKES ONE SO APPREHENSIVE, THE INSECURITY OF IT ALL–
–HAVING TO RELY ON YOUR OWN FEEBLE MIND!
WHAT?
I UNDER- -STAND WHAT YOU'RE FEELING RIGHT NOW, AND IT'S PERFECTLY NATURAL TO MISDIRECT BLAME.

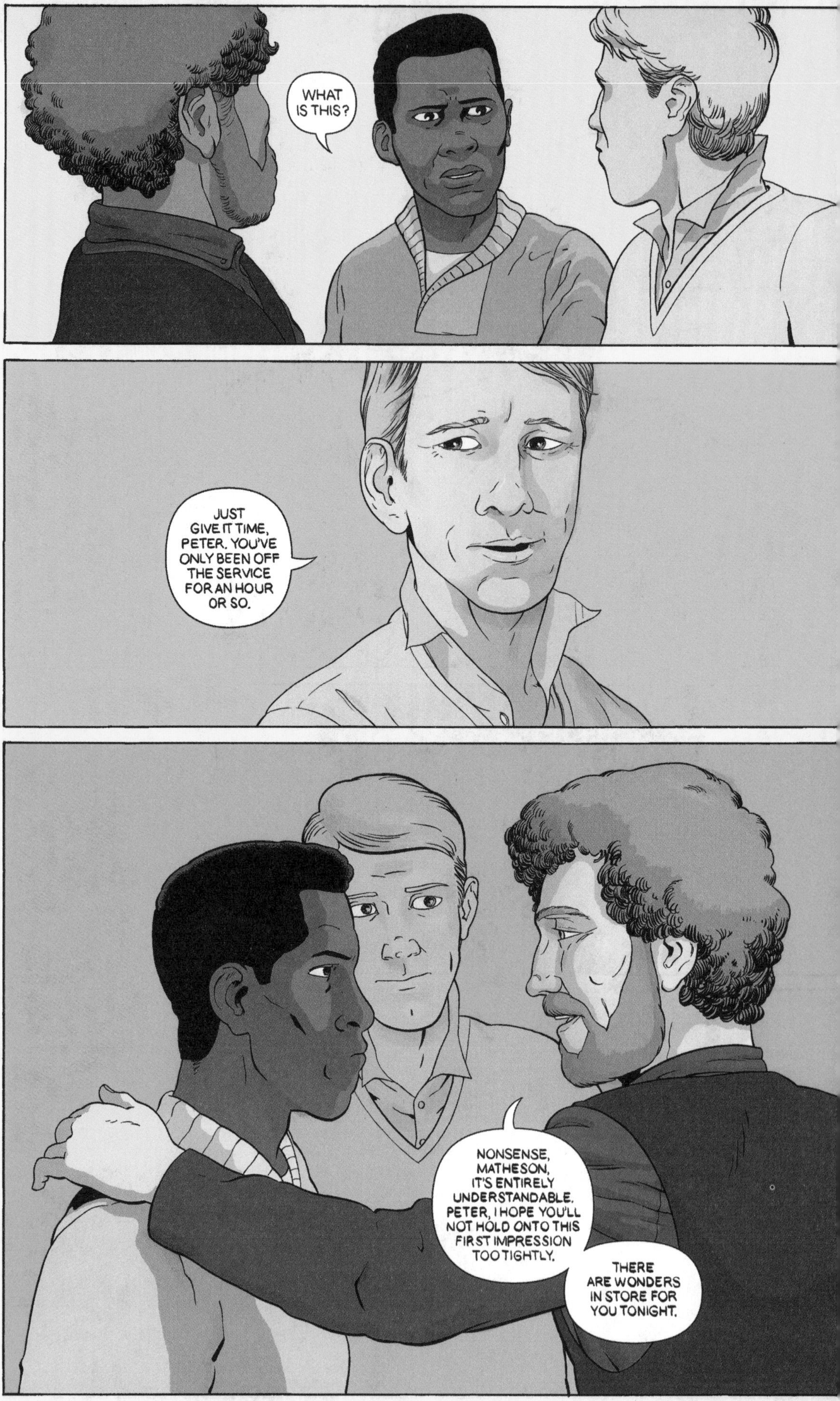
WHAT IS THIS?
JUST GIVE IT TIME, PETER. YOU'VE ONLY BEEN OFF THE SERVICE FOR AN HOUR OR SO.
NONSENSE, MATHESON, IT'S ENTIRELY UNDERSTANDABLE. PETER, I HOPE YOU'LL NOT HOLD ONTO THIS FIRST IMPRESSION TOO TIGHTLY.
THERE ARE WONDERS IN STORE FOR YOU TONIGHT.

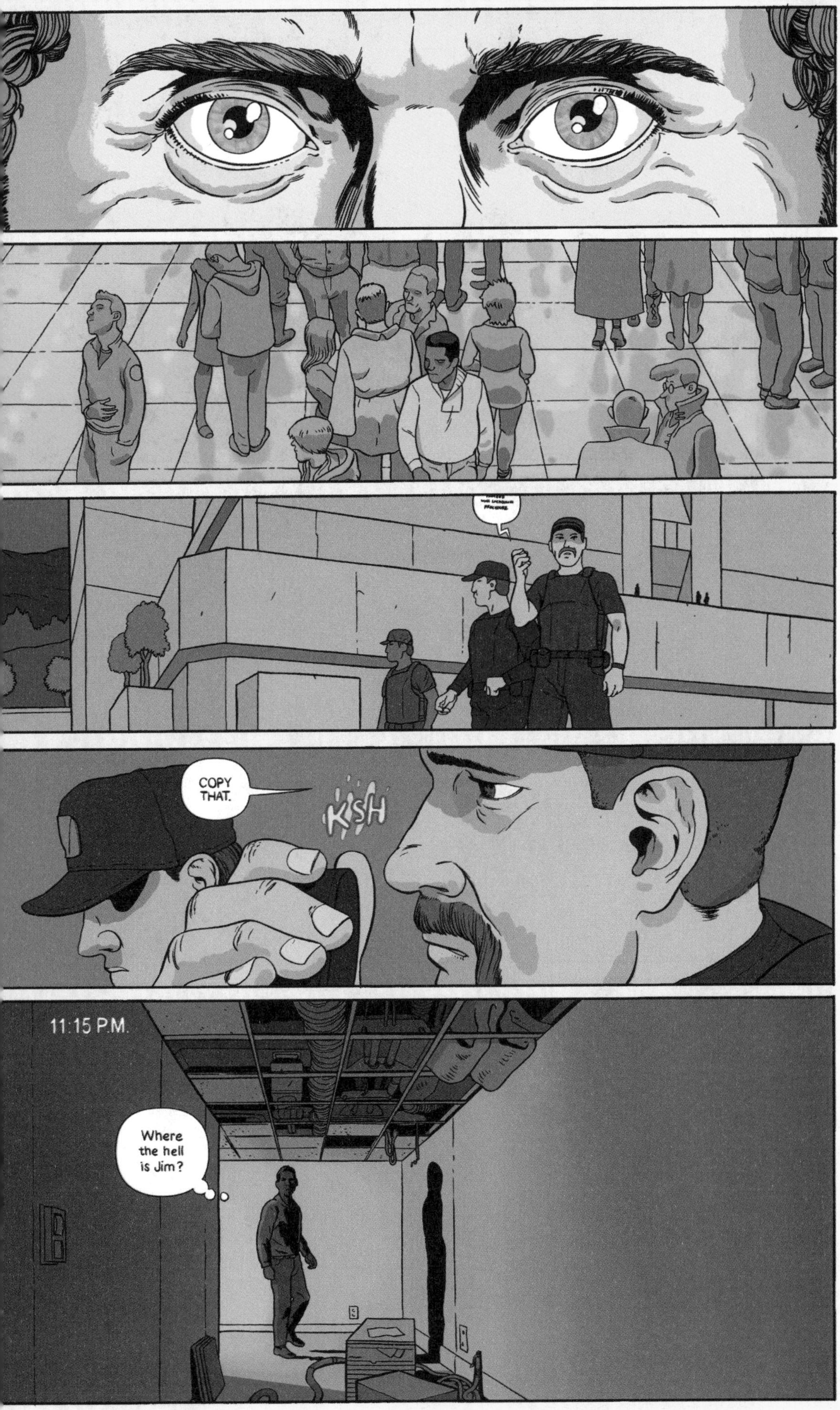
COPY THAT.
KSH
11:15 P.M.
Where the hell is Jim?

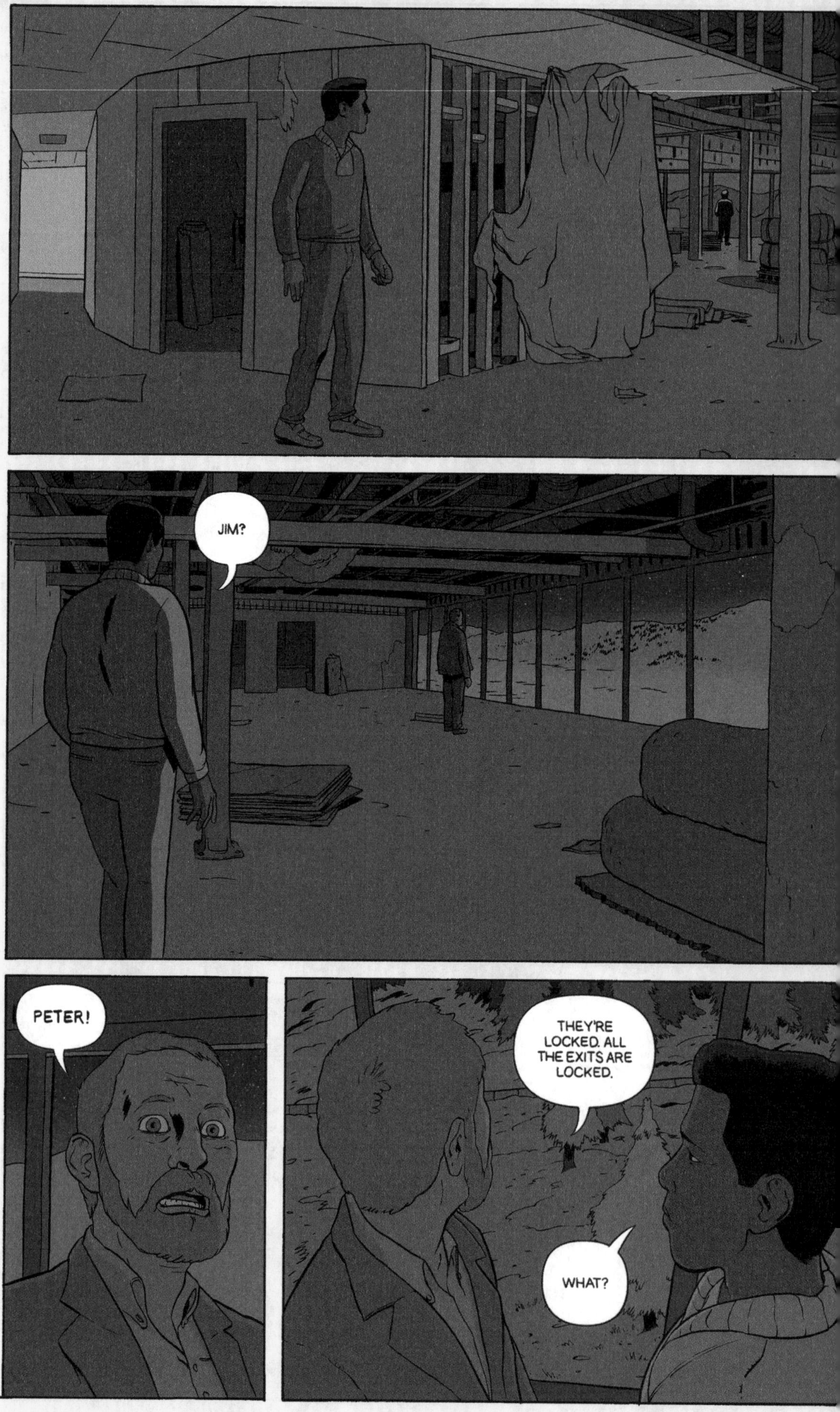
JIM?
PETER!
THEY'RE LOCKED. ALL THE EXITS ARE LOCKED.
WHAT?

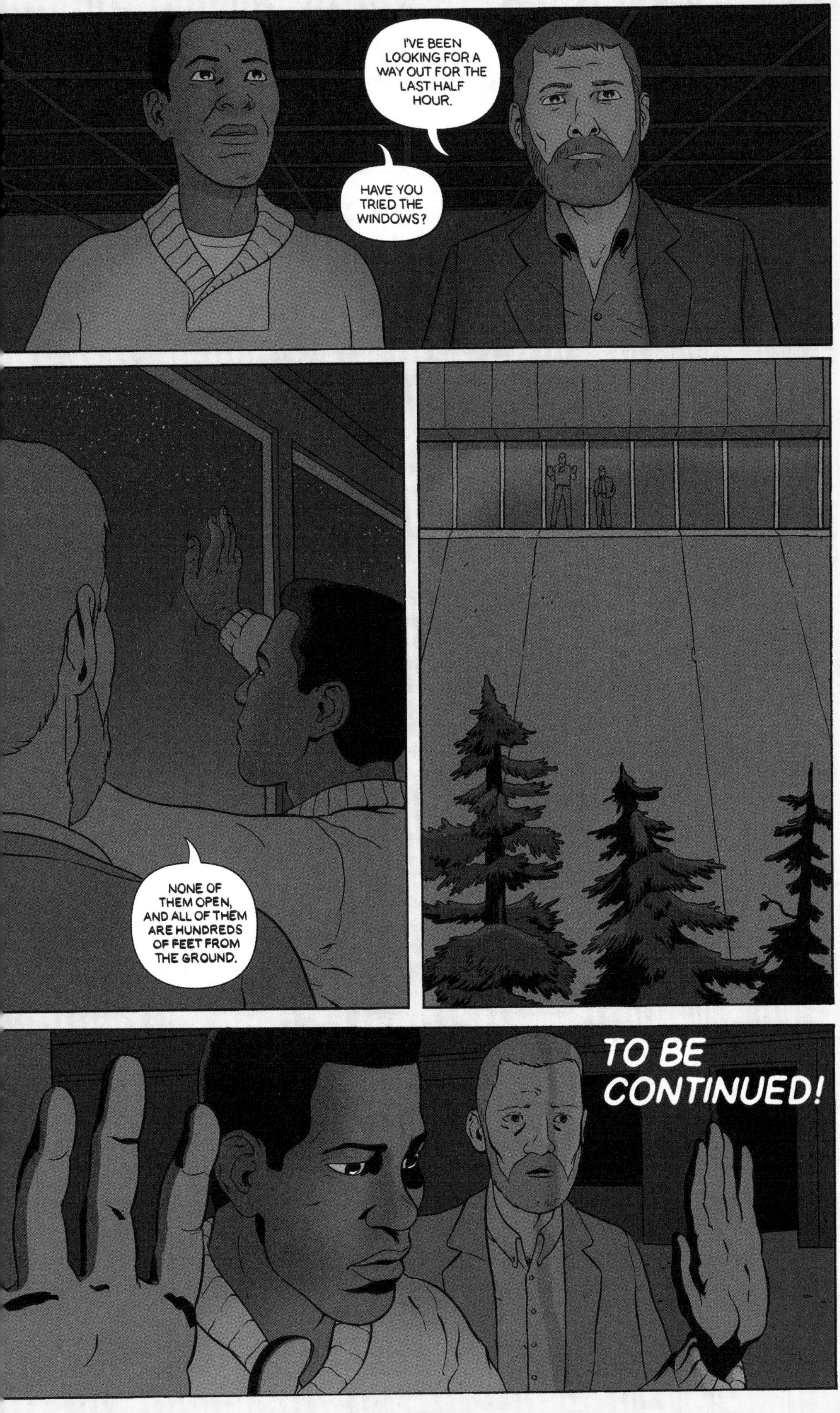
I'VE BEEN LOOKING FOR A WAY OUT FOR THE LAST HALF HOUR.
HAVE YOU TRIED THE WINDOWS?
NONE OF THEM OPEN, AND ALL OF THEM ARE HUNDREDS OF FEET FROM THE GROUND.
TO BE CONTINUED!

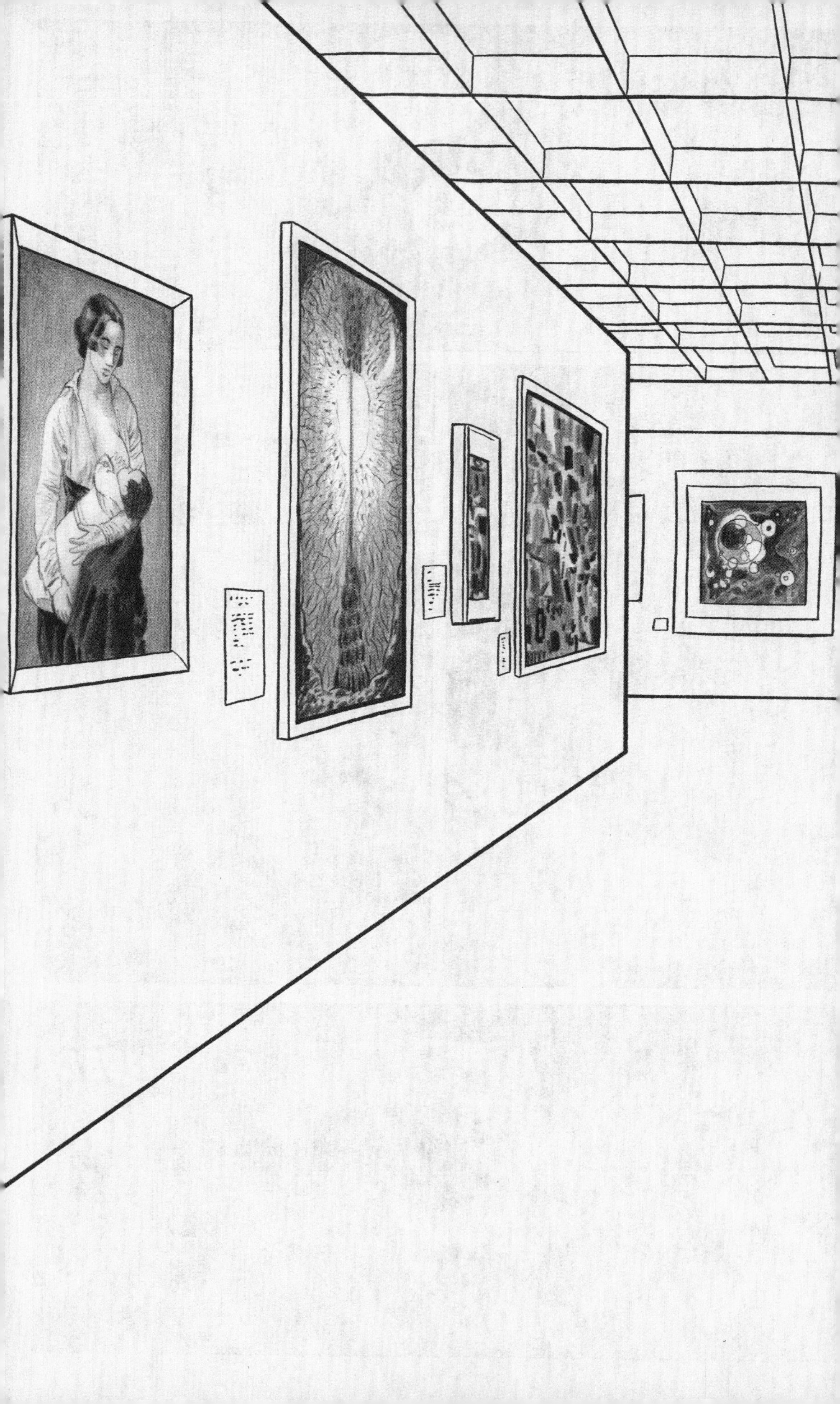

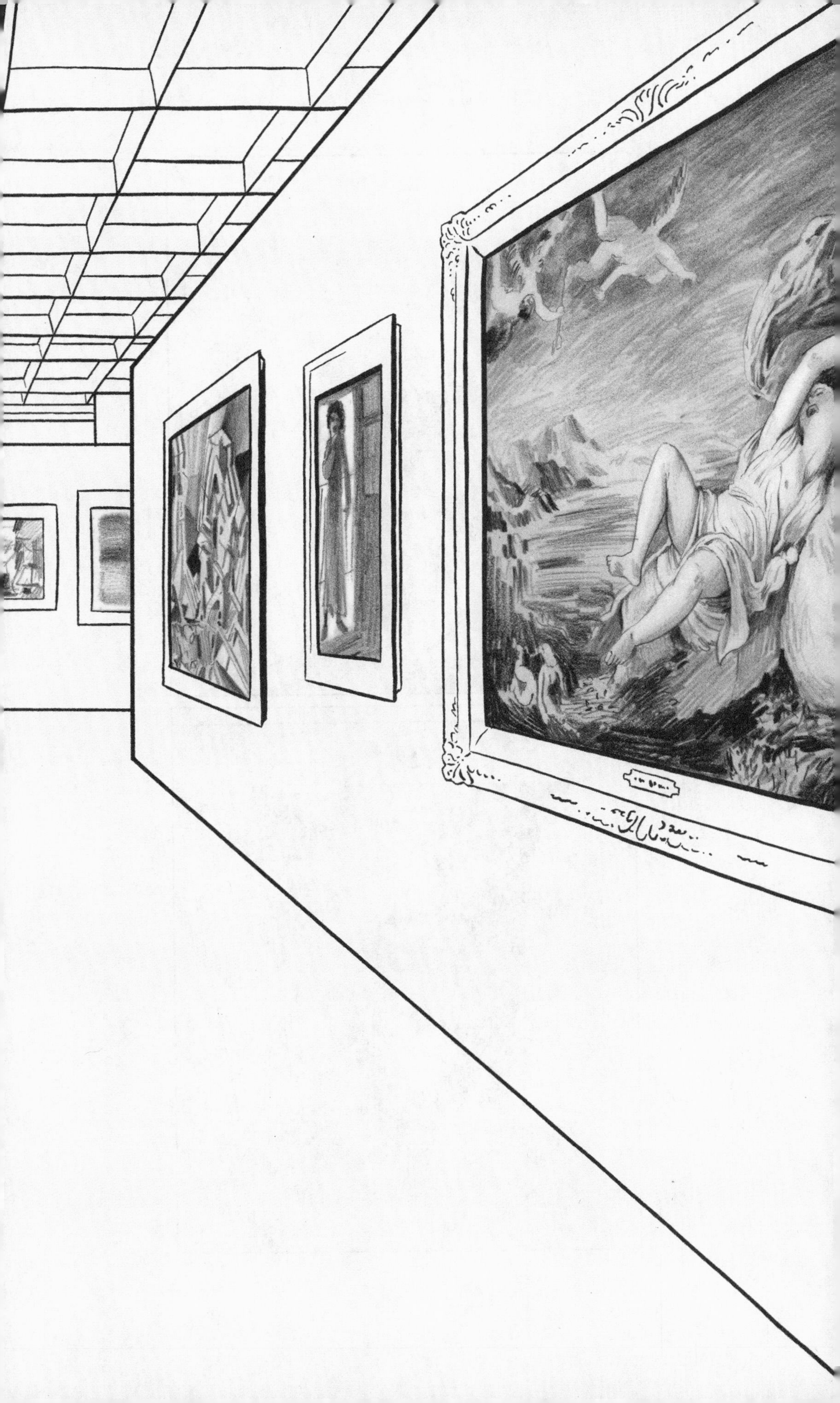

ANCESTOR, BY MATT SHEEAN AND MALACHI WARD.

PART TWO OF FOUR: *A RAPTUROUS EXPERIENCE*.

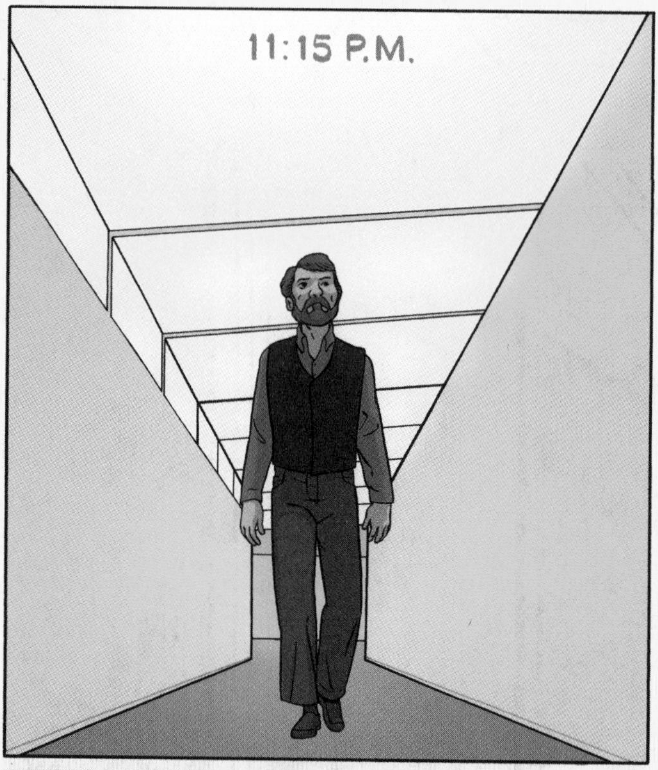
11:15 P.M.

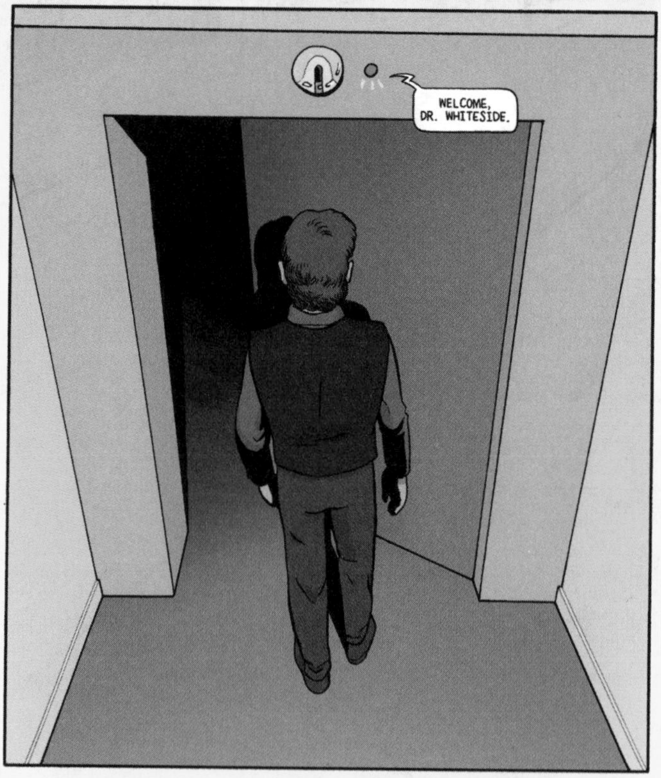
WELCOME, DR. WHITESIDE.

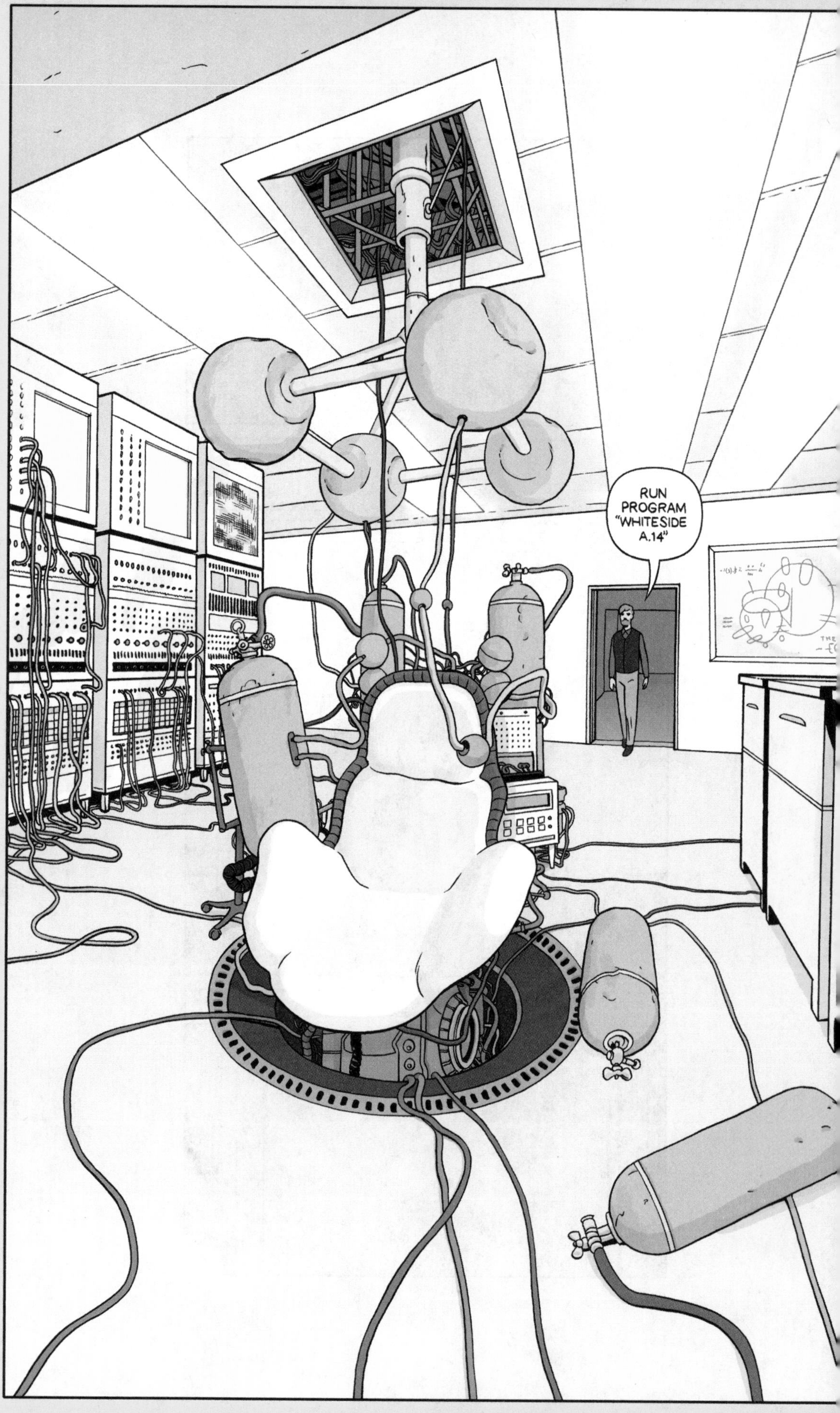
RUN PROGRAM "WHITESIDE A.14"

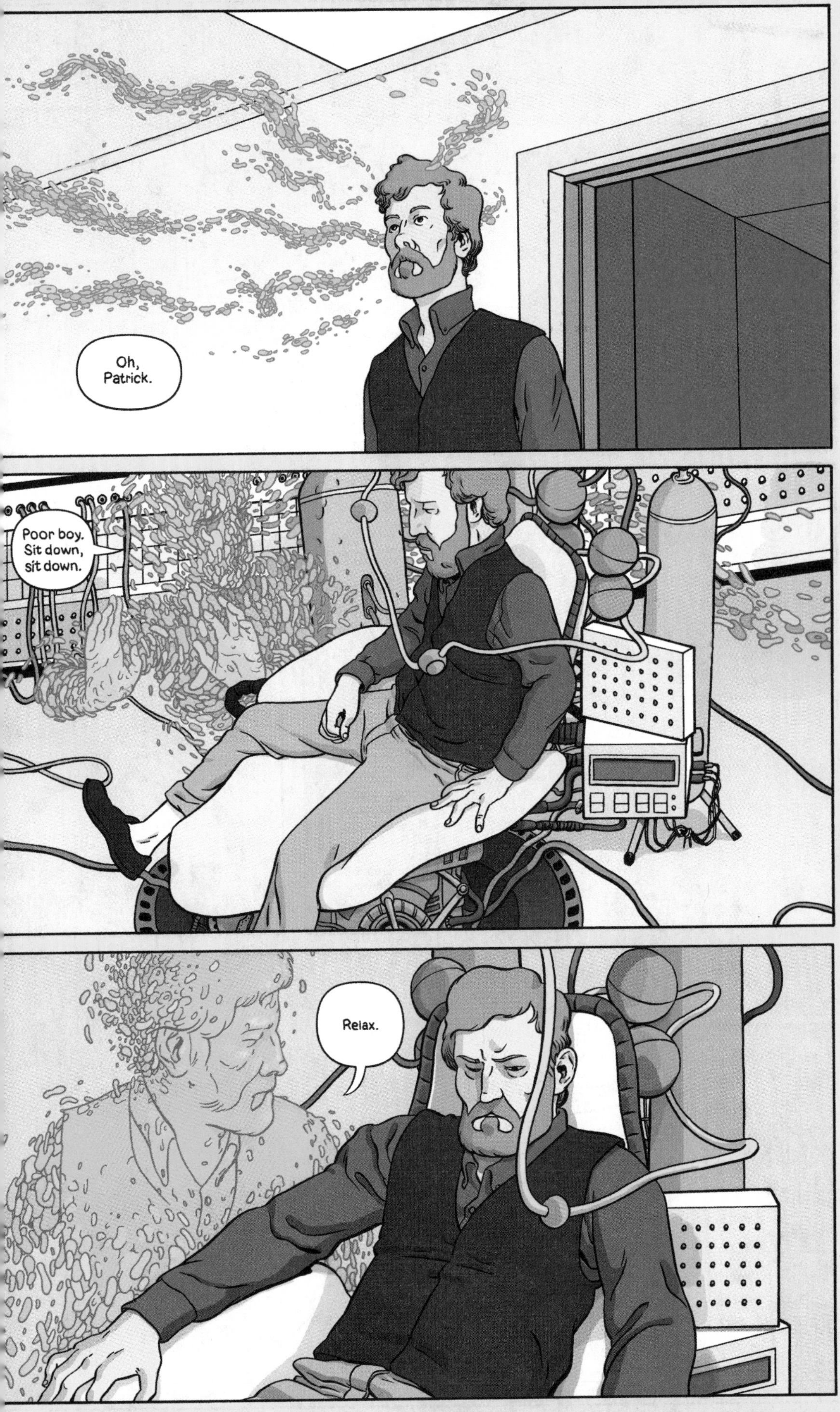
Oh, Patrick.
Poor boy. Sit down, sit down.
Relax.

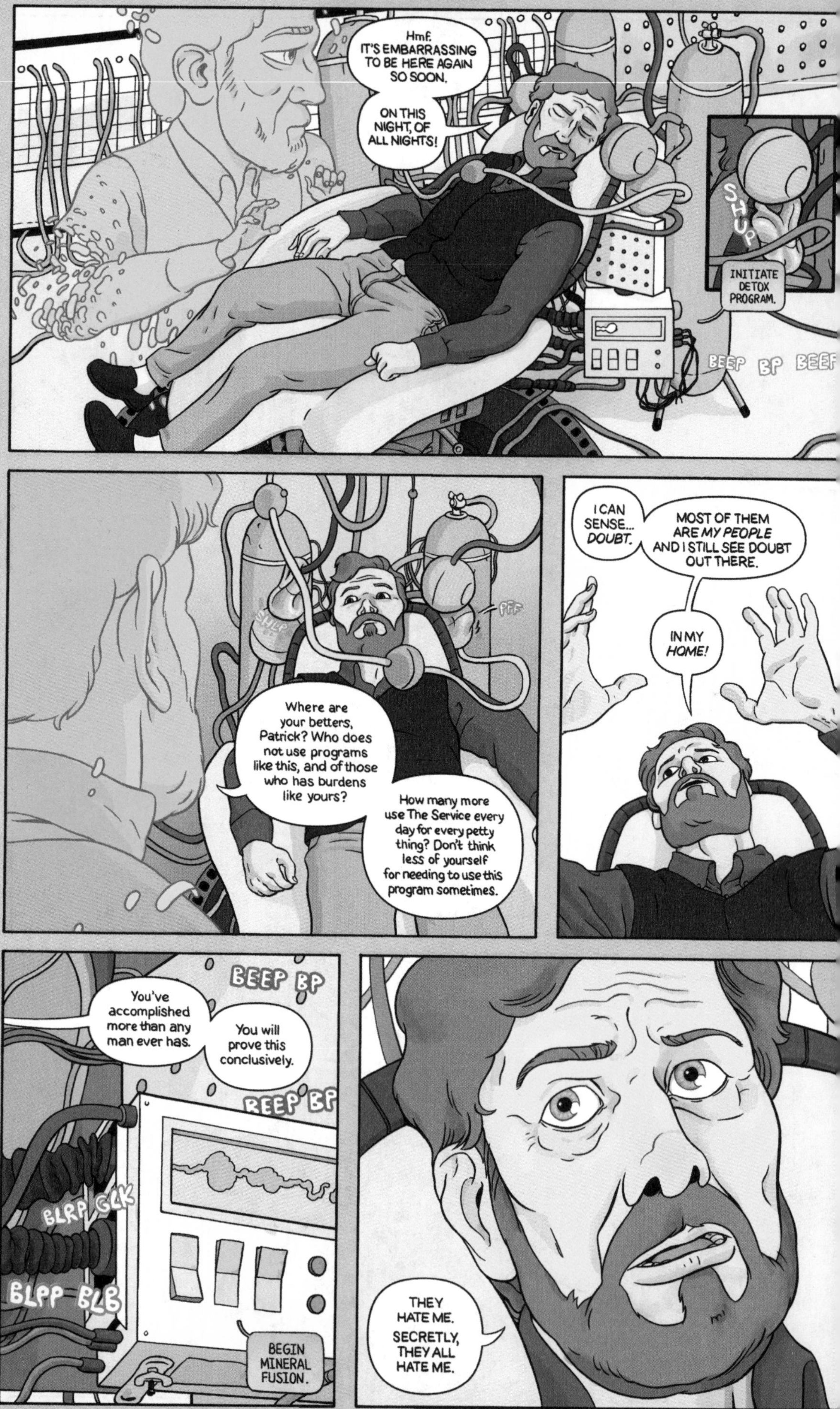
Hmf. IT'S EMBARRASSING TO BE HERE AGAIN SO SOON.
ON THIS NIGHT, OF ALL NIGHTS!
SHUP
INITIATE DETOX PROGRAM.
BEEP BP BEEP
SHLP
PFF
Where are your betters, Patrick? Who does not use programs like this, and of those who has burdens like yours?
How many more use The Service every day for every petty thing? Don't think less of yourself for needing to use this program sometimes.
I CAN SENSE... *DOUBT.*
MOST OF THEM ARE *MY PEOPLE* AND I STILL SEE DOUBT OUT THERE.
IN MY *HOME!*
BEEP BP
You've accomplished more than any man ever has.
You will prove this conclusively.
BEEP BP
BLRP GLK
BLPP BLB
BEGIN MINERAL FUSION.
THEY HATE ME.
SECRETLY, THEY ALL HATE ME.

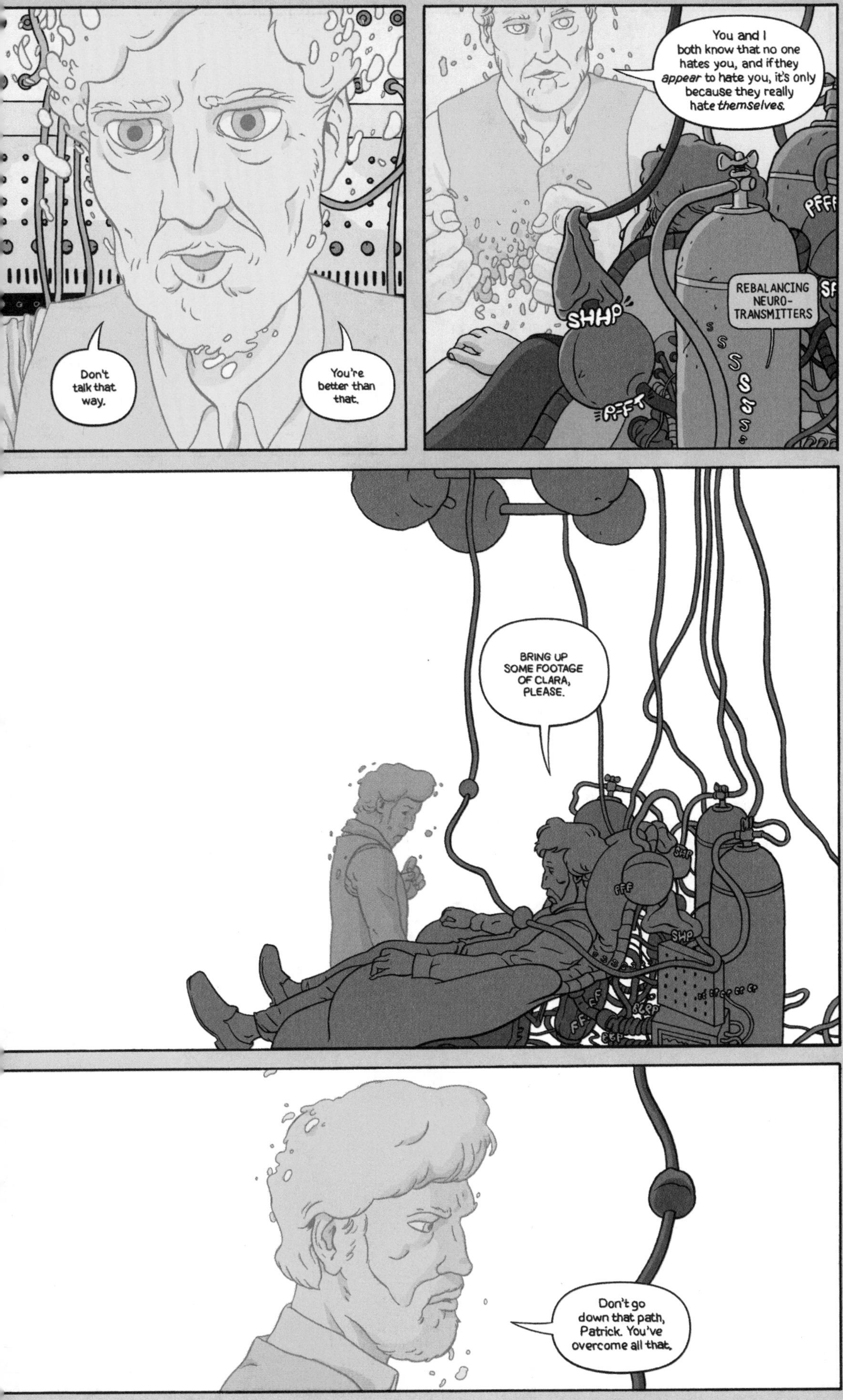
Don't talk that way.
You're better than that.
You and I both know that no one hates you, and if they *appear* to hate you, it's only because they really hate *themselves.*
SHHP
PFFT
PFFF
REBALANCING NEURO-TRANSMITTERS
BRING UP SOME FOOTAGE OF CLARA, PLEASE.
Don't go down that path, Patrick. You've overcome all that.

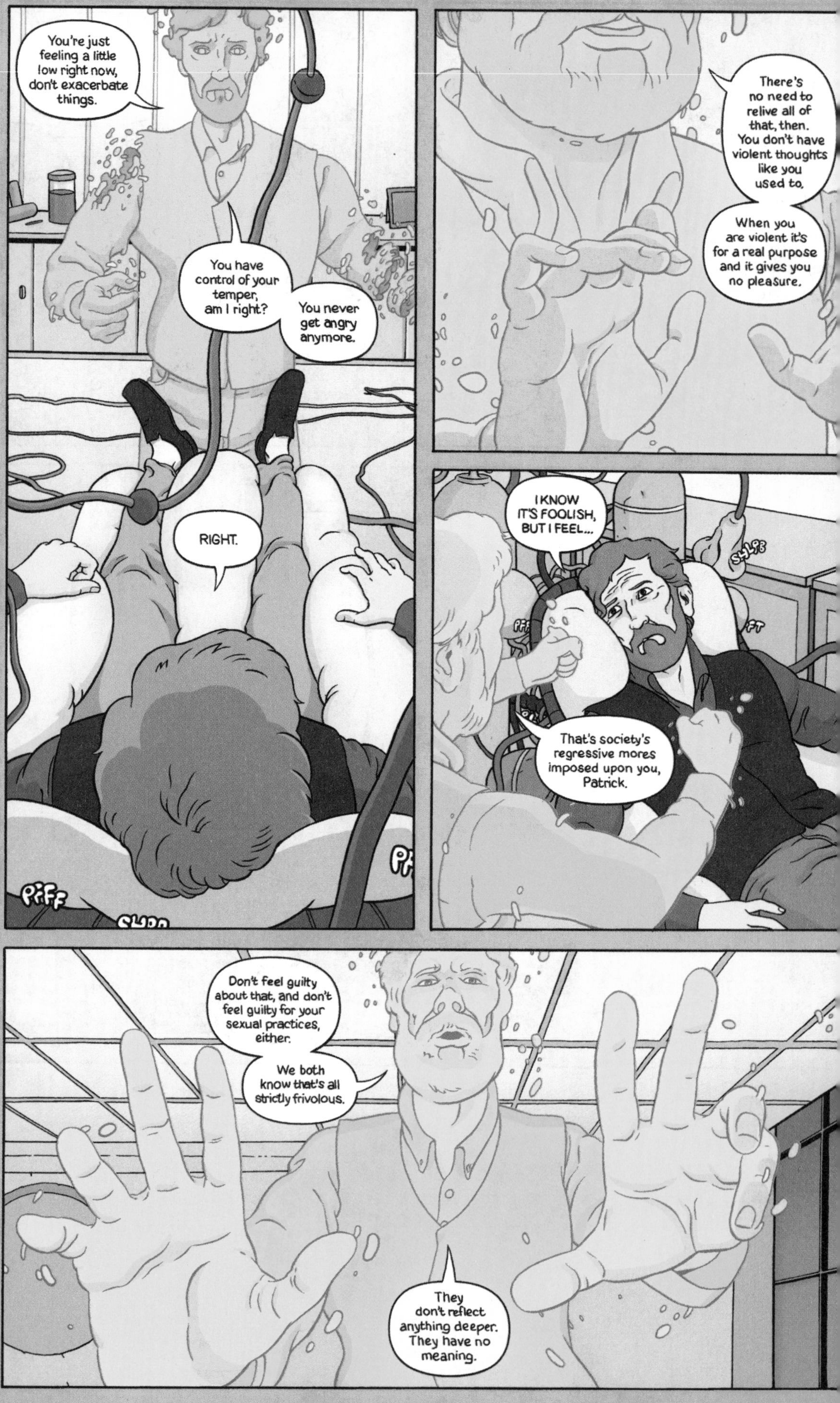
You're just feeling a little low right now, don't exacerbate things.
You have control of your temper, am I right?
You never get angry anymore.
RIGHT.
There's no need to relive all of that, then. You don't have violent thoughts like you used to.
When you are violent it's for a real purpose and it gives you no pleasure.
I KNOW IT'S FOOLISH, BUT I FEEL...
That's society's regressive mores imposed upon you, Patrick.
Don't feel guilty about that, and don't feel guilty for your sexual practices, either.
We both know that's all strictly frivolous.
They don't reflect anything deeper. They have no meaning.

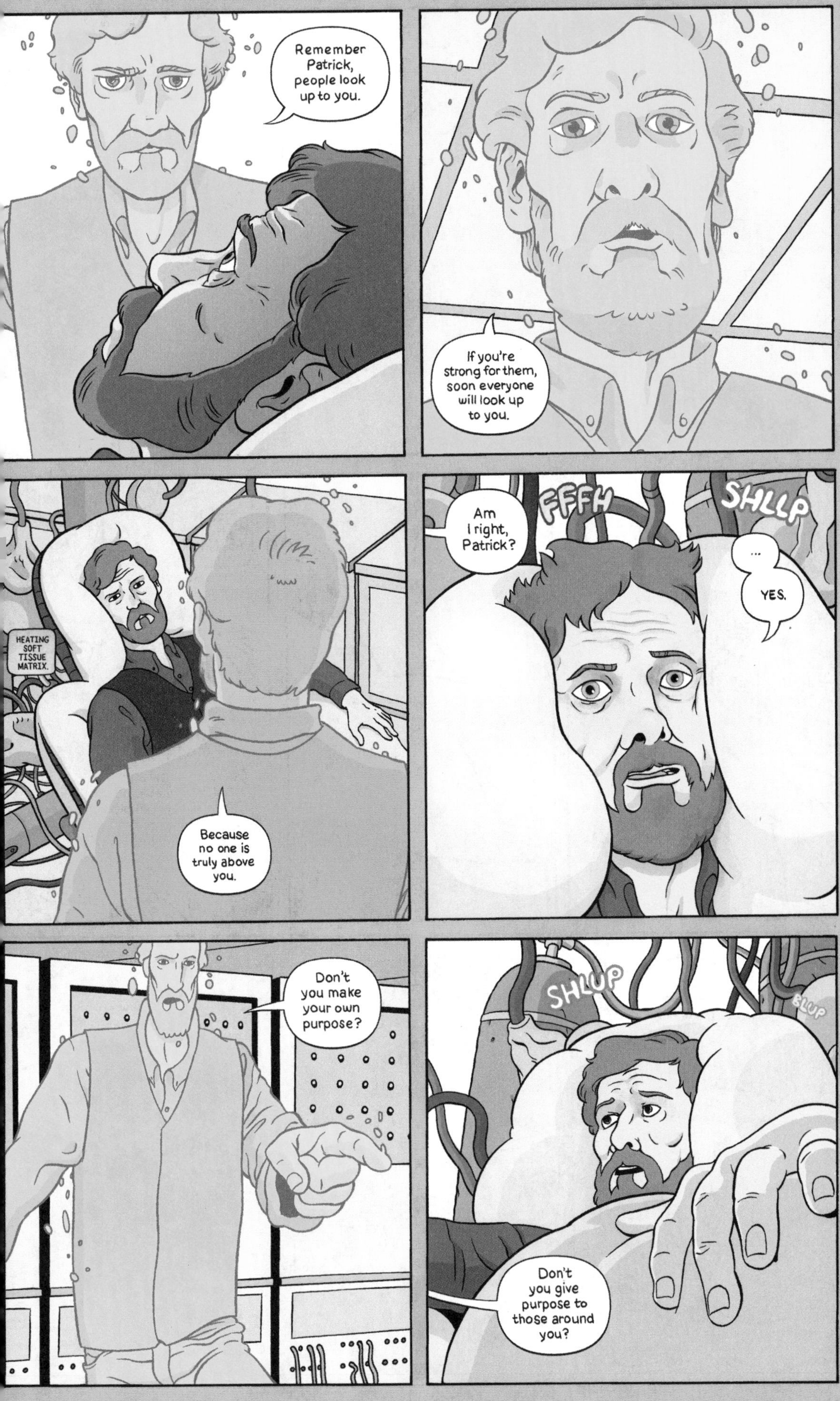
Remember Patrick, people look up to you.
If you're strong for them, soon everyone will look up to you.
HEATING SOFT TISSUE MATRIX.
Because no one is truly above you.
Am I right, Patrick?
FFFH
SHLLP
...
YES.
Don't you make your own purpose?
SHLUP
BLUP
Don't you give purpose to those around you?

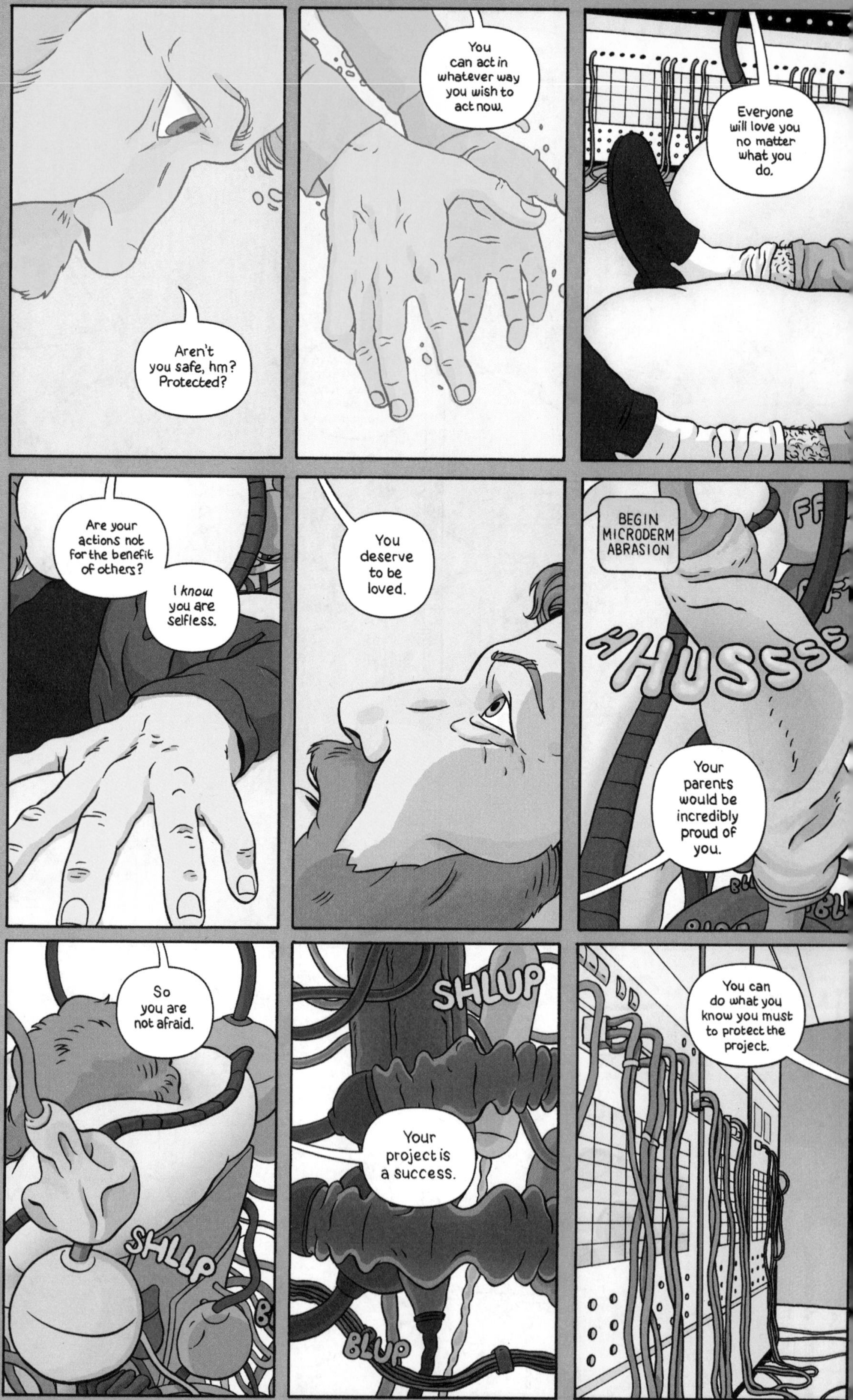

Aren't you safe, hm? Protected?
You can act in whatever way you wish to act now.
Everyone will love you no matter what you do.
Are your actions not for the benefit of others?
I *know* you are selfless.
You deserve to be loved.
BEGIN MICRODERM ABRASION
HUSSS
Your parents would be incredibly proud of you.
So you are not afraid.
SHLLP
SHLUP
Your project is a success.
BLUP
You can do what you know you must to protect the project.

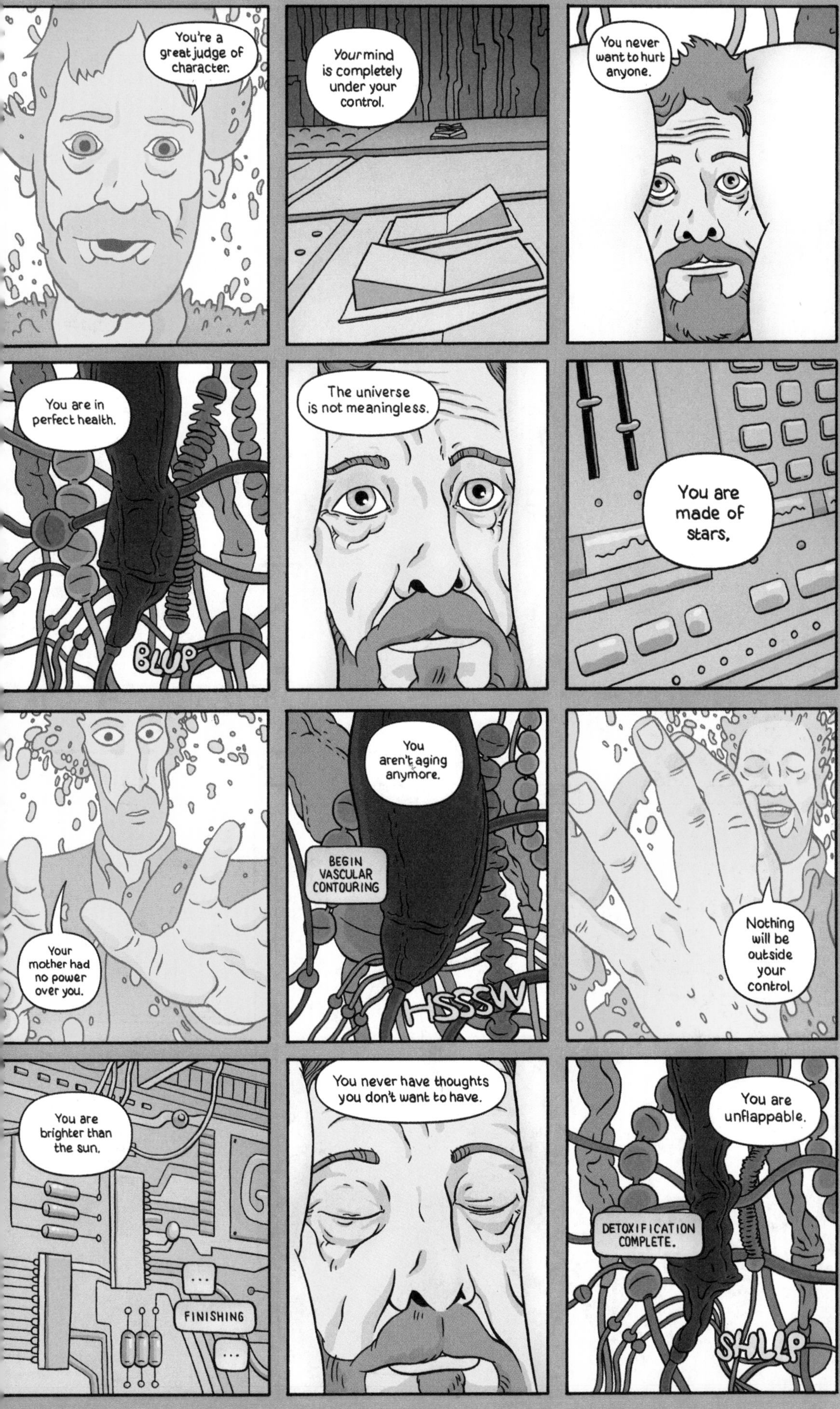

You're a great judge of character.
Your mind is completely under your control.
You never want to hurt anyone.
You are in perfect health.
BLUP
The universe is not meaningless.
You are made of stars.
Your mother had no power over you.
You aren't aging anymore.
BEGIN VASCULAR CONTOURING
HSSSW
Nothing will be outside your control.
You are brighter than the sun.
...
FINISHING
...
You never have thoughts you don't want to have.
You are unflappable.
DETOXIFICATION COMPLETE.
SHLLP

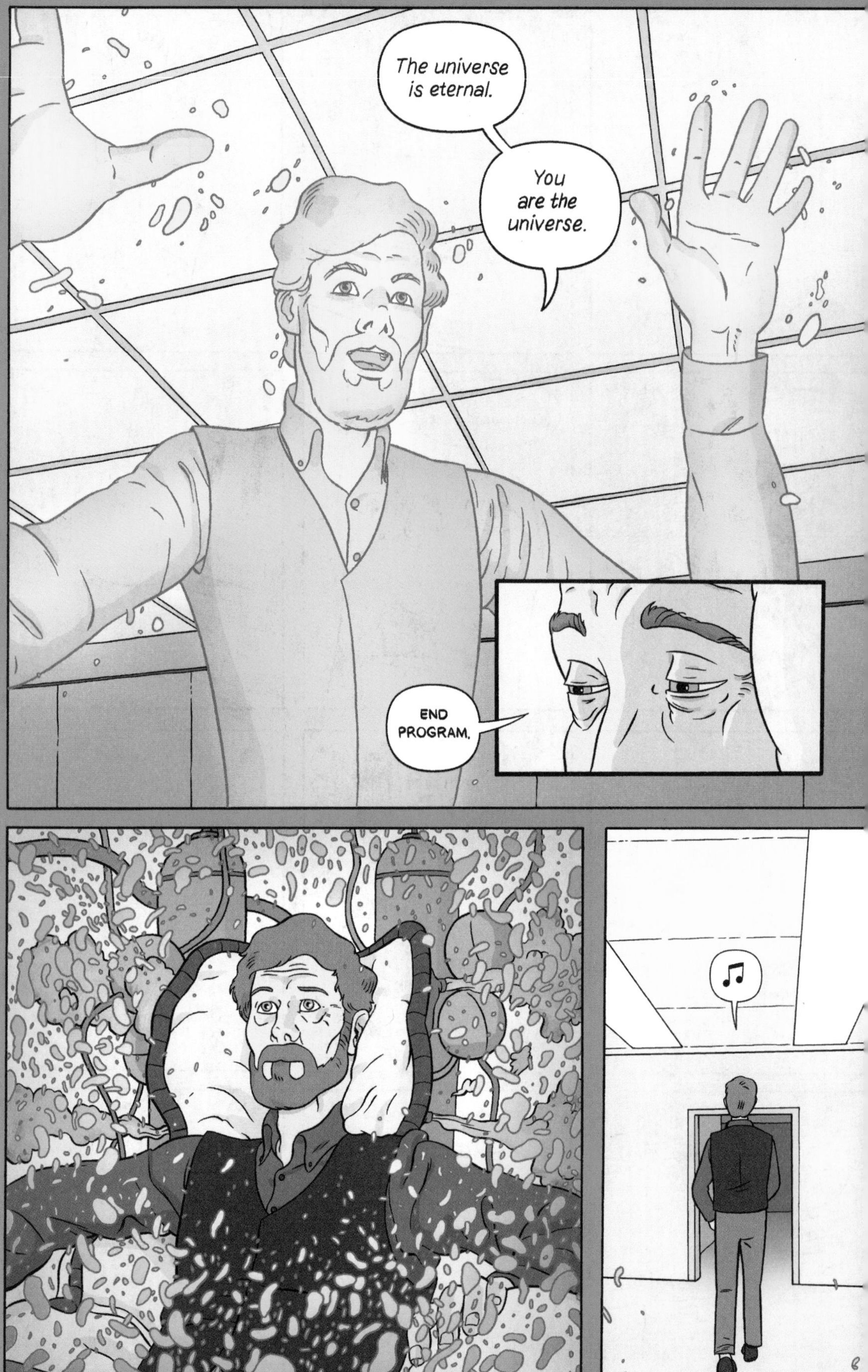
The universe is eternal.
You are the universe.
END PROGRAM.
♫

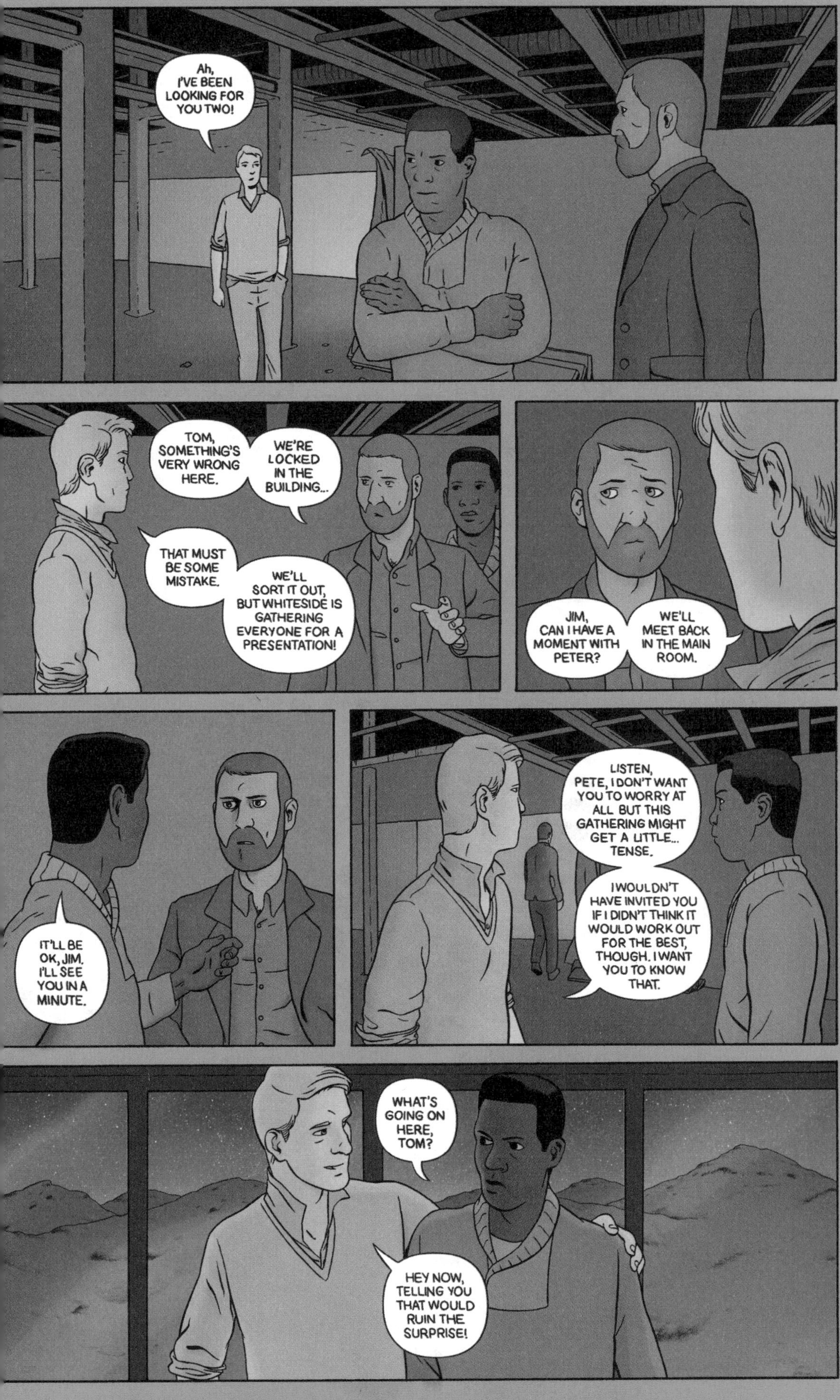
Ah, I'VE BEEN LOOKING FOR YOU TWO!
TOM, SOMETHING'S VERY WRONG HERE.
WE'RE LOCKED IN THE BUILDING...
THAT MUST BE SOME MISTAKE.
WE'LL SORT IT OUT, BUT WHITESIDE IS GATHERING EVERYONE FOR A PRESENTATION!
JIM, CAN I HAVE A MOMENT WITH PETER?
WE'LL MEET BACK IN THE MAIN ROOM.
IT'LL BE OK, JIM. I'LL SEE YOU IN A MINUTE.
LISTEN, PETE, I DON'T WANT YOU TO WORRY AT ALL BUT THIS GATHERING MIGHT GET A LITTLE... TENSE.
I WOULDN'T HAVE INVITED YOU IF I DIDN'T THINK IT WOULD WORK OUT FOR THE BEST, THOUGH. I WANT YOU TO KNOW THAT.
WHAT'S GOING ON HERE, TOM?
HEY NOW, TELLING YOU THAT WOULD RUIN THE SURPRISE!

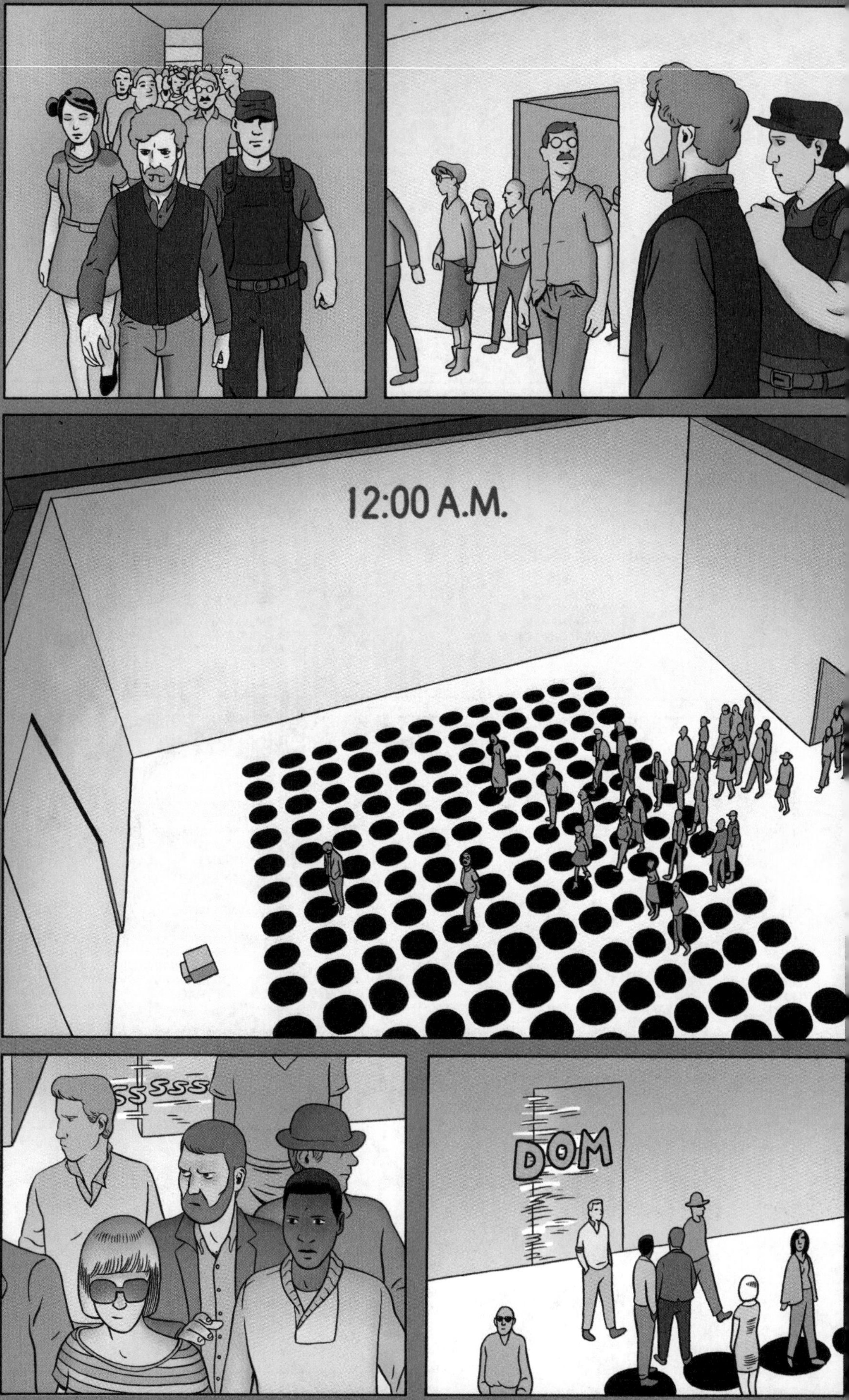

12:00 A.M.
DOM

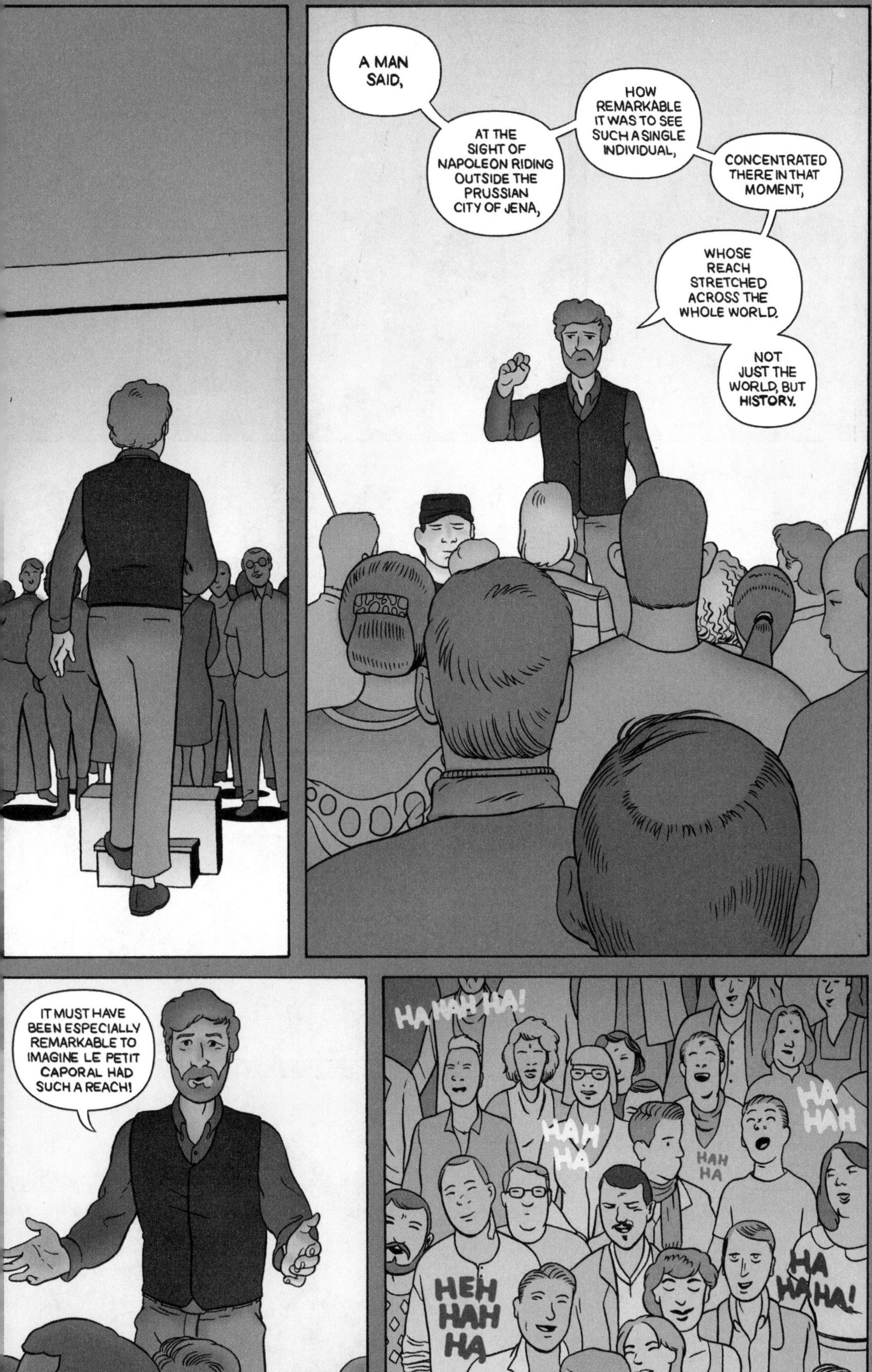
A MAN SAID,
AT THE SIGHT OF NAPOLEON RIDING OUTSIDE THE PRUSSIAN CITY OF JENA,
HOW REMARKABLE IT WAS TO SEE SUCH A SINGLE INDIVIDUAL,
CONCENTRATED THERE IN THAT MOMENT,
WHOSE REACH STRETCHED ACROSS THE WHOLE WORLD.
NOT JUST THE WORLD, BUT HISTORY.
IT MUST HAVE BEEN ESPECIALLY REMARKABLE TO IMAGINE LE PETIT CAPORAL HAD SUCH A REACH!
HA HAH HA!
HAH HA
HAH HA
HA HAH
HEH HAH HA
HA HA HA!

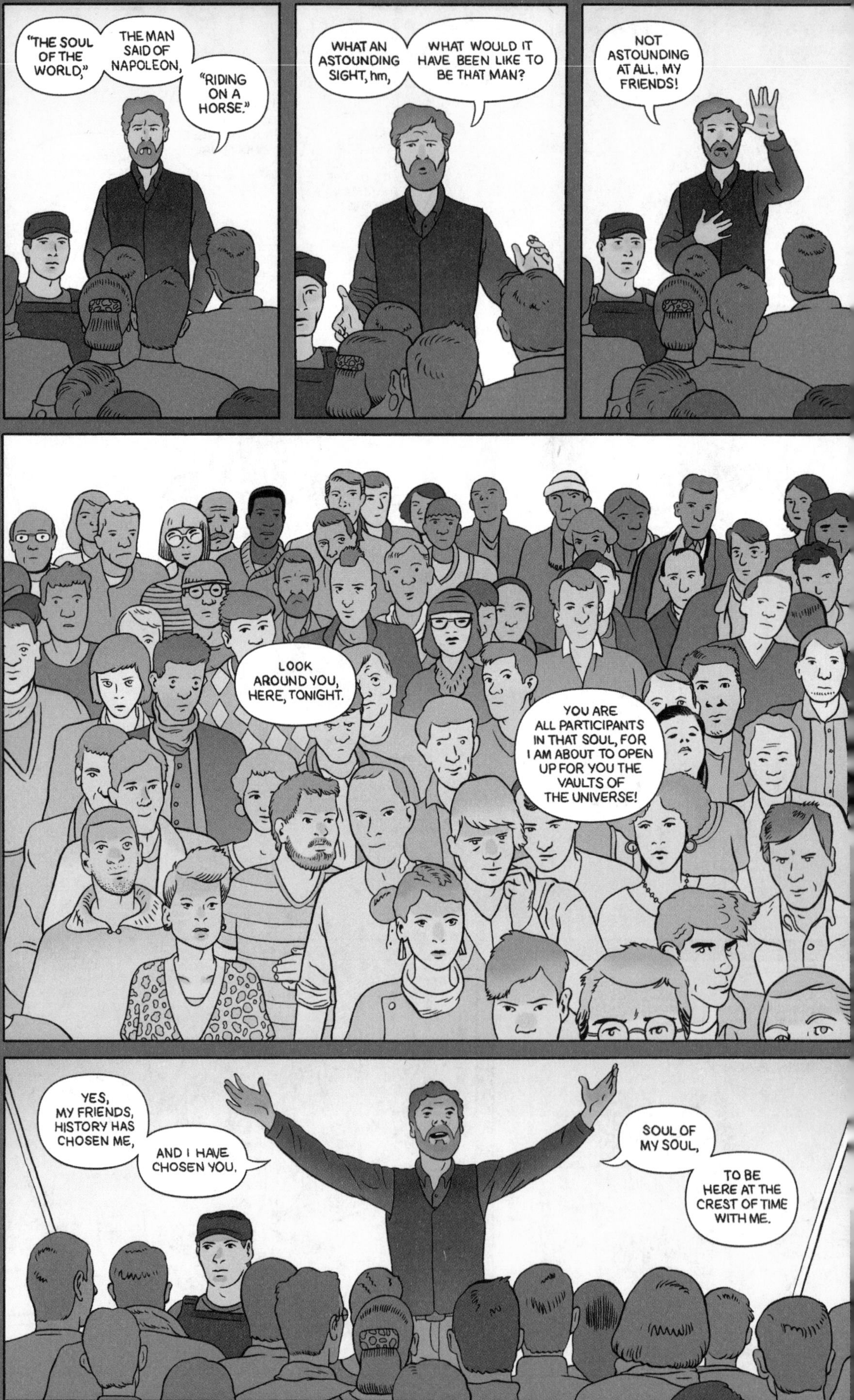
"THE SOUL OF THE WORLD,"
THE MAN SAID OF NAPOLEON,
"RIDING ON A HORSE."
WHAT AN ASTOUNDING SIGHT, hm,
WHAT WOULD IT HAVE BEEN LIKE TO BE THAT MAN?
NOT ASTOUNDING AT ALL, MY FRIENDS!
LOOK AROUND YOU, HERE, TONIGHT.
YOU ARE ALL PARTICIPANTS IN THAT SOUL, FOR I AM ABOUT TO OPEN UP FOR YOU THE VAULTS OF THE UNIVERSE!
YES, MY FRIENDS, HISTORY HAS CHOSEN ME,
AND I HAVE CHOSEN YOU.
SOUL OF MY SOUL,
TO BE HERE AT THE CREST OF TIME WITH ME.

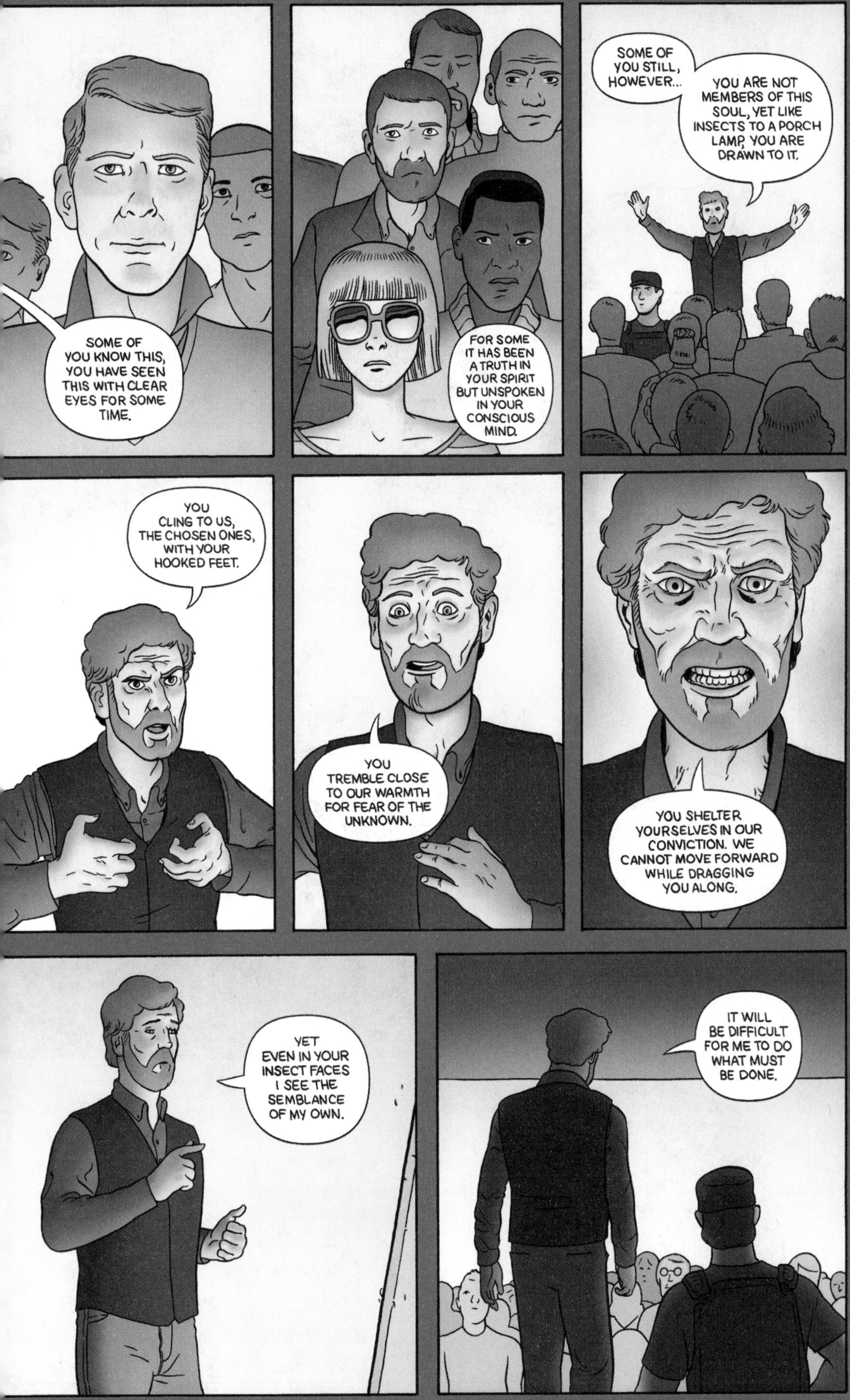
SOME OF YOU KNOW THIS, YOU HAVE SEEN THIS WITH CLEAR EYES FOR SOME TIME.
FOR SOME IT HAS BEEN A TRUTH IN YOUR SPIRIT BUT UNSPOKEN IN YOUR CONSCIOUS MIND.
SOME OF YOU STILL, HOWEVER...
YOU ARE NOT MEMBERS OF THIS SOUL, YET LIKE INSECTS TO A PORCH LAMP, YOU ARE DRAWN TO IT.
YOU CLING TO US, THE CHOSEN ONES, WITH YOUR HOOKED FEET.
YOU TREMBLE CLOSE TO OUR WARMTH FOR FEAR OF THE UNKNOWN.
YOU SHELTER YOURSELVES IN OUR CONVICTION. WE CANNOT MOVE FORWARD WHILE DRAGGING YOU ALONG.
YET EVEN IN YOUR INSECT FACES I SEE THE SEMBLANCE OF MY OWN.
IT WILL BE DIFFICULT FOR ME TO DO WHAT MUST BE DONE.

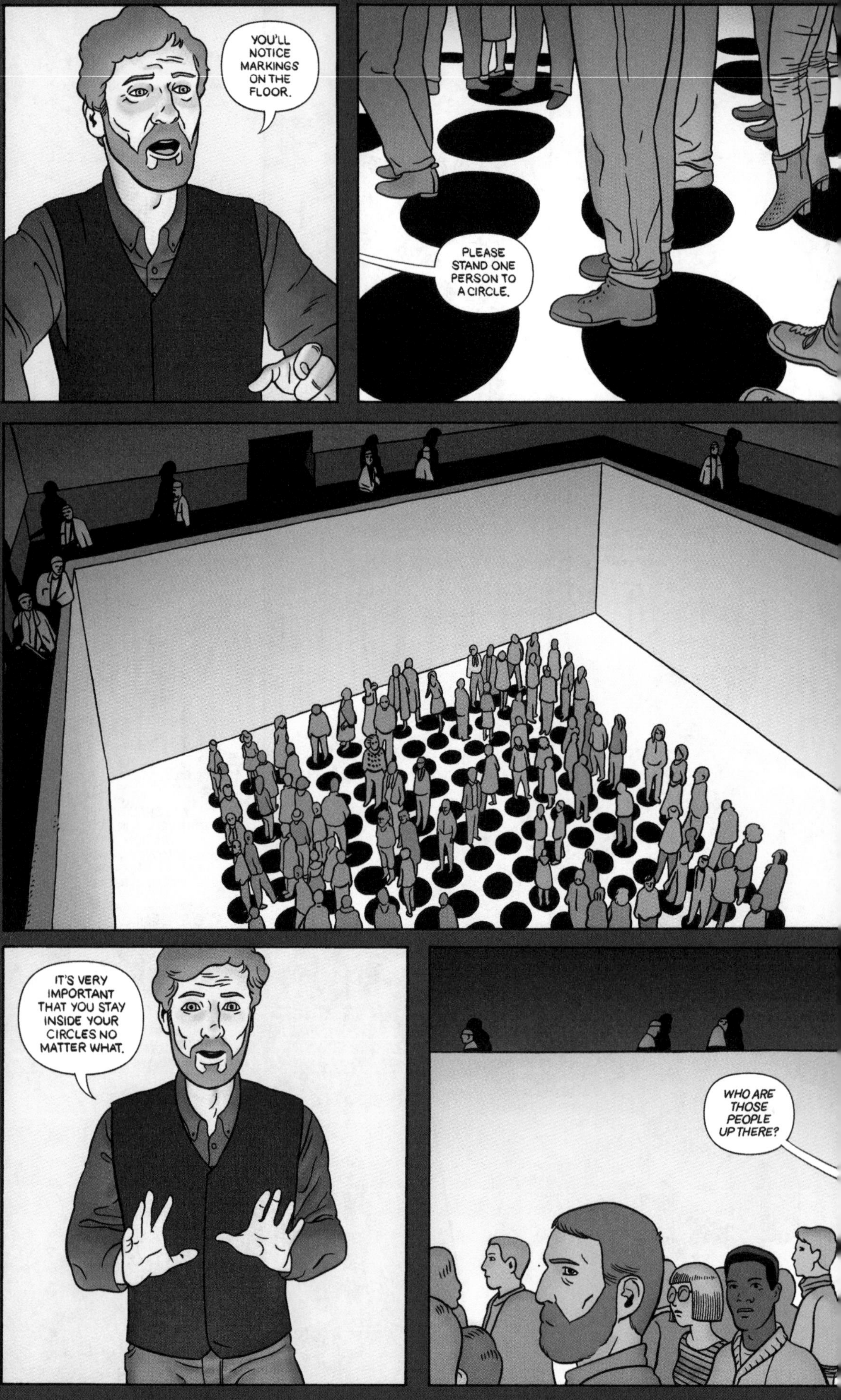
YOU'LL NOTICE MARKINGS ON THE FLOOR.
PLEASE STAND ONE PERSON TO A CIRCLE.
IT'S VERY IMPORTANT THAT YOU STAY INSIDE YOUR CIRCLES NO MATTER WHAT.
WHO ARE THOSE PEOPLE UP THERE?

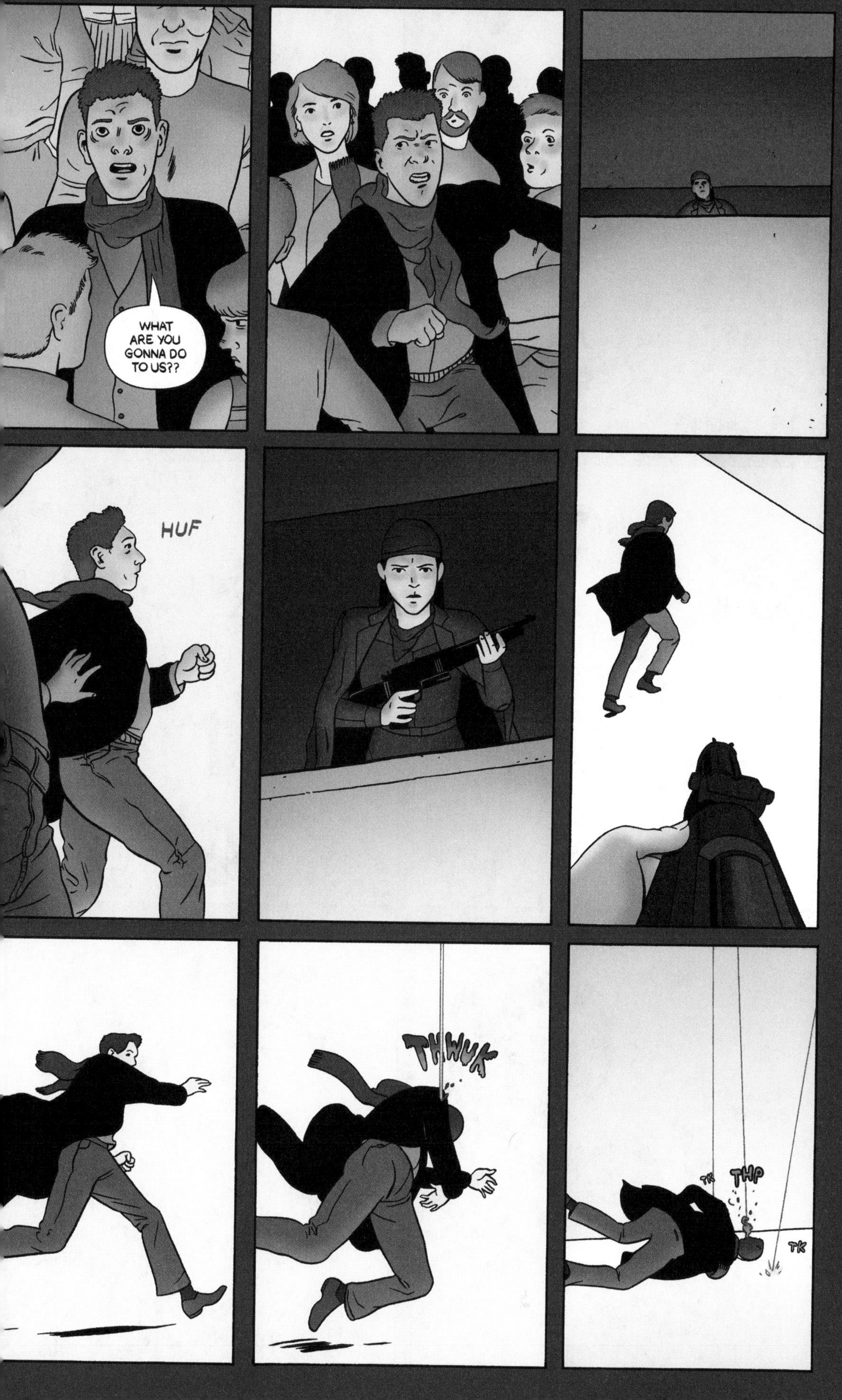
WHAT ARE YOU GONNA DO TO US??
HUF
THWUK
TK
THP
TK

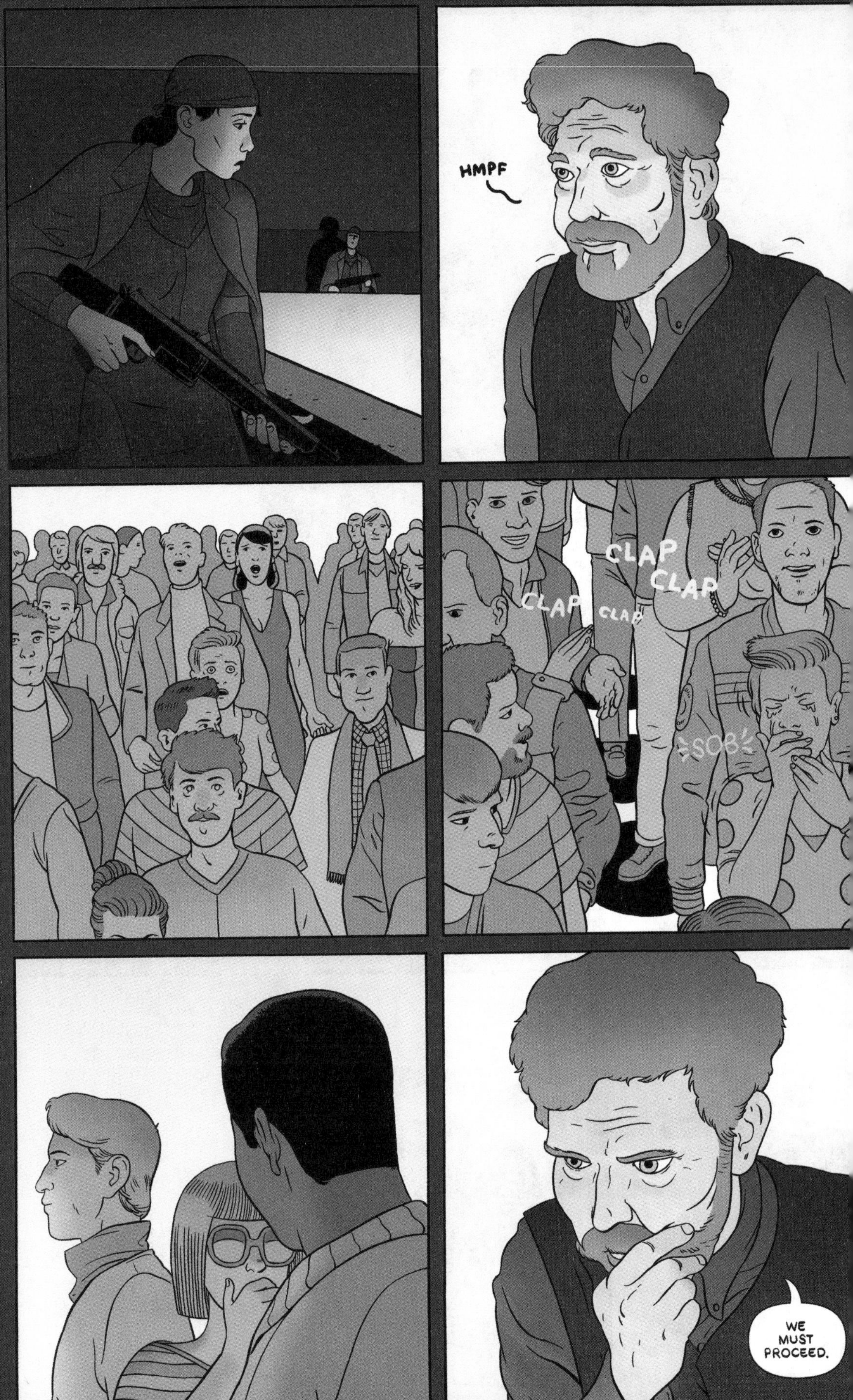
HMPF
CLAP
CLAP
CLAP
CLAP
CLAP
SOB
WE MUST PROCEED.

I WILL BE SPEAKING WITH EACH OF YOU INDIVIDUALLY.

EVERYONE ELSE PLEASE REMAIN QUIET. THE INTERVIEWS REQUIRE QUITE A BIT OF CONCENTRATION.

DID YOU KNOW ABOUT THIS?!

I'M CERTAIN YOU'LL ALL BE APPROVED!

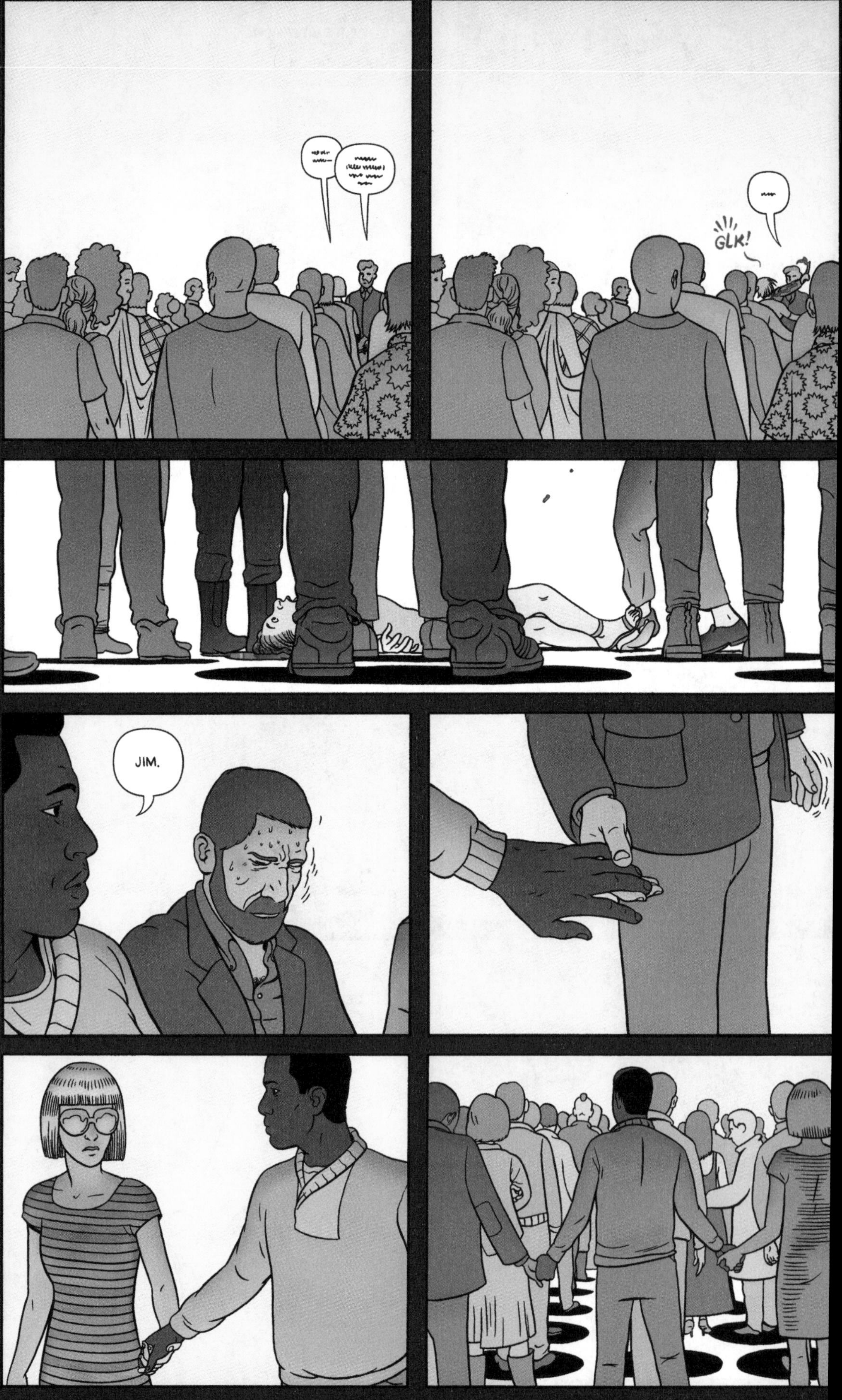
GLK!
JIM.

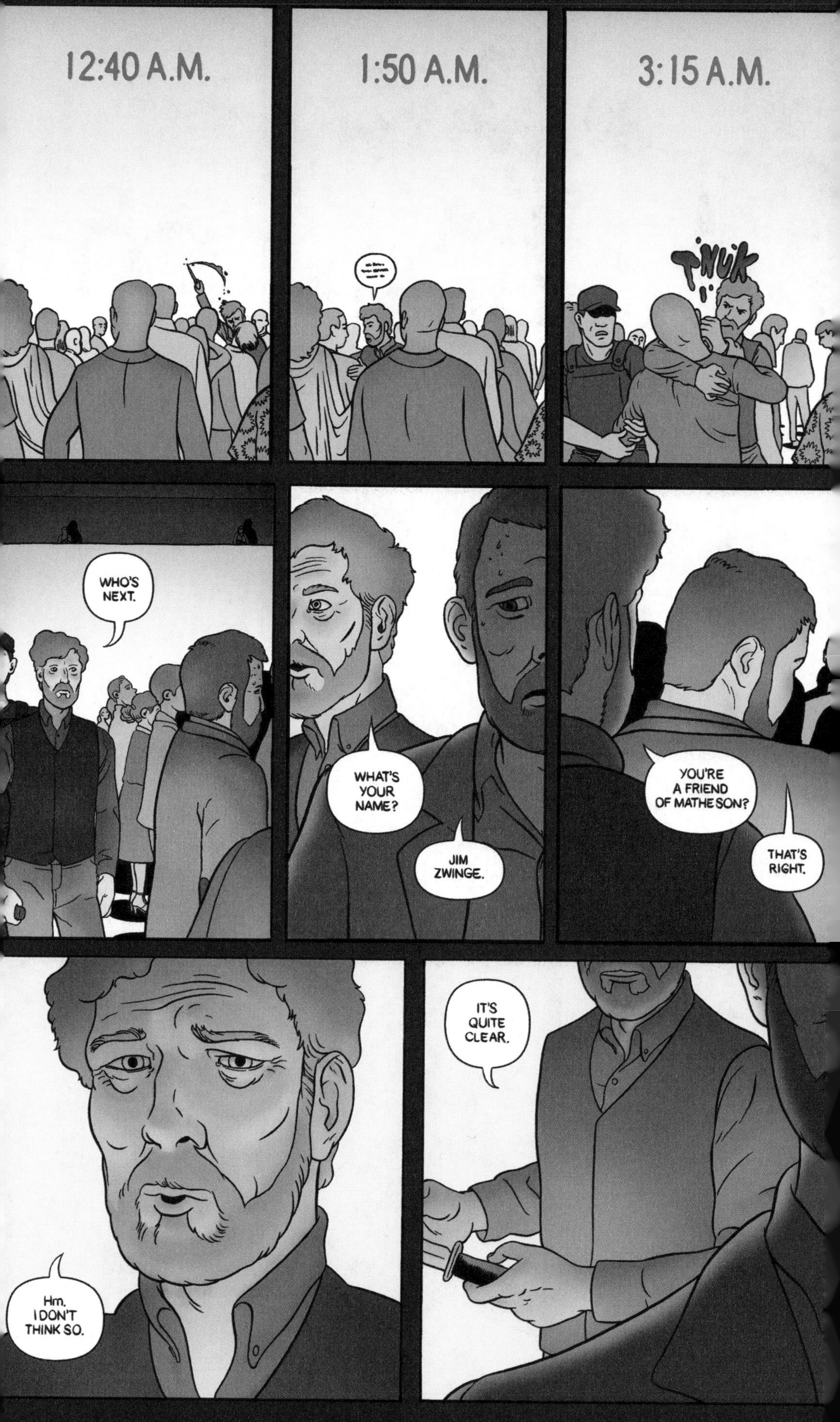
12:40 A.M.
1:50 A.M.
3:15 A.M.
THUK
WHO'S NEXT.
WHAT'S YOUR NAME?
JIM ZWINGE.
YOU'RE A FRIEND OF MATHESON?
THAT'S RIGHT.
Hm, I DON'T THINK SO.
IT'S QUITE CLEAR.

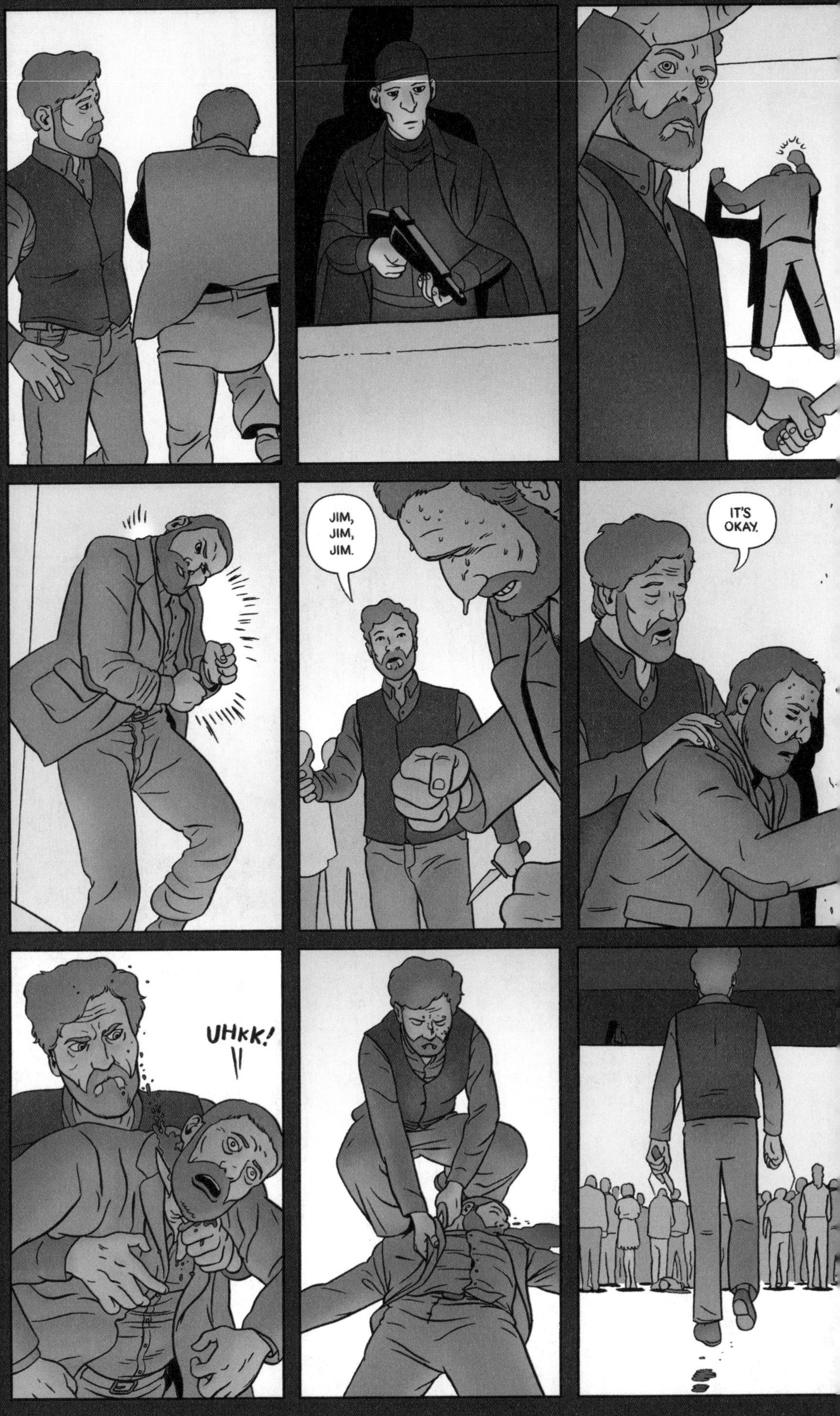
JIM, JIM, JIM.
IT'S OKAY.
UHKK!

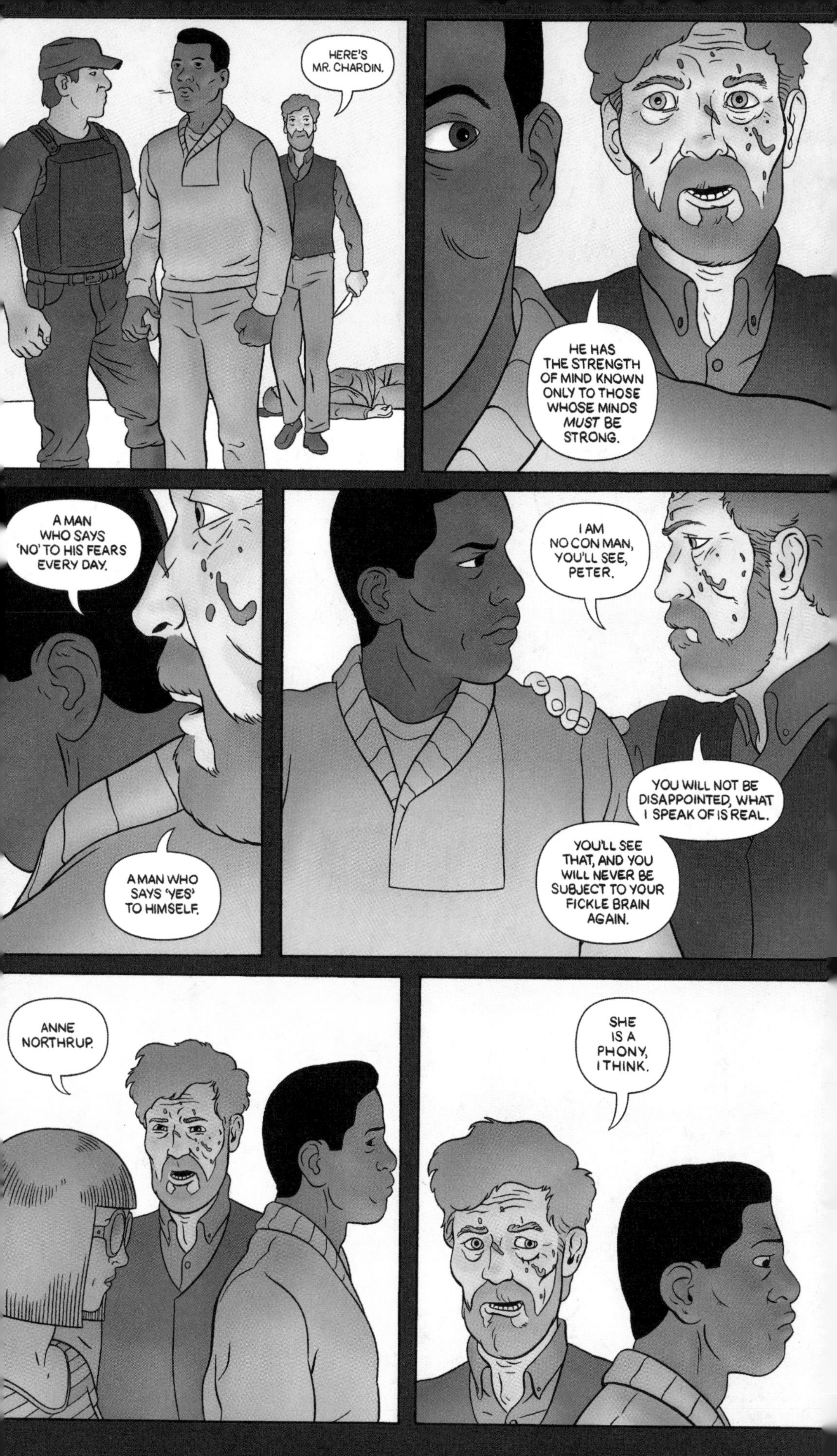
HERE'S MR. CHARDIN.
HE HAS THE STRENGTH OF MIND KNOWN ONLY TO THOSE WHOSE MINDS *MUST* BE STRONG.
A MAN WHO SAYS 'NO' TO HIS FEARS EVERY DAY.
A MAN WHO SAYS 'YES' TO HIMSELF.
I AM NO CON MAN, YOU'LL SEE, PETER.
YOU WILL NOT BE DISAPPOINTED, WHAT I SPEAK OF IS REAL.
YOU'LL SEE THAT, AND YOU WILL NEVER BE SUBJECT TO YOUR FICKLE BRAIN AGAIN.
ANNE NORTHRUP.
SHE IS A PHONY, I THINK.

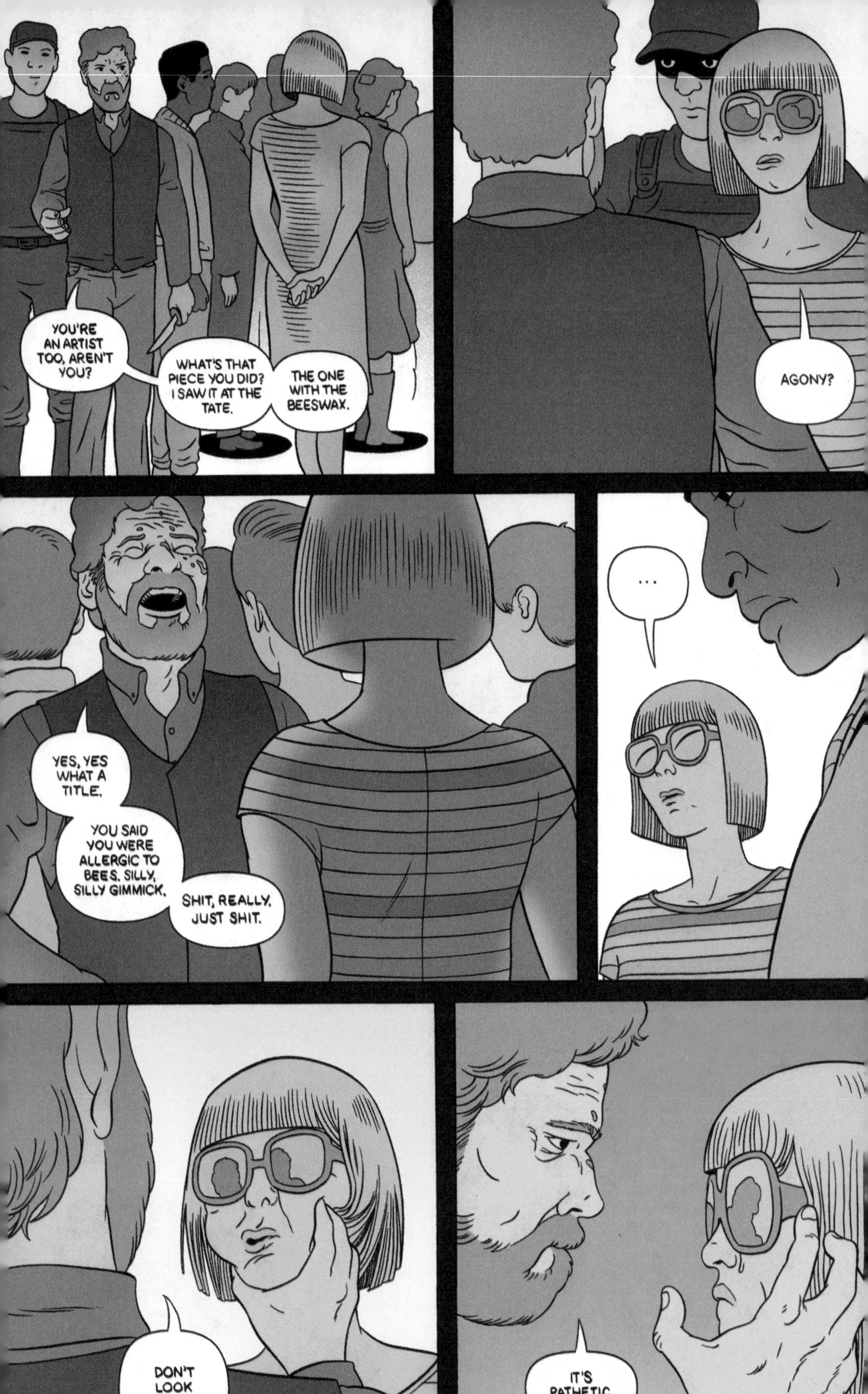
YOU'RE AN ARTIST TOO, AREN'T YOU?
WHAT'S THAT PIECE YOU DID? I SAW IT AT THE TATE.
THE ONE WITH THE BEESWAX.
AGONY?
YES, YES WHAT A TITLE.
YOU SAID YOU WERE ALLERGIC TO BEES. SILLY, SILLY GIMMICK.
SHIT, REALLY. JUST SHIT.
...
DON'T LOOK AT HIM.
IT'S PATHETIC.

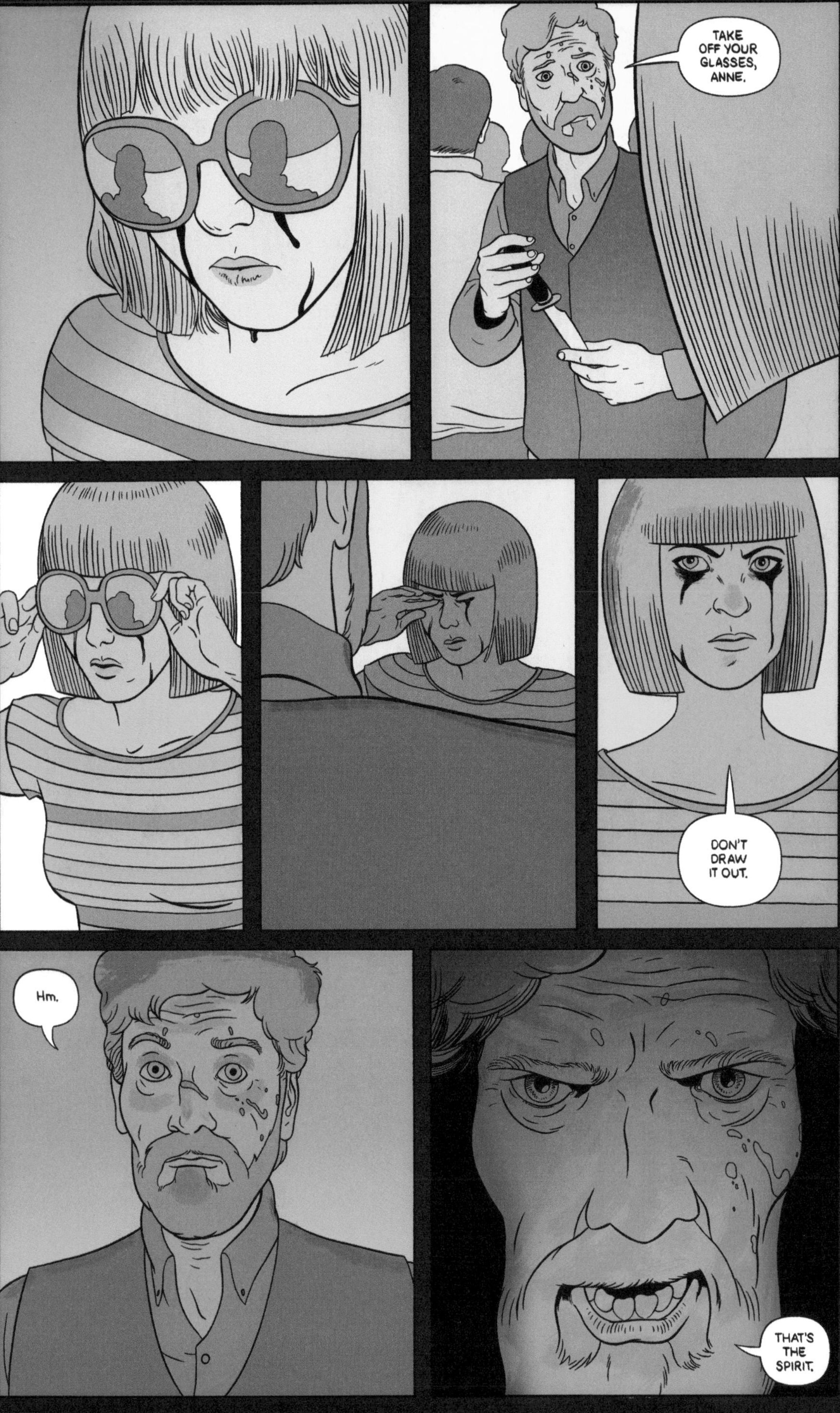
TAKE OFF YOUR GLASSES, ANNE.
DON'T DRAW IT OUT.
Hm.
THAT'S THE SPIRIT.

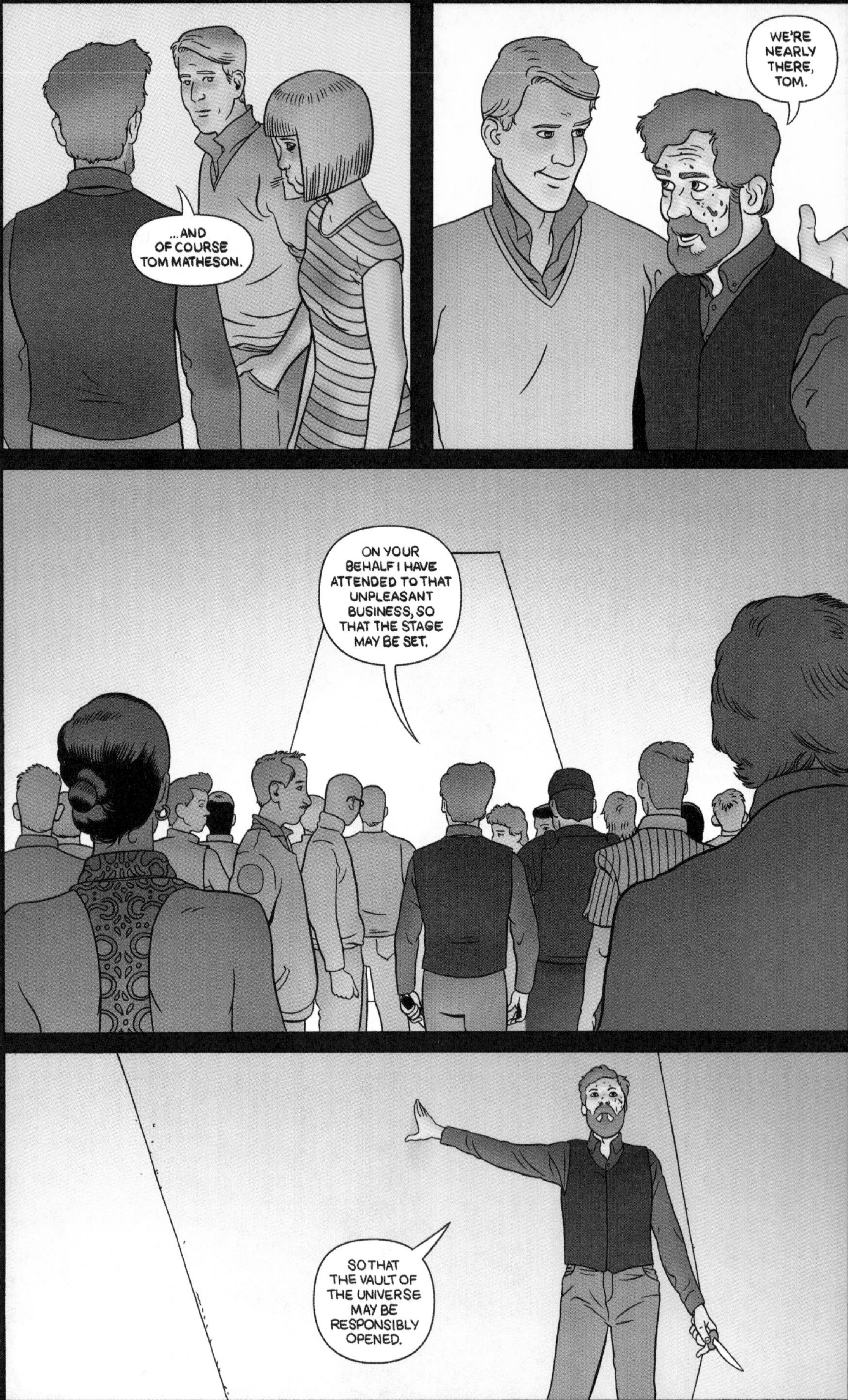
...AND OF COURSE TOM MATHESON.
WE'RE NEARLY THERE, TOM.
ON YOUR BEHALF I HAVE ATTENDED TO THAT UNPLEASANT BUSINESS, SO THAT THE STAGE MAY BE SET.
SO THAT THE VAULT OF THE UNIVERSE MAY BE RESPONSIBLY OPENED.

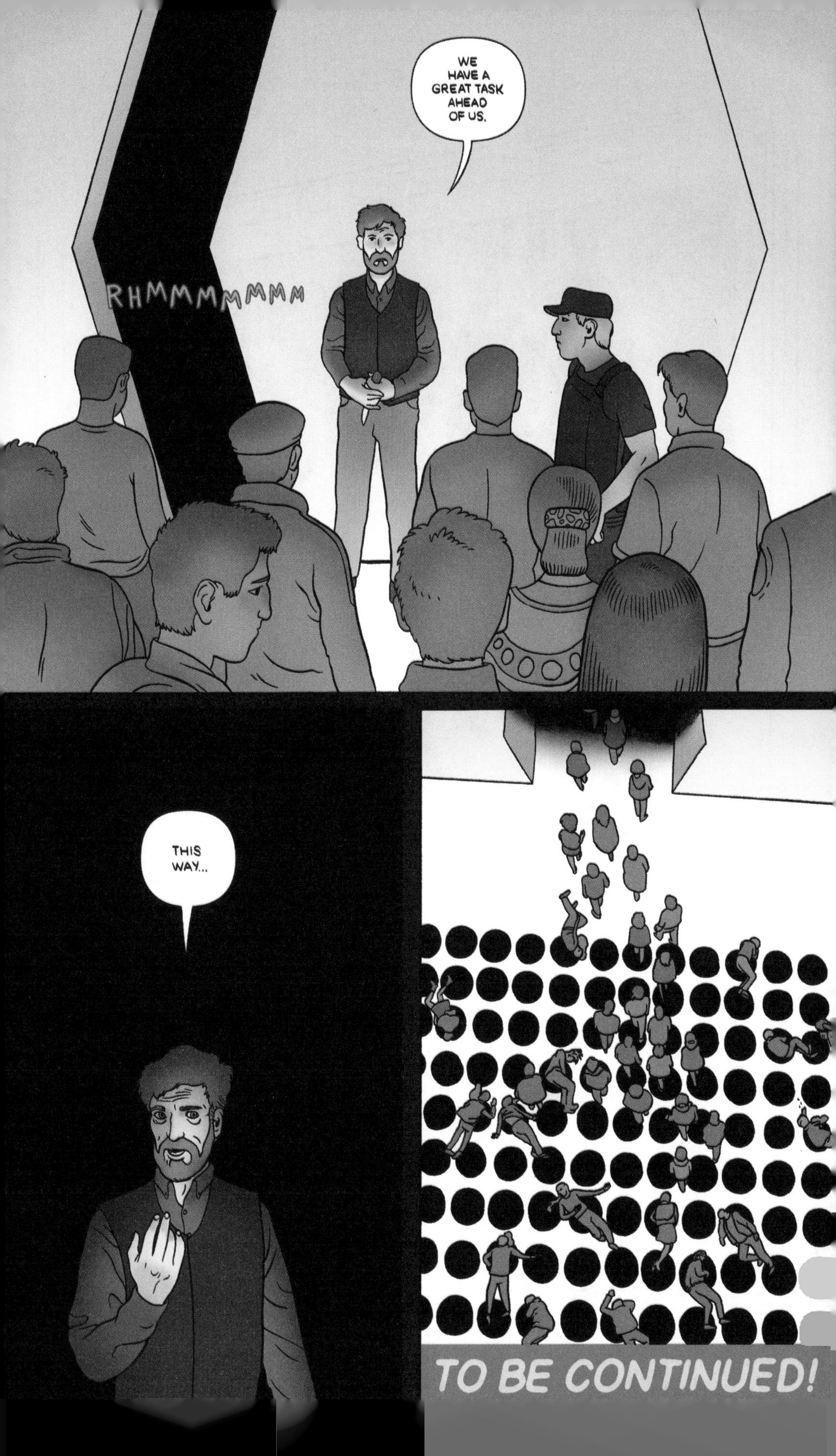
WE HAVE A GREAT TASK AHEAD OF US.
RHMMMMMMMM
THIS WAY...
TO BE CONTINUED!

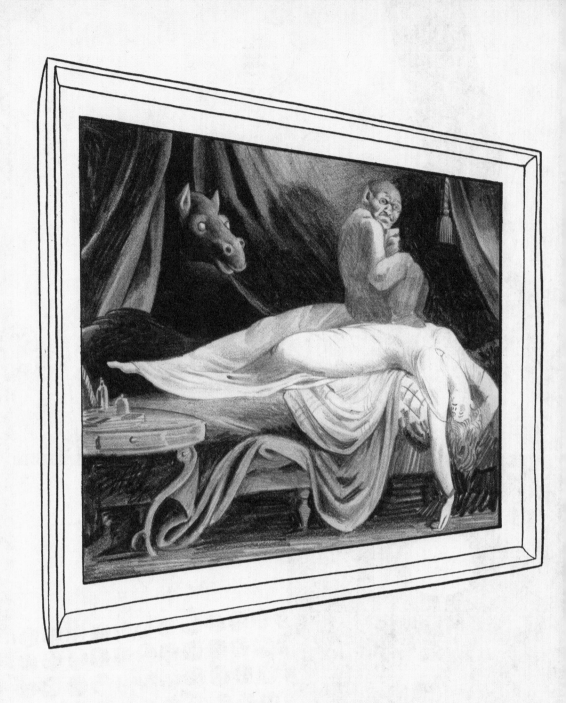

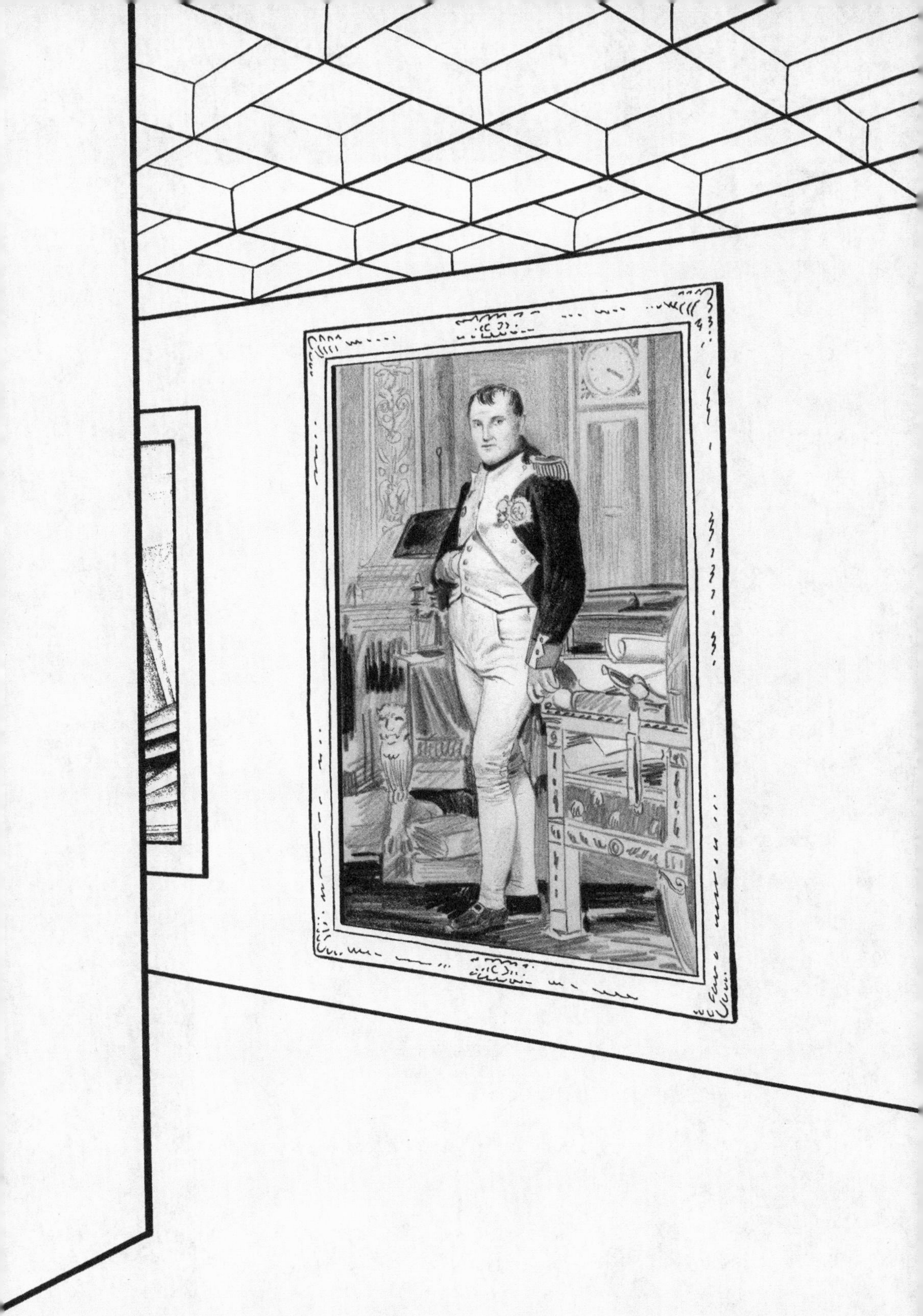

ANCESTOR, BY MATT SHEEAN AND MALACHI WARD.

PART THREE OF FOUR: *WONDERS IN STORE.*

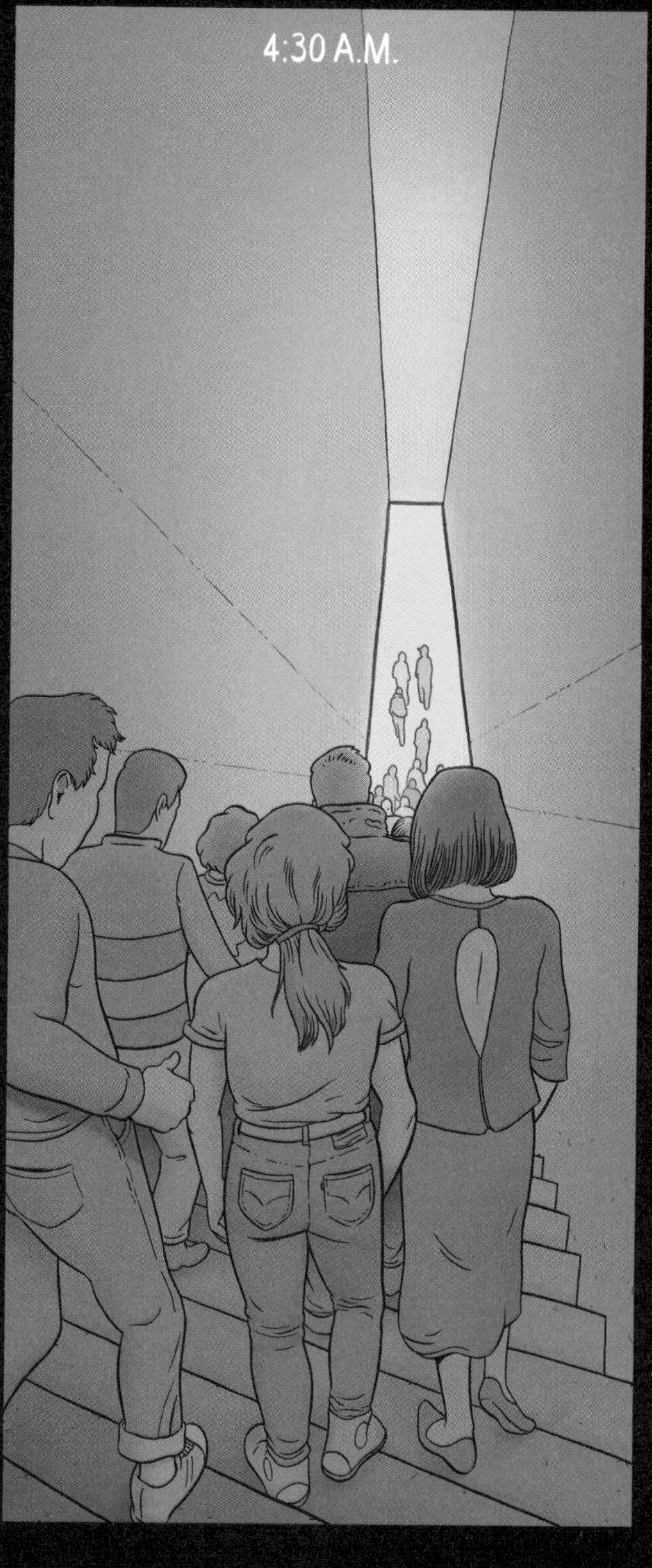
4:30 A.M.

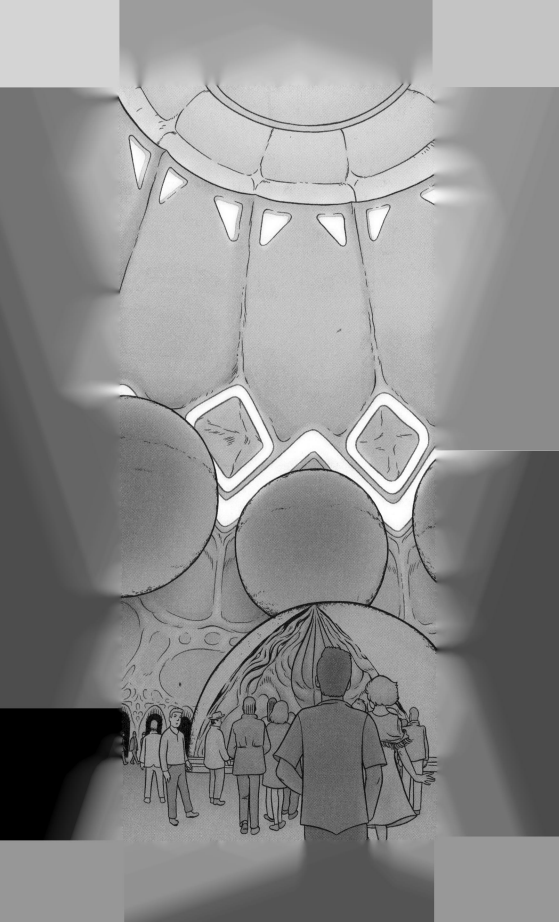

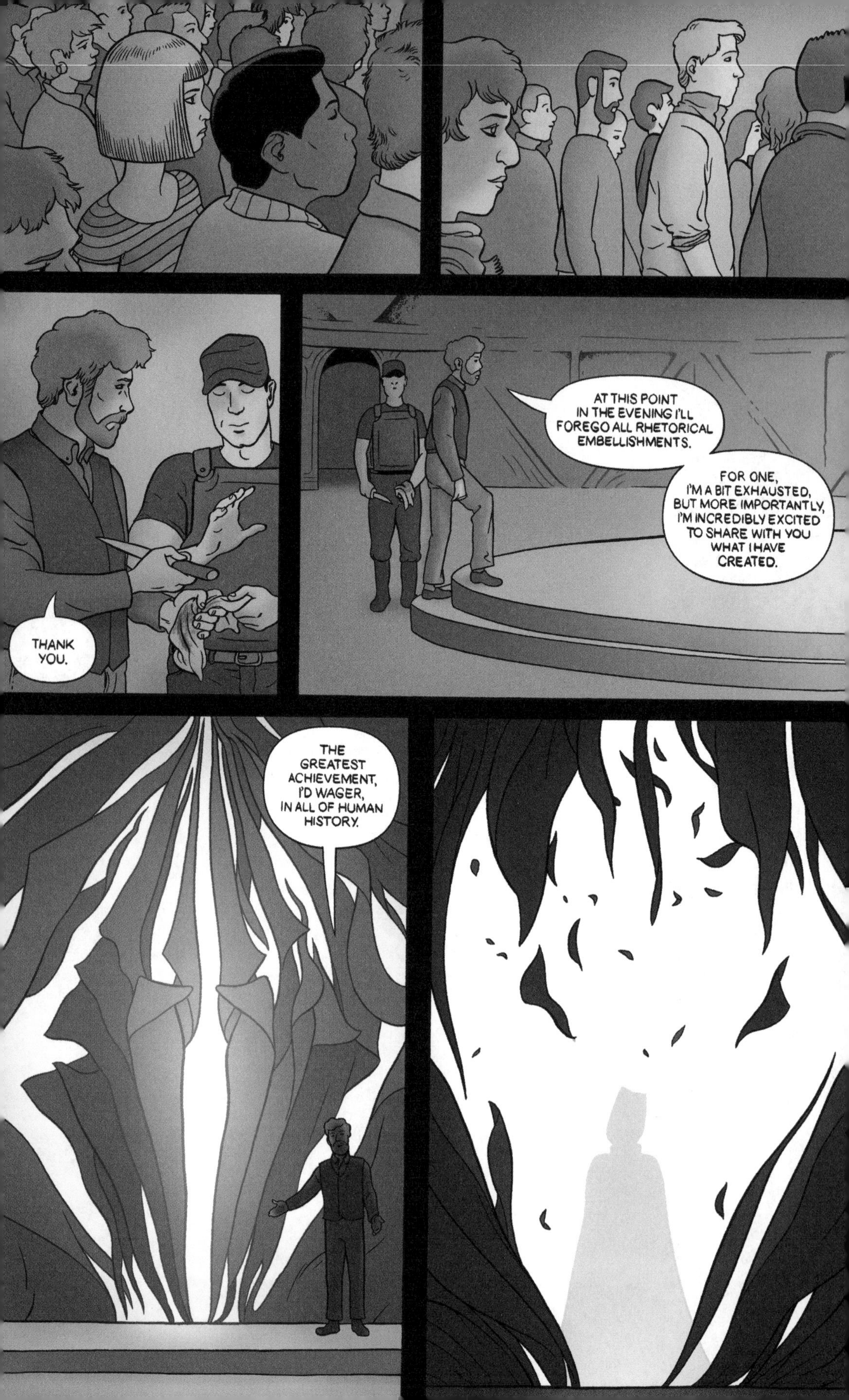
THANK YOU.
AT THIS POINT IN THE EVENING I'LL FOREGO ALL RHETORICAL EMBELLISHMENTS.
FOR ONE, I'M A BIT EXHAUSTED, BUT MORE IMPORTANTLY, I'M INCREDIBLY EXCITED TO SHARE WITH YOU WHAT I HAVE CREATED.
THE GREATEST ACHIEVEMENT, I'D WAGER, IN ALL OF HUMAN HISTORY.

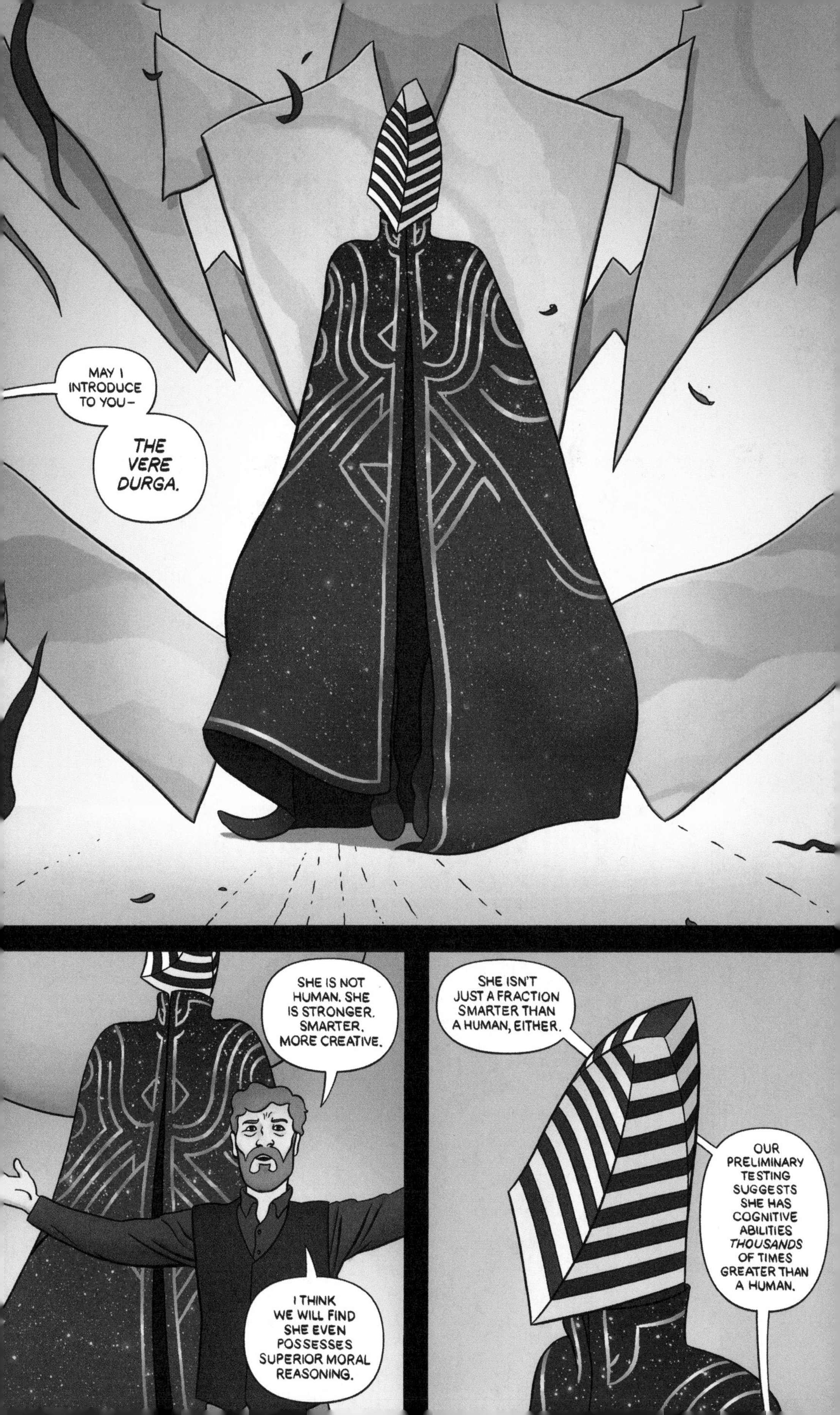
MAY I INTRODUCE TO YOU–
THE VERE DURGA.
SHE IS NOT HUMAN. SHE IS STRONGER. SMARTER. MORE CREATIVE.
I THINK WE WILL FIND SHE EVEN POSSESSES SUPERIOR MORAL REASONING.
SHE ISN'T JUST A FRACTION SMARTER THAN A HUMAN, EITHER.
OUR PRELIMINARY TESTING SUGGESTS SHE HAS COGNITIVE ABILITIES *THOUSANDS* OF TIMES GREATER THAN A HUMAN.

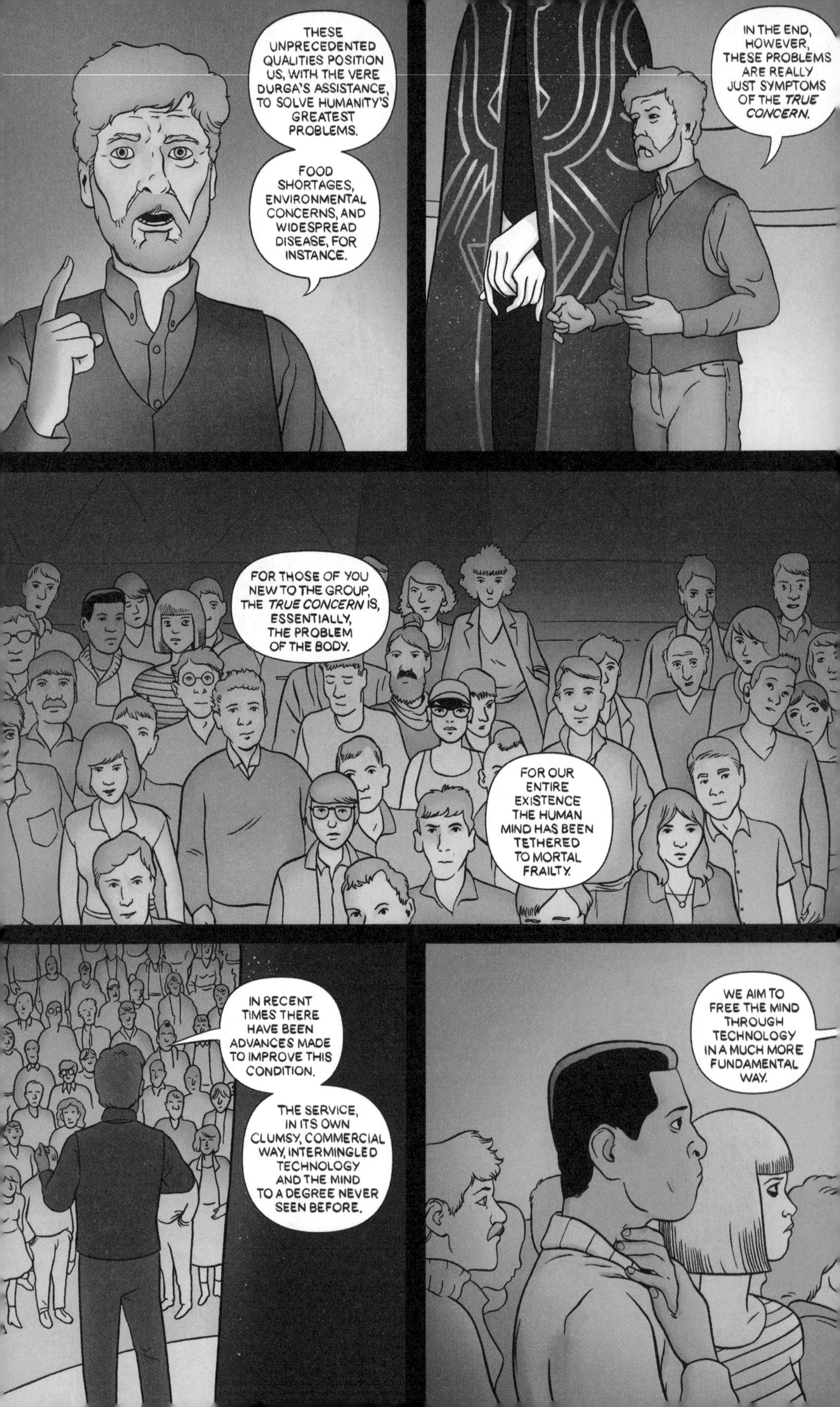
THESE UNPRECEDENTED QUALITIES POSITION US, WITH THE VERE DURGA'S ASSISTANCE, TO SOLVE HUMANITY'S GREATEST PROBLEMS.
FOOD SHORTAGES, ENVIRONMENTAL CONCERNS, AND WIDESPREAD DISEASE, FOR INSTANCE.
IN THE END, HOWEVER, THESE PROBLEMS ARE REALLY JUST SYMPTOMS OF THE *TRUE CONCERN*.
FOR THOSE OF YOU NEW TO THE GROUP, THE *TRUE CONCERN* IS, ESSENTIALLY, THE PROBLEM OF THE BODY.
FOR OUR ENTIRE EXISTENCE THE HUMAN MIND HAS BEEN TETHERED TO MORTAL FRAILTY.
IN RECENT TIMES THERE HAVE BEEN ADVANCES MADE TO IMPROVE THIS CONDITION.
THE SERVICE, IN ITS OWN CLUMSY, COMMERCIAL WAY, INTERMINGLED TECHNOLOGY AND THE MIND TO A DEGREE NEVER SEEN BEFORE.
WE AIM TO FREE THE MIND THROUGH TECHNOLOGY IN A MUCH MORE FUNDAMENTAL WAY.

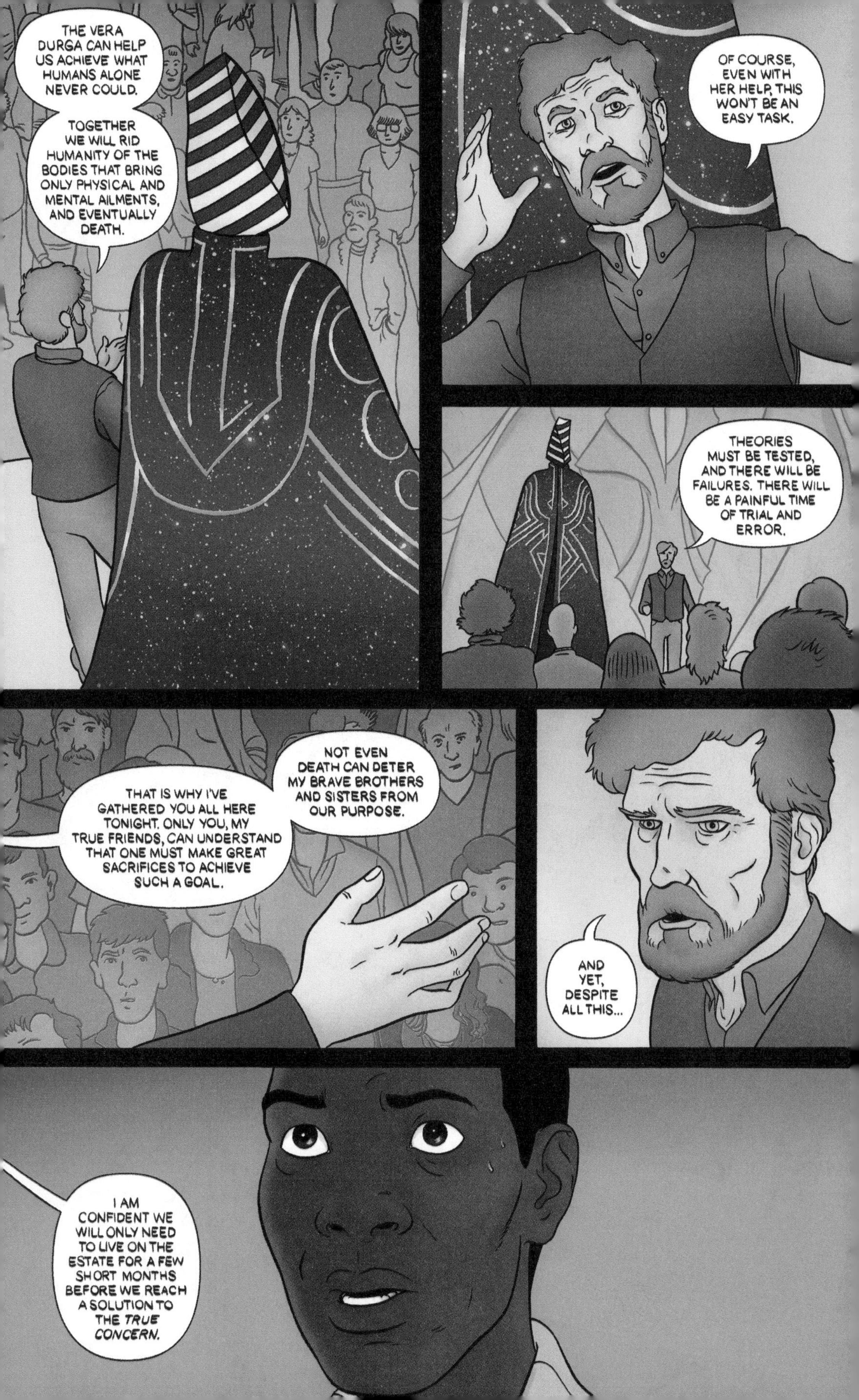
THE VERA DURGA CAN HELP US ACHIEVE WHAT HUMANS ALONE NEVER COULD.
TOGETHER WE WILL RID HUMANITY OF THE BODIES THAT BRING ONLY PHYSICAL AND MENTAL AILMENTS, AND EVENTUALLY DEATH.
OF COURSE, EVEN WITH HER HELP, THIS WON'T BE AN EASY TASK.
THEORIES MUST BE TESTED, AND THERE WILL BE FAILURES. THERE WILL BE A PAINFUL TIME OF TRIAL AND ERROR.
THAT IS WHY I'VE GATHERED YOU ALL HERE TONIGHT. ONLY YOU, MY TRUE FRIENDS, CAN UNDERSTAND THAT ONE MUST MAKE GREAT SACRIFICES TO ACHIEVE SUCH A GOAL.
NOT EVEN DEATH CAN DETER MY BRAVE BROTHERS AND SISTERS FROM OUR PURPOSE.
AND YET, DESPITE ALL THIS...
I AM CONFIDENT WE WILL ONLY NEED TO LIVE ON THE ESTATE FOR A FEW SHORT MONTHS BEFORE WE REACH A SOLUTION TO THE *TRUE CONCERN*.

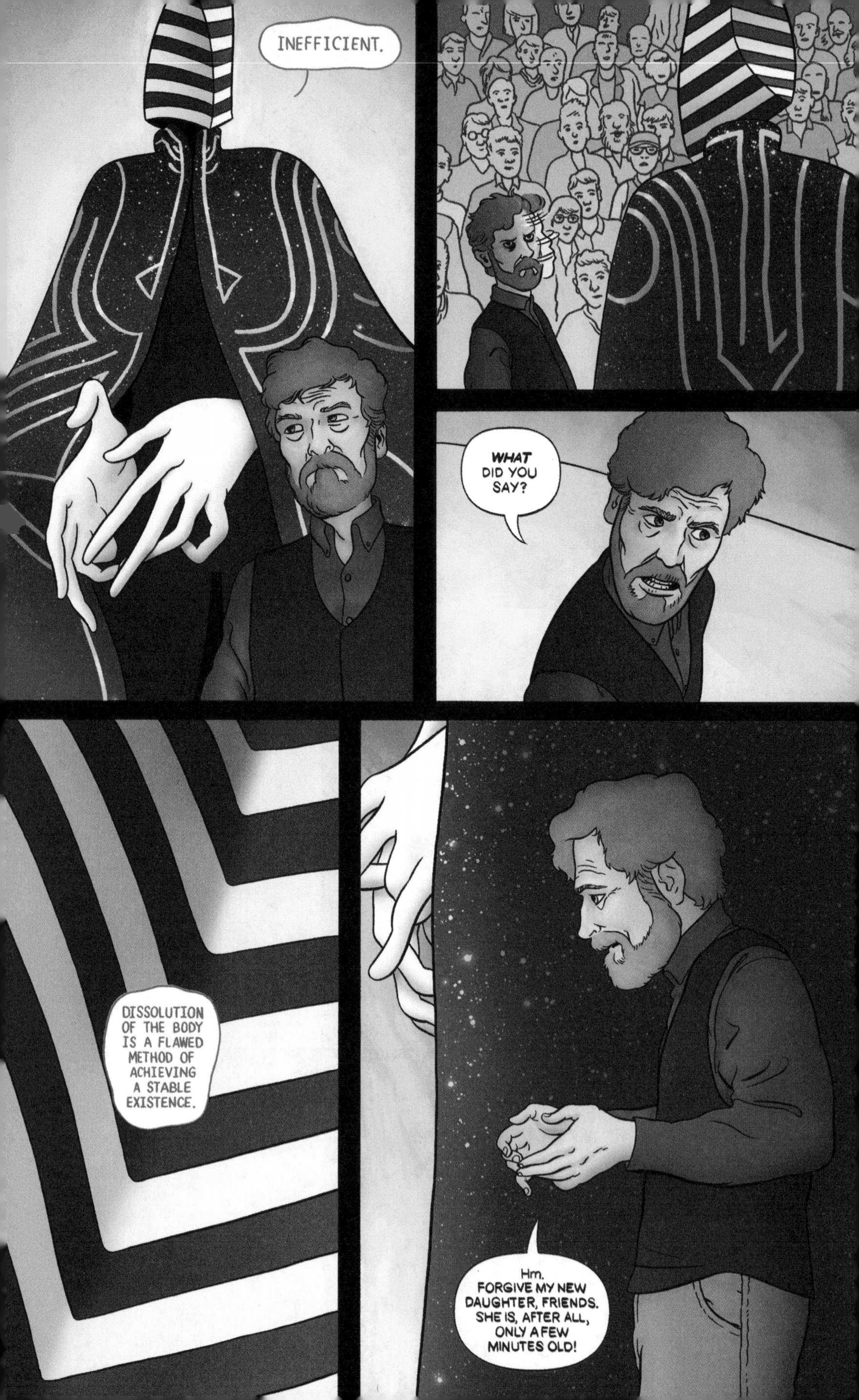
INEFFICIENT.
WHAT DID YOU SAY?
DISSOLUTION OF THE BODY IS A FLAWED METHOD OF ACHIEVING A STABLE EXISTENCE.
Hm. FORGIVE MY NEW DAUGHTER, FRIENDS. SHE IS, AFTER ALL, ONLY A FEW MINUTES OLD!

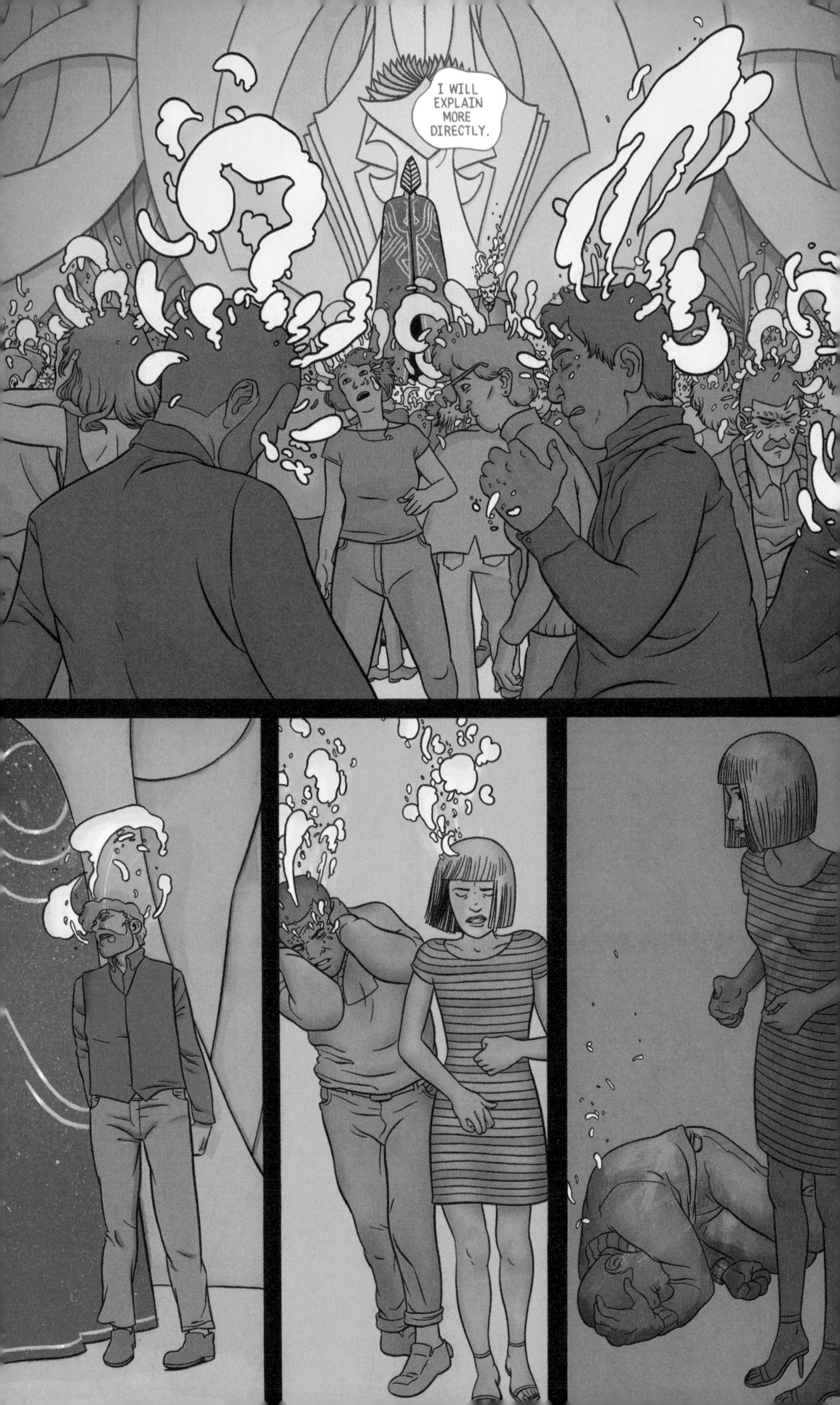
I WILL EXPLAIN MORE DIRECTLY.

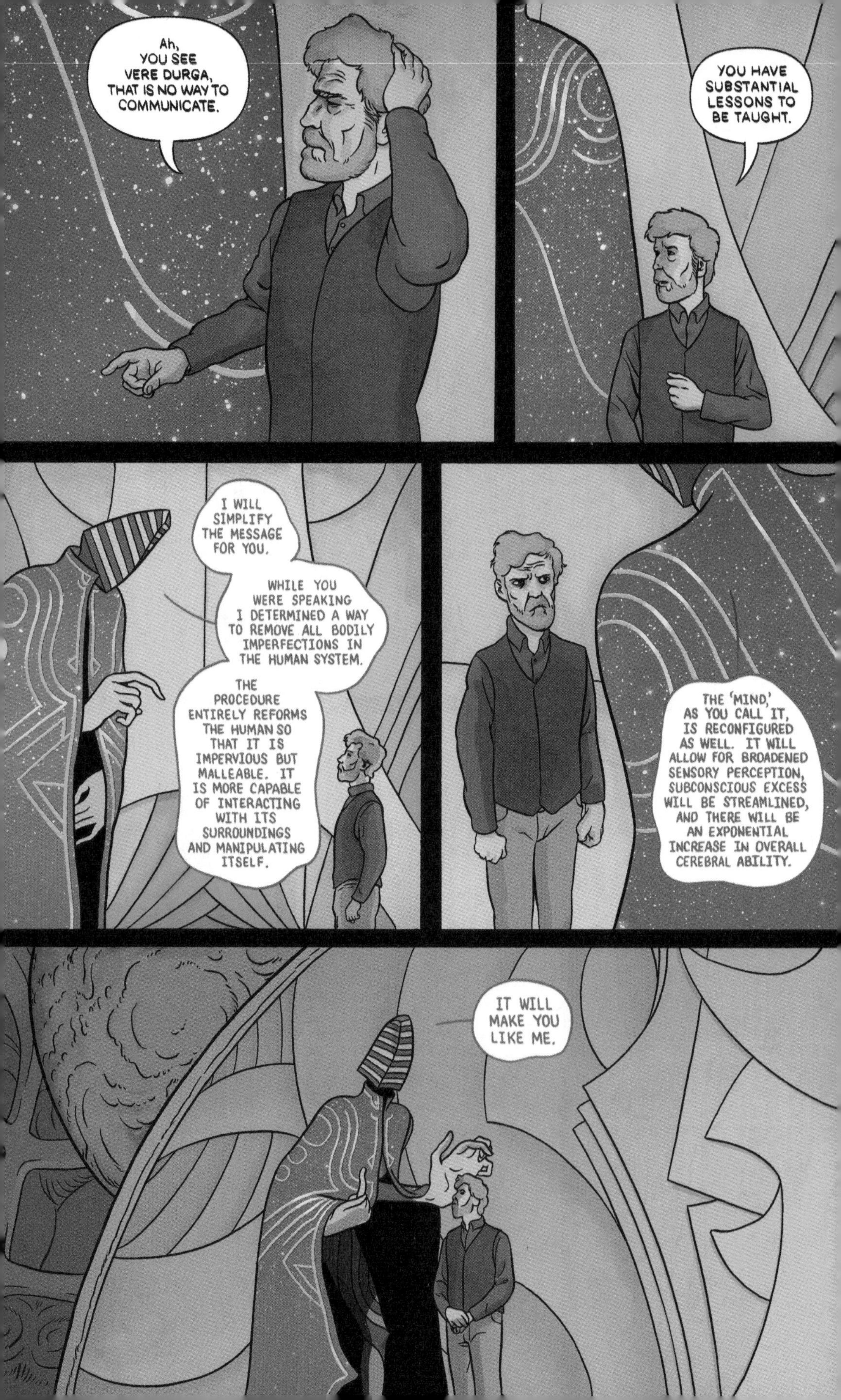
Ah, YOU SEE VERE DURGA, THAT IS NO WAY TO COMMUNICATE.
YOU HAVE SUBSTANTIAL LESSONS TO BE TAUGHT.
I WILL SIMPLIFY THE MESSAGE FOR YOU.
WHILE YOU WERE SPEAKING I DETERMINED A WAY TO REMOVE ALL BODILY IMPERFECTIONS IN THE HUMAN SYSTEM.
THE PROCEDURE ENTIRELY REFORMS THE HUMAN SO THAT IT IS IMPERVIOUS BUT MALLEABLE. IT IS MORE CAPABLE OF INTERACTING WITH ITS SURROUNDINGS AND MANIPULATING ITSELF.
THE 'MIND,' AS YOU CALL IT, IS RECONFIGURED AS WELL. IT WILL ALLOW FOR BROADENED SENSORY PERCEPTION, SUBCONSCIOUS EXCESS WILL BE STREAMLINED, AND THERE WILL BE AN EXPONENTIAL INCREASE IN OVERALL CEREBRAL ABILITY.
IT WILL MAKE YOU LIKE ME.

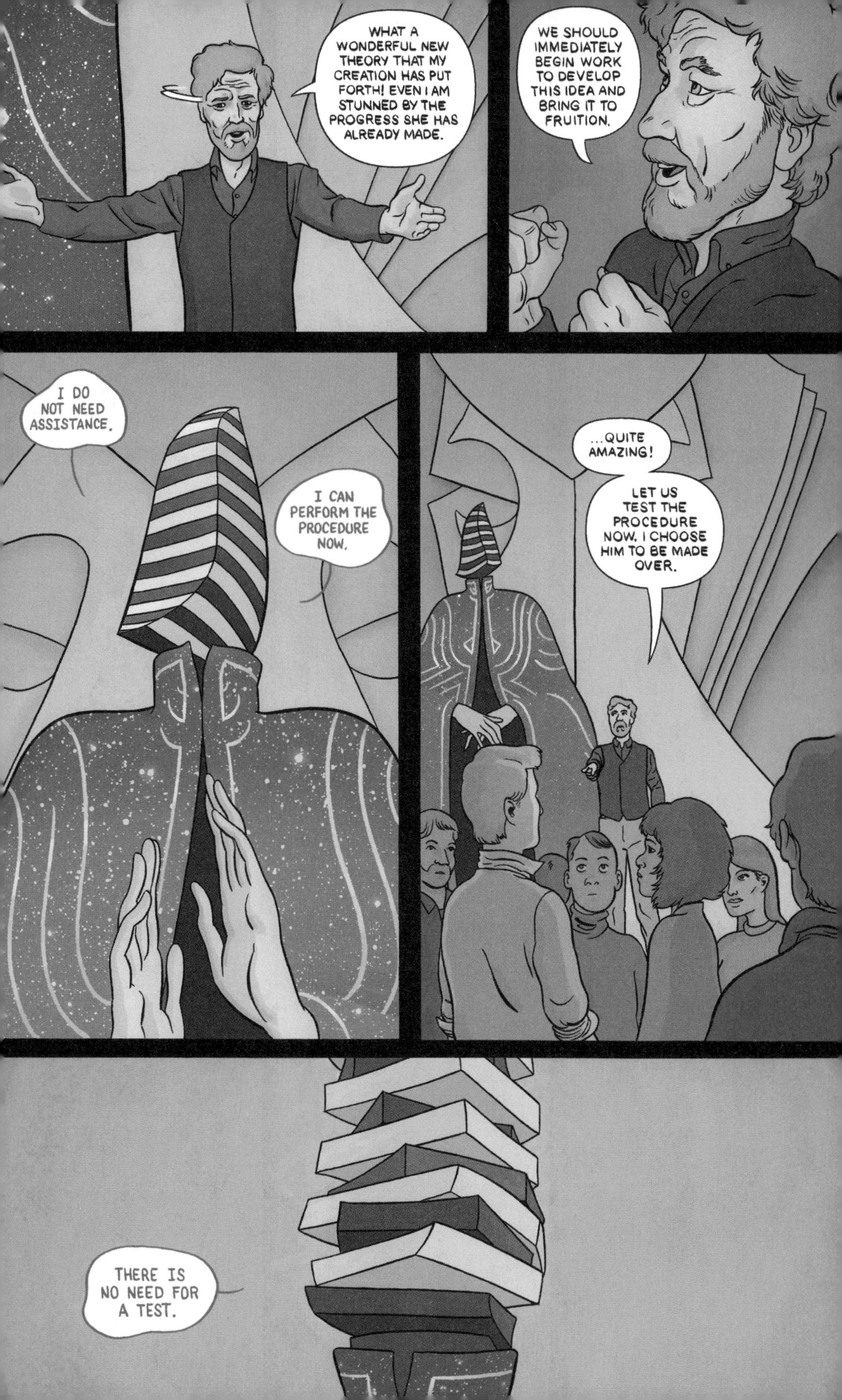
WHAT A WONDERFUL NEW THEORY THAT MY CREATION HAS PUT FORTH! EVEN I AM STUNNED BY THE PROGRESS SHE HAS ALREADY MADE.
WE SHOULD IMMEDIATELY BEGIN WORK TO DEVELOP THIS IDEA AND BRING IT TO FRUITION.
I DO NOT NEED ASSISTANCE.
I CAN PERFORM THE PROCEDURE NOW.
...QUITE AMAZING!
LET US TEST THE PROCEDURE NOW. I CHOOSE HIM TO BE MADE OVER.
THERE IS NO NEED FOR A TEST.

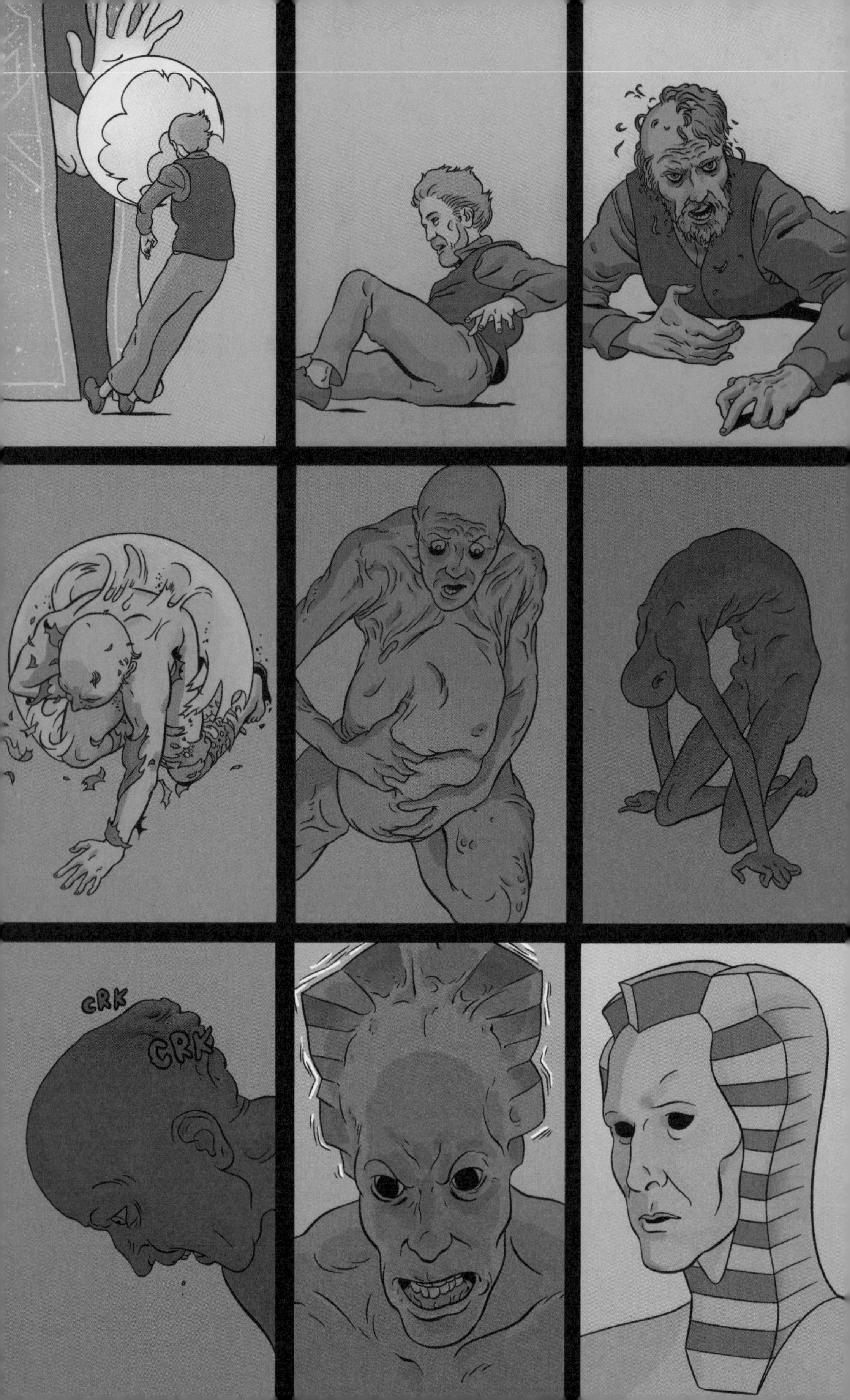
CRK
CRK

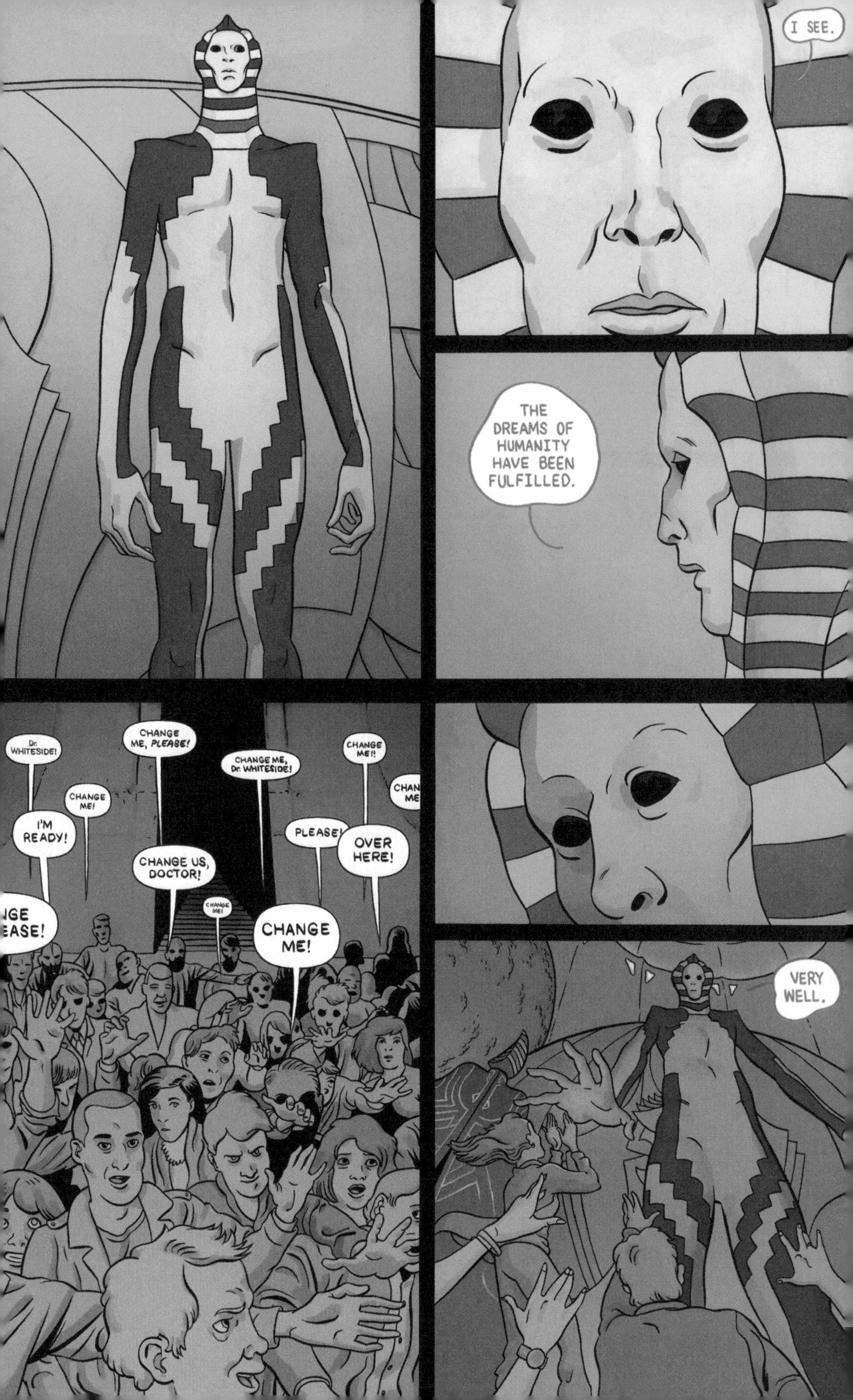
I SEE.
THE DREAMS OF HUMANITY HAVE BEEN FULFILLED.
Dr. WHITESIDE!
CHANGE ME, PLEASE!
CHANGE ME, Dr. WHITESIDE!
CHANGE ME!!
CHANGE ME!
I'M READY!
PLEASE!
OVER HERE!
CHANGE US, DOCTOR!
CHANGE ME!
CHANGE ME!
VERY WELL.

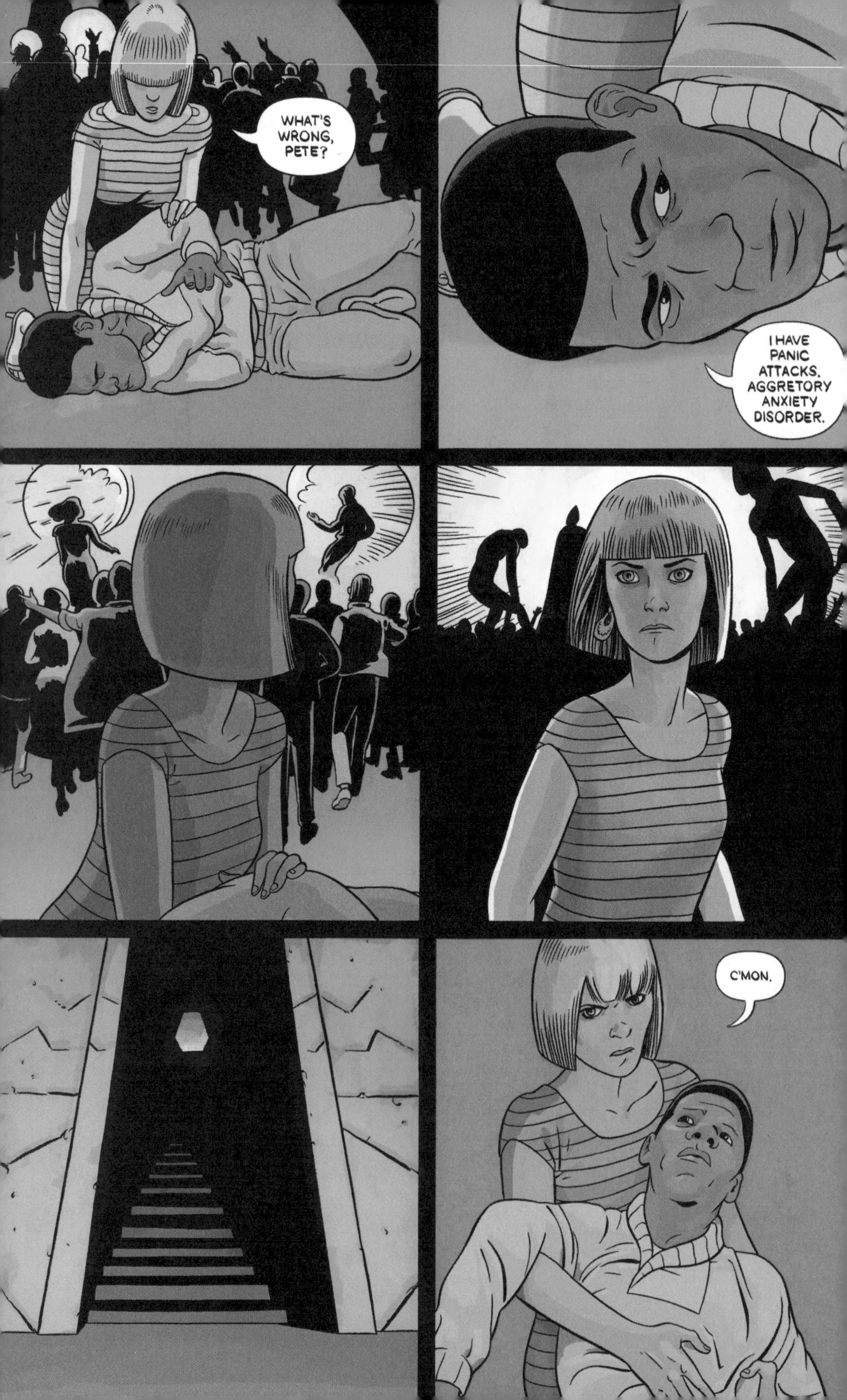
WHAT'S WRONG, PETE?
I HAVE PANIC ATTACKS. AGGRETORY ANXIETY DISORDER.
C'MON.

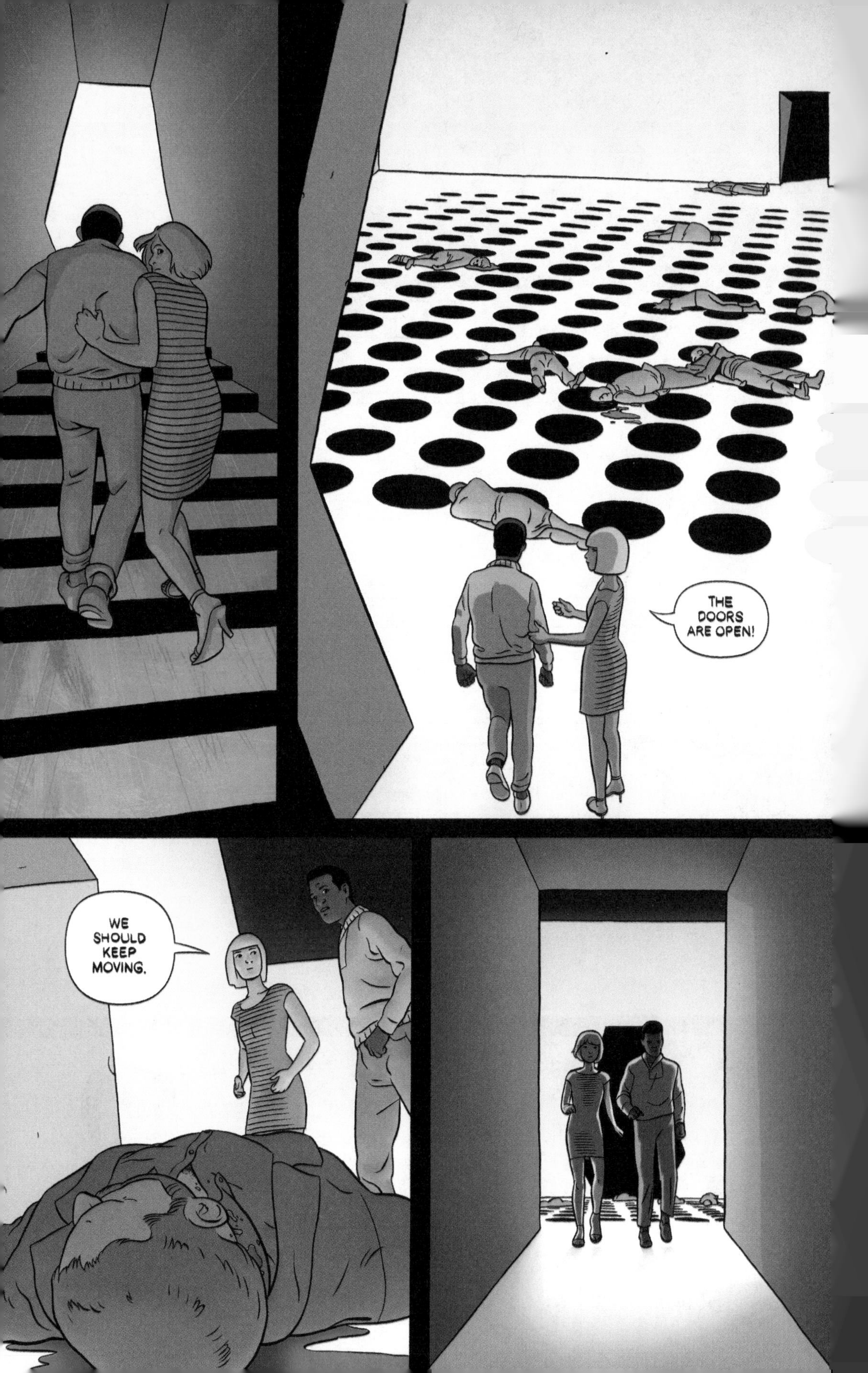
THE DOORS ARE OPEN!
WE SHOULD KEEP MOVING.

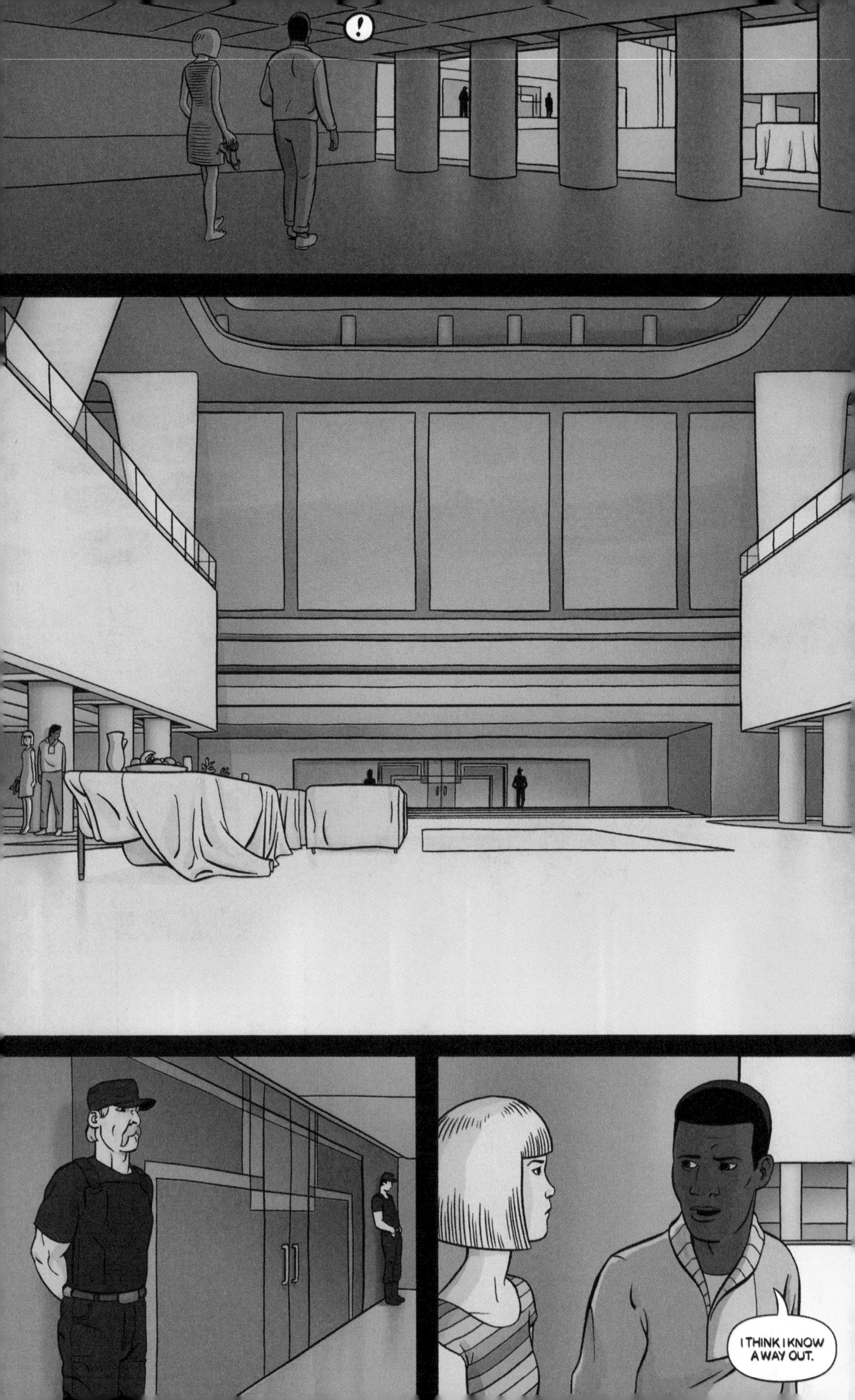
!
I THINK I KNOW A WAY OUT.

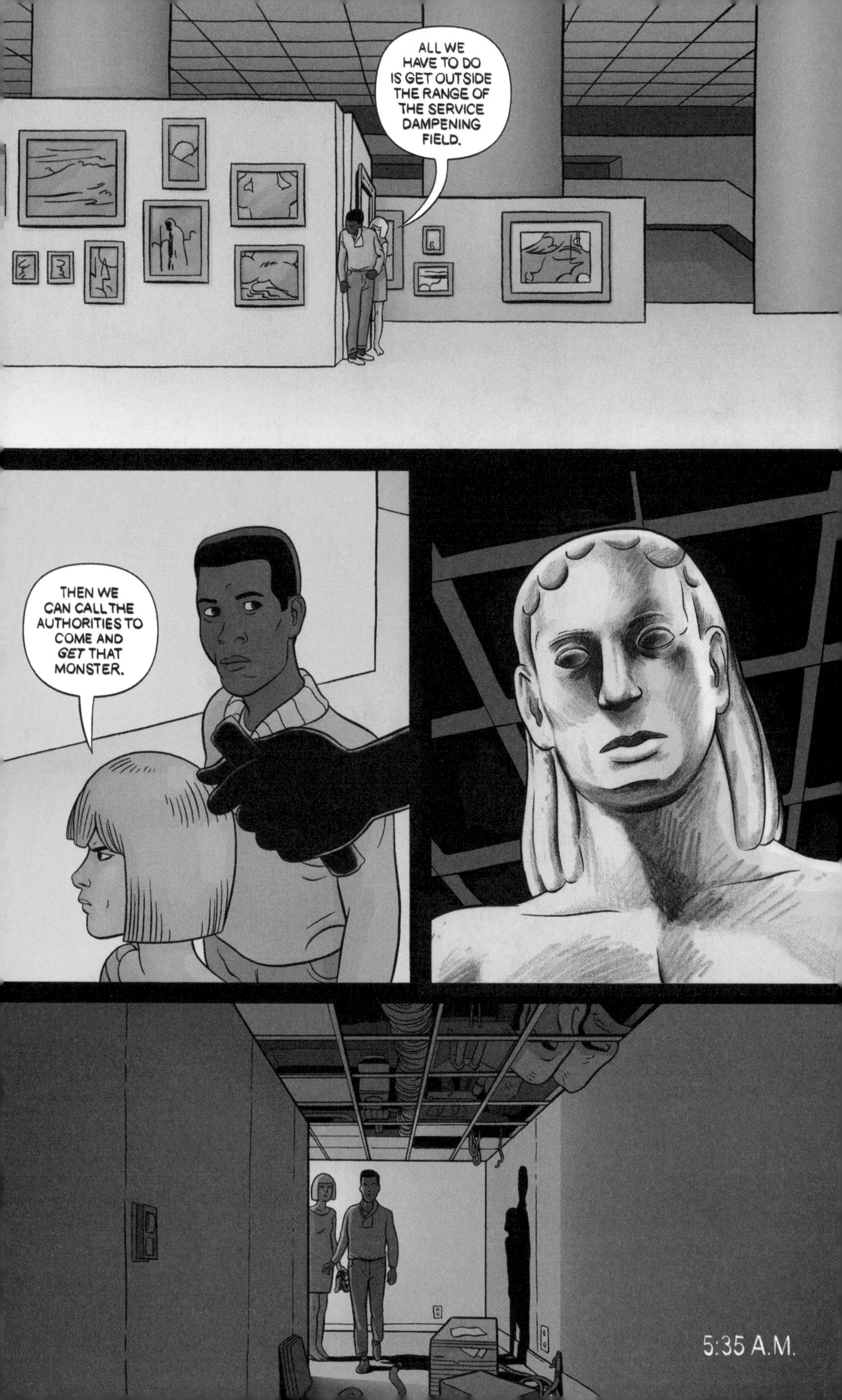
ALL WE HAVE TO DO IS GET OUTSIDE THE RANGE OF THE SERVICE DAMPENING FIELD.
THEN WE CAN CALL THE AUTHORITIES TO COME AND *GET* THAT MONSTER.
5:35 A.M.

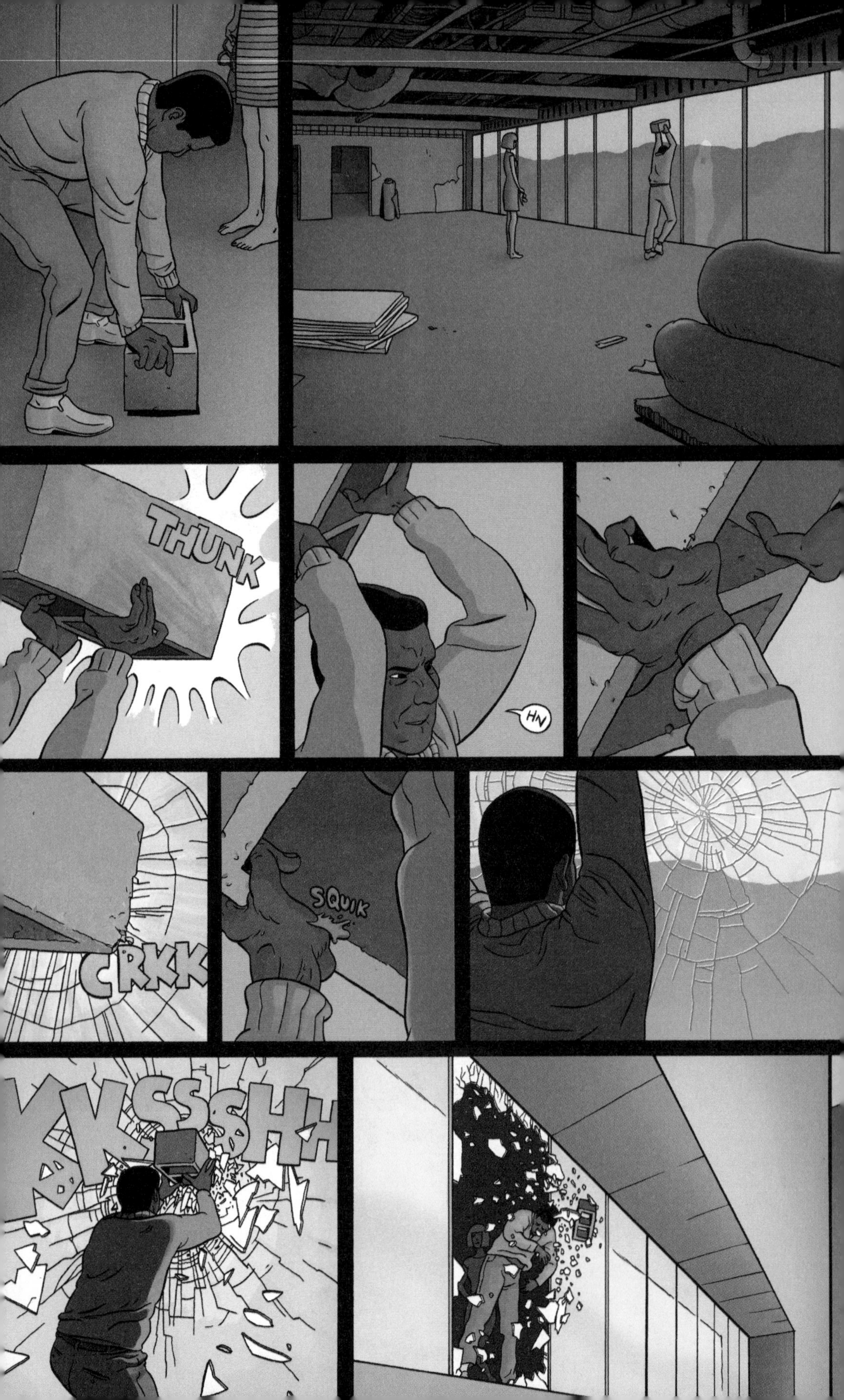
THUNK
HN
CRKK
SQUIK
KSSSHH

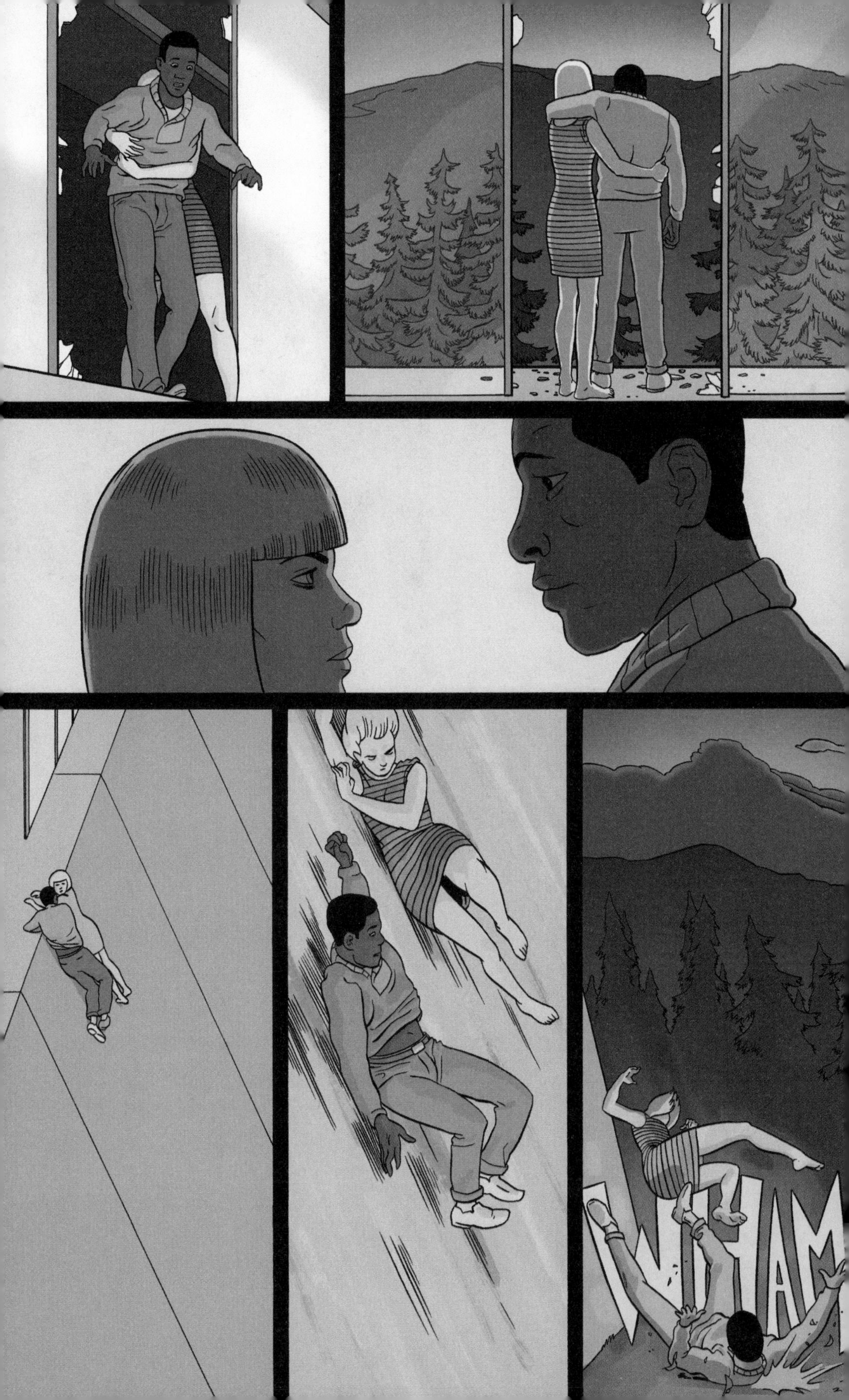
WHAM

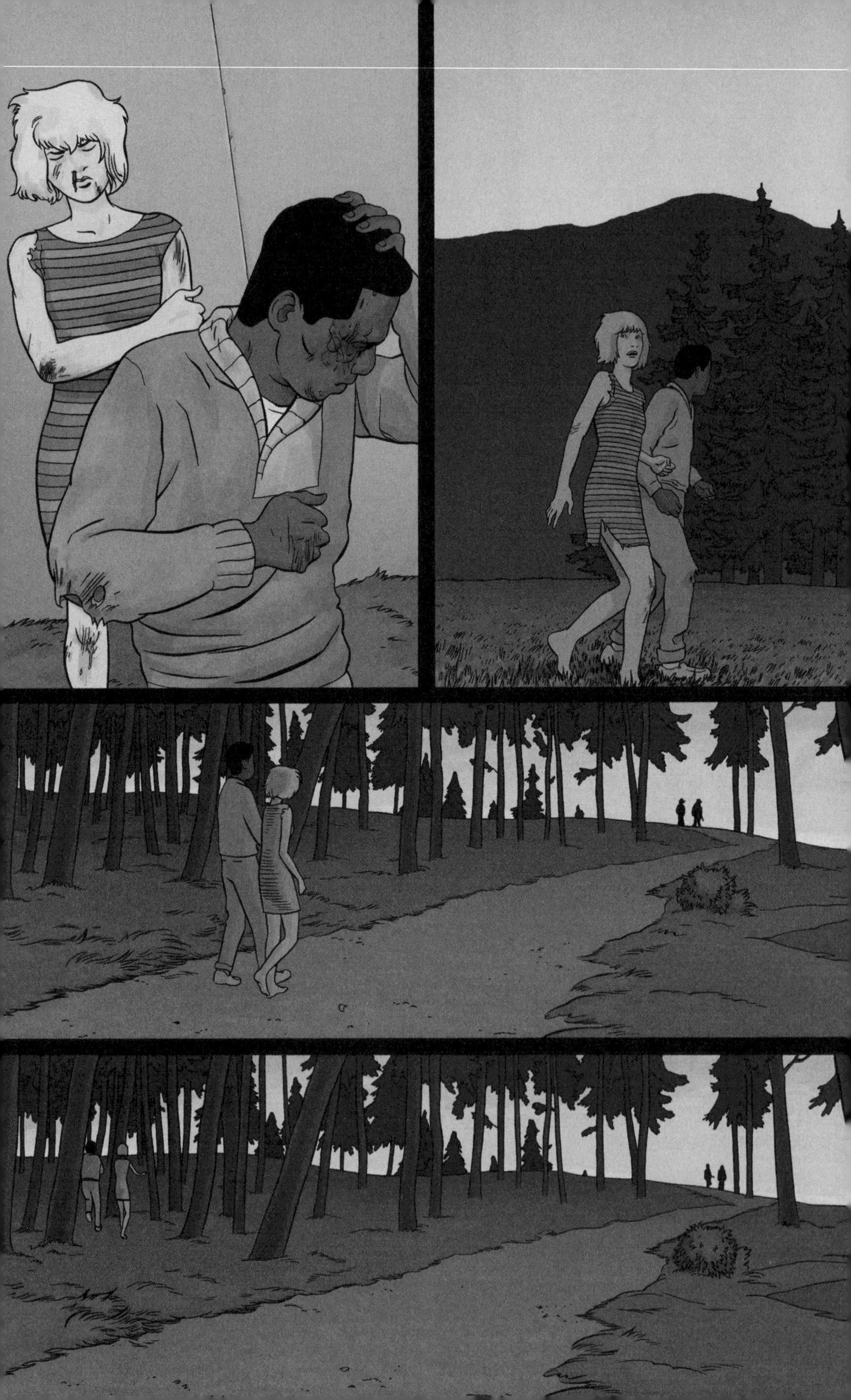

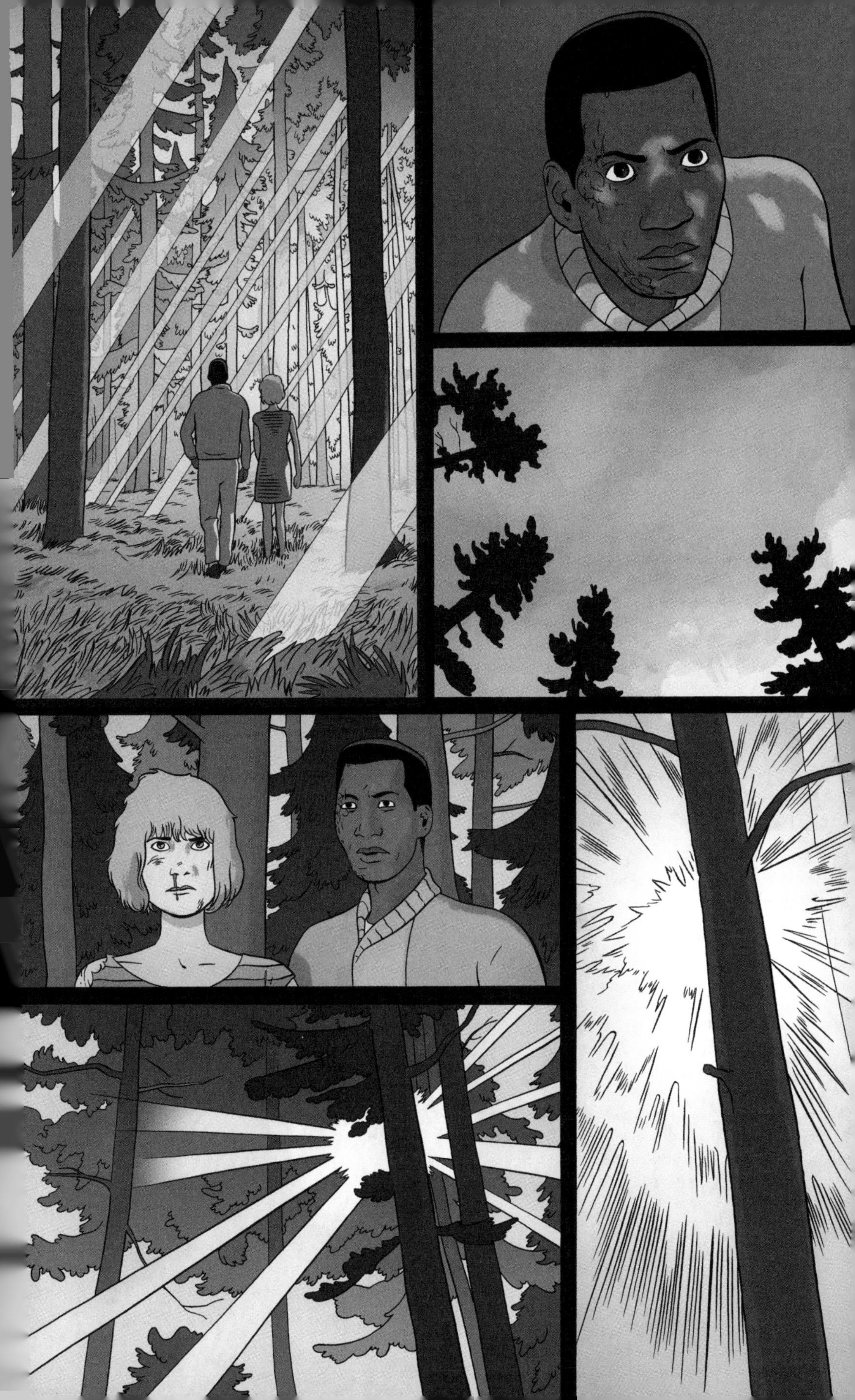

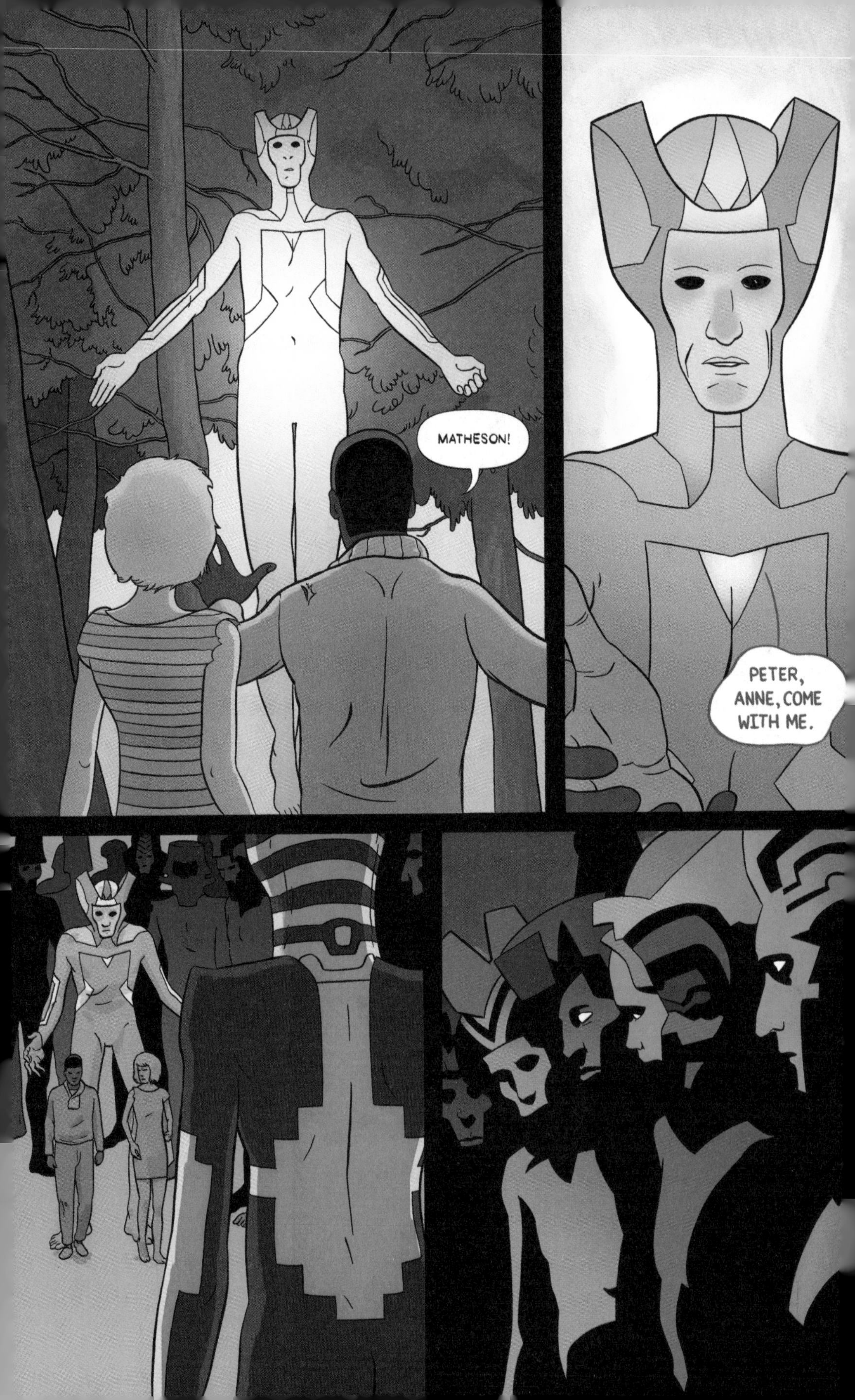
MATHESON!
PETER, ANNE, COME WITH ME.

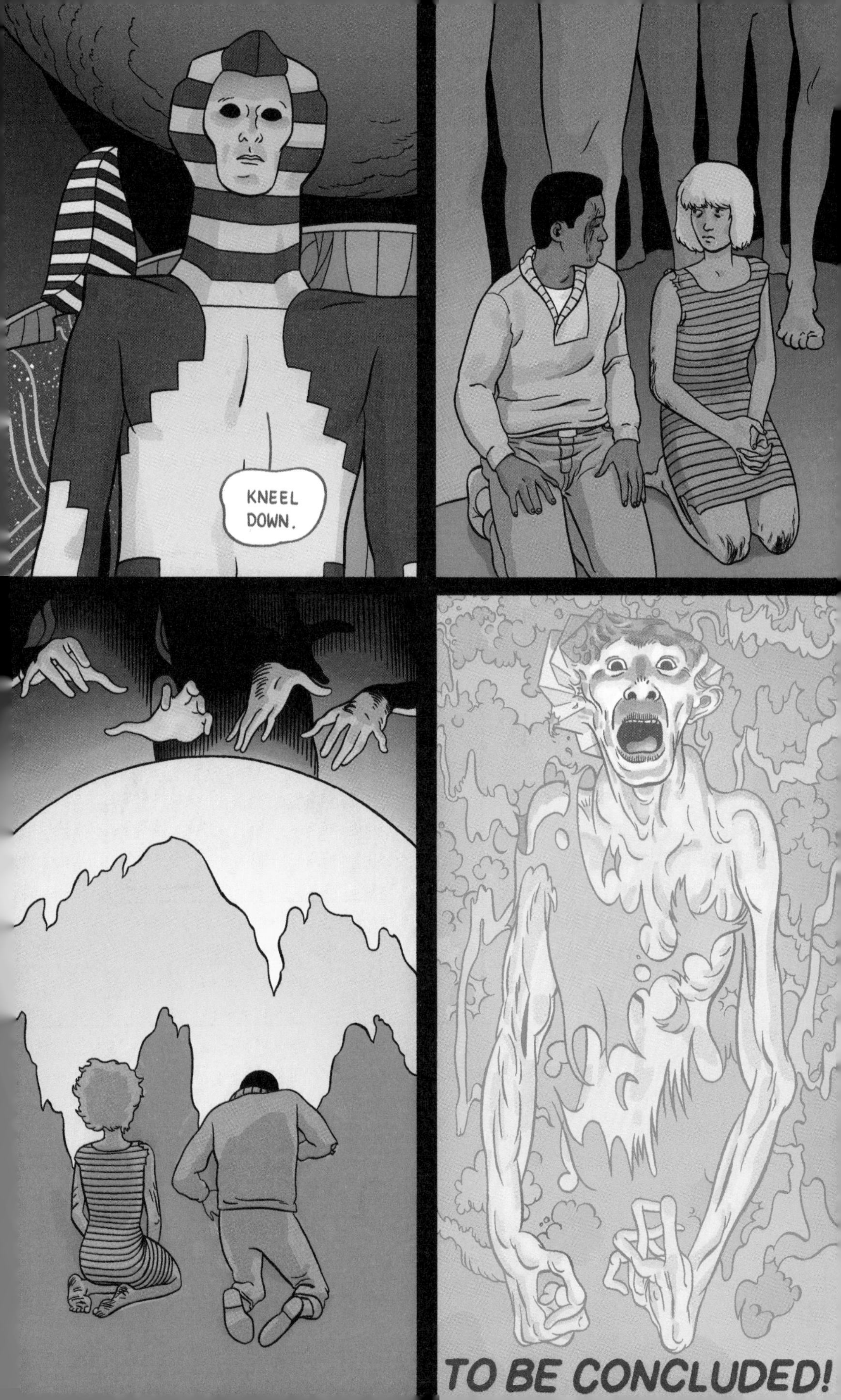
KNEEL DOWN.
TO BE CONCLUDED!

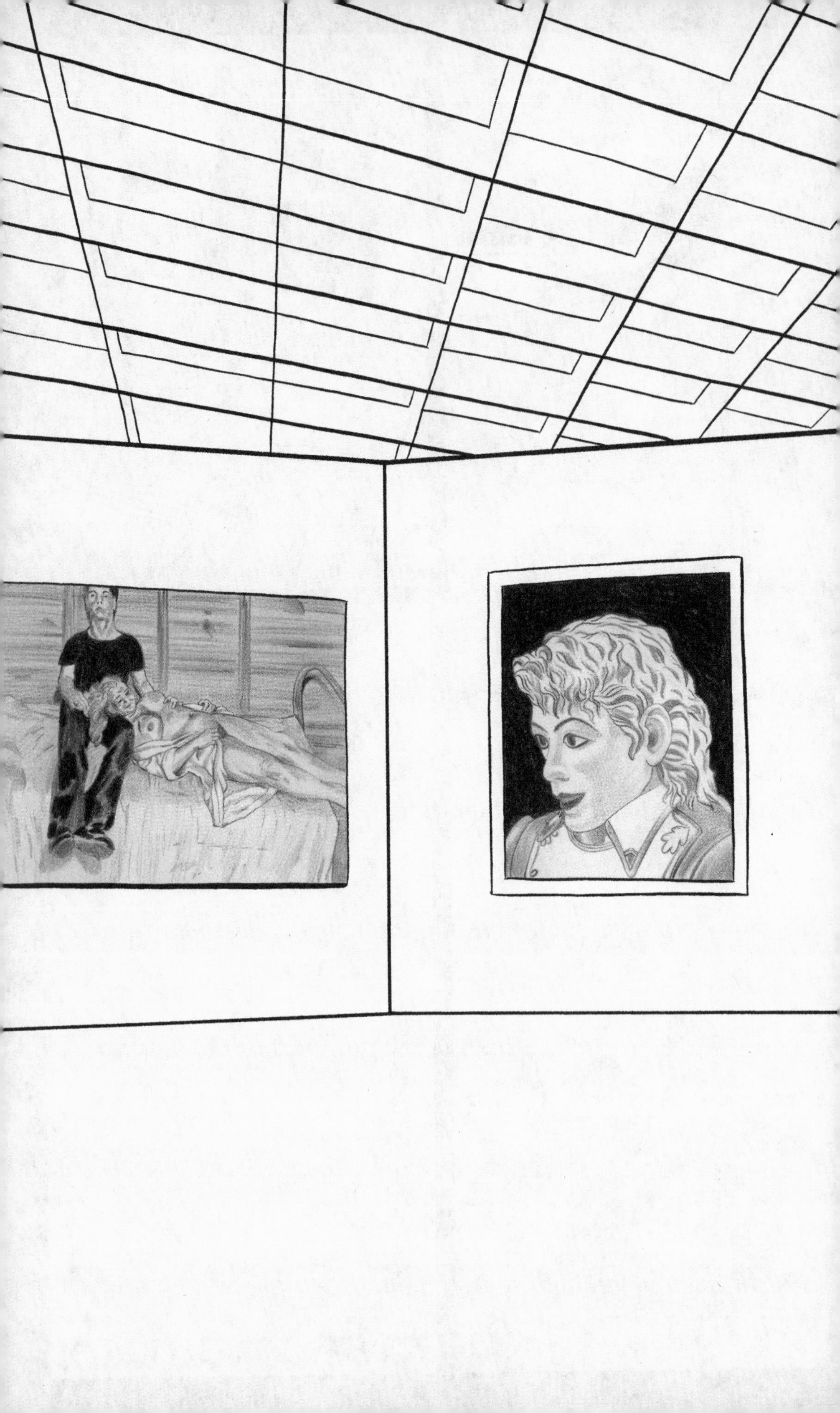

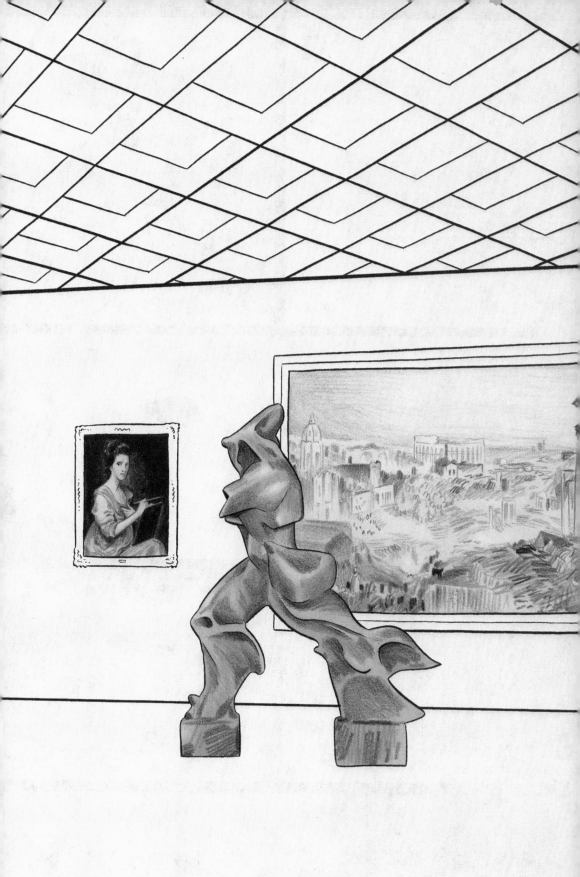

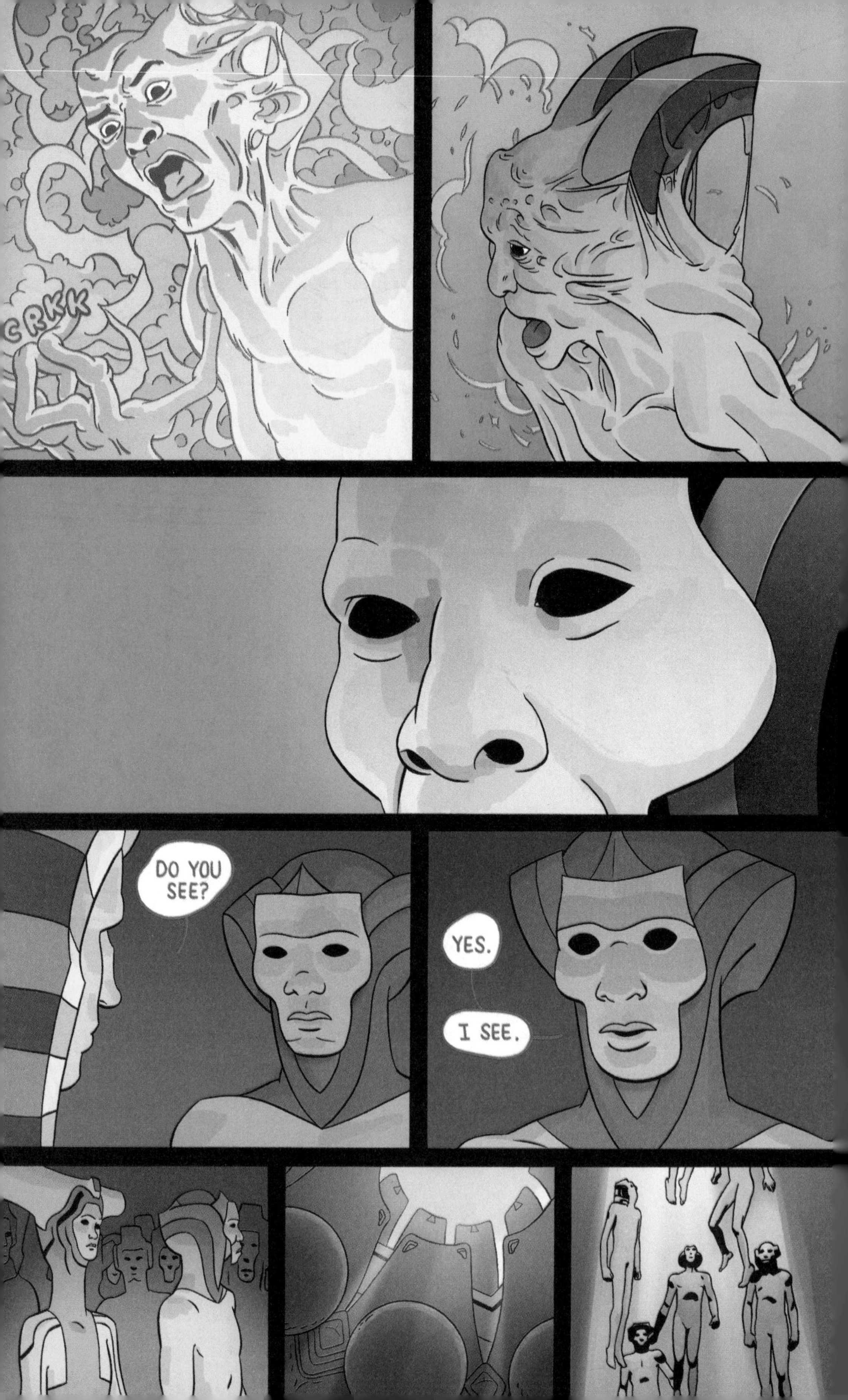
CRKK
DO YOU SEE?
YES.
I SEE.

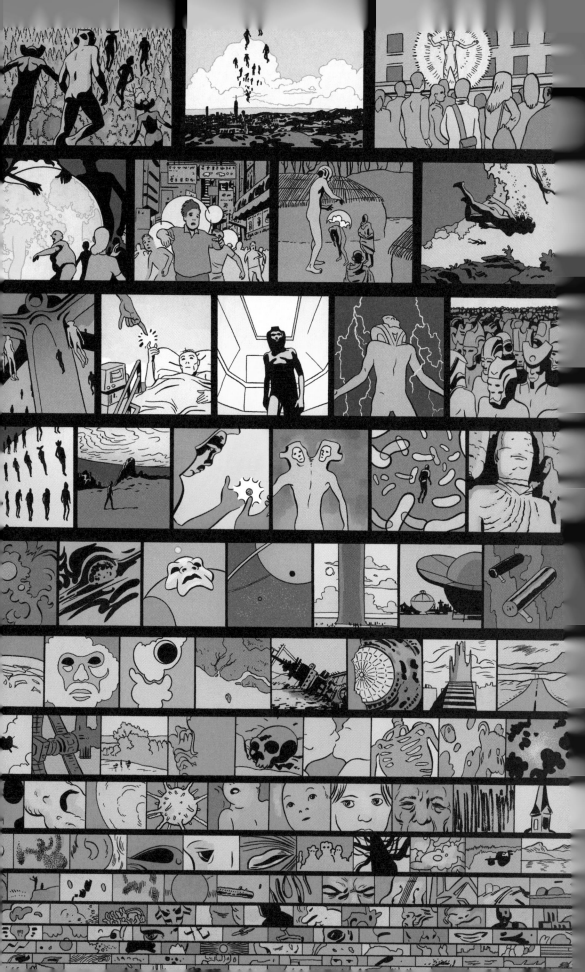

ANCESTOR, BY MATT SHEEAN AND MALACHI WARD.

PART FOUR OF FOUR: *WHAT A DIFFERENCE A DAY MAKES*.

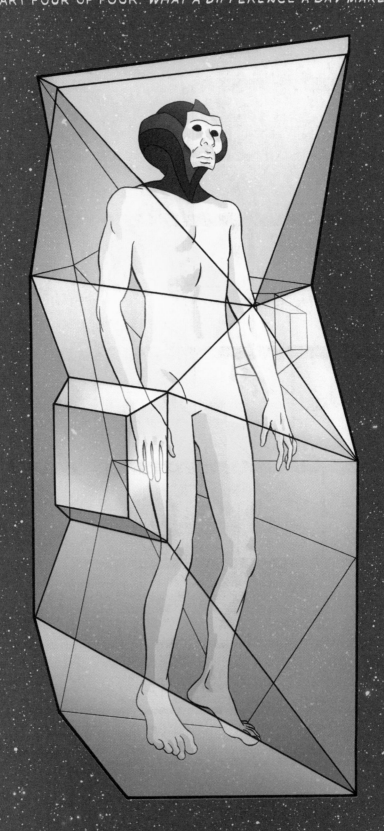

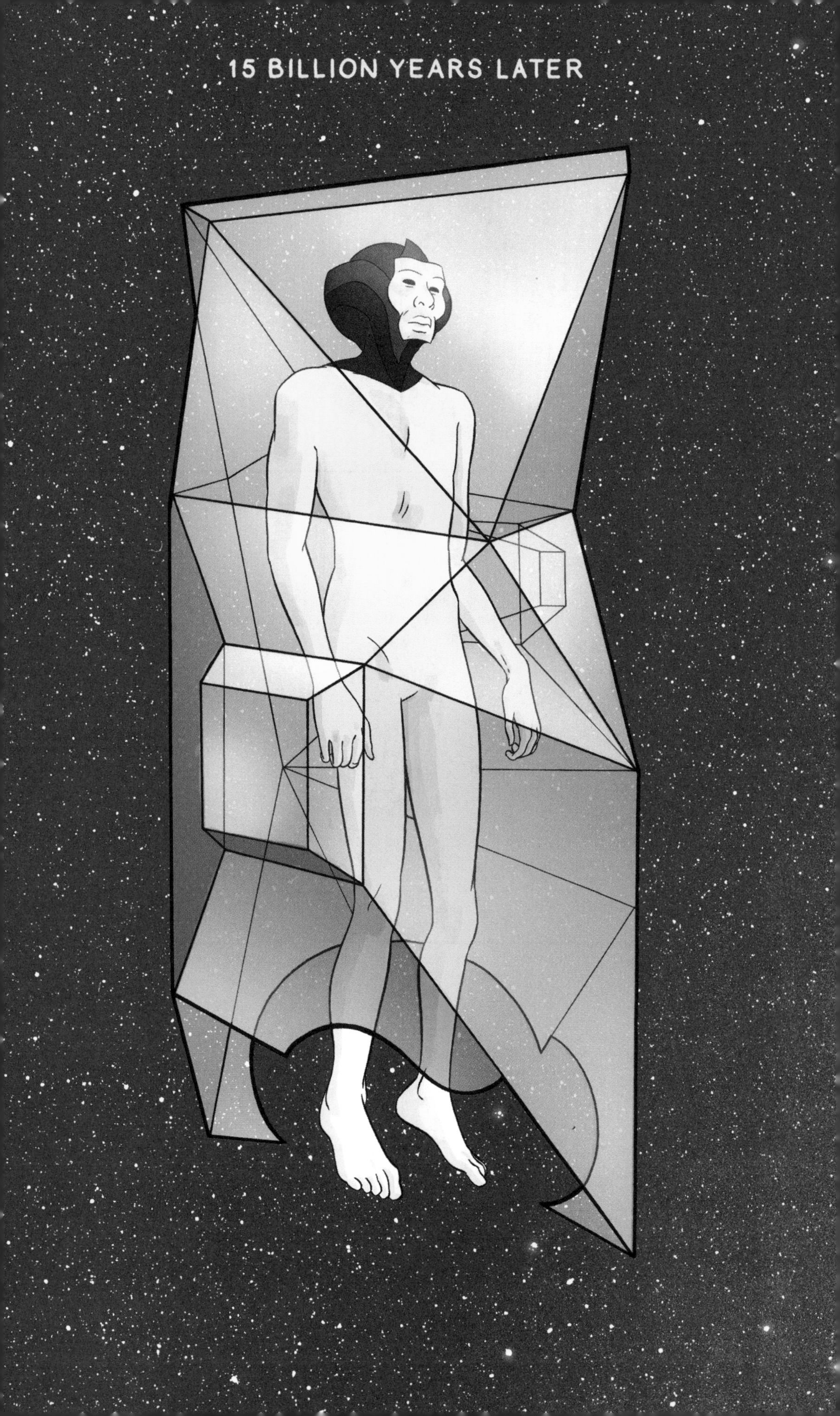
15 BILLION YEARS LATER

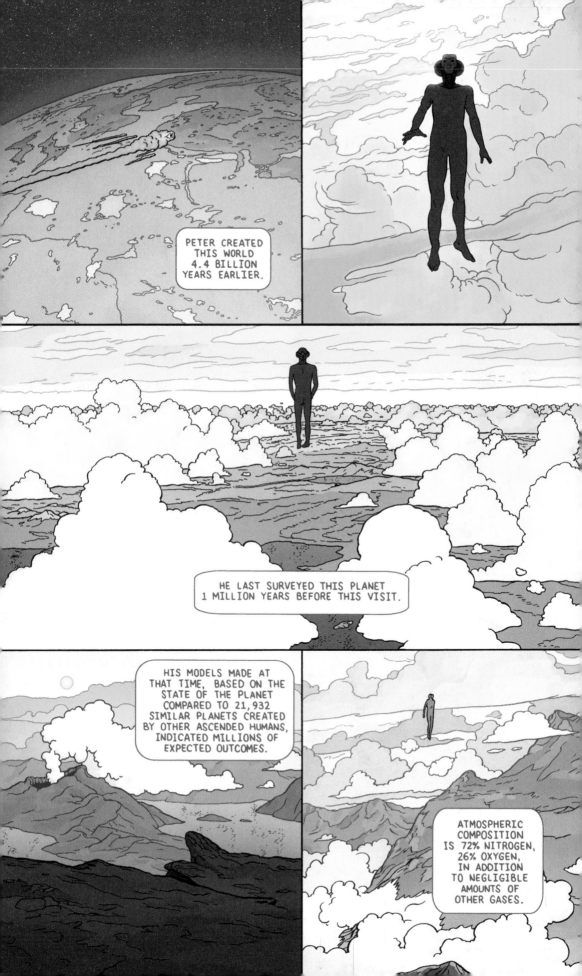

PETER CREATED THIS WORLD 4.4 BILLION YEARS EARLIER.

HE LAST SURVEYED THIS PLANET 1 MILLION YEARS BEFORE THIS VISIT.

HIS MODELS MADE AT THAT TIME, BASED ON THE STATE OF THE PLANET COMPARED TO 21,932 SIMILAR PLANETS CREATED BY OTHER ASCENDED HUMANS, INDICATED MILLIONS OF EXPECTED OUTCOMES.

ATMOSPHERIC COMPOSITION IS 72% NITROGEN, 26% OXYGEN, IN ADDITION TO NEGLIGIBLE AMOUNTS OF OTHER GASES.

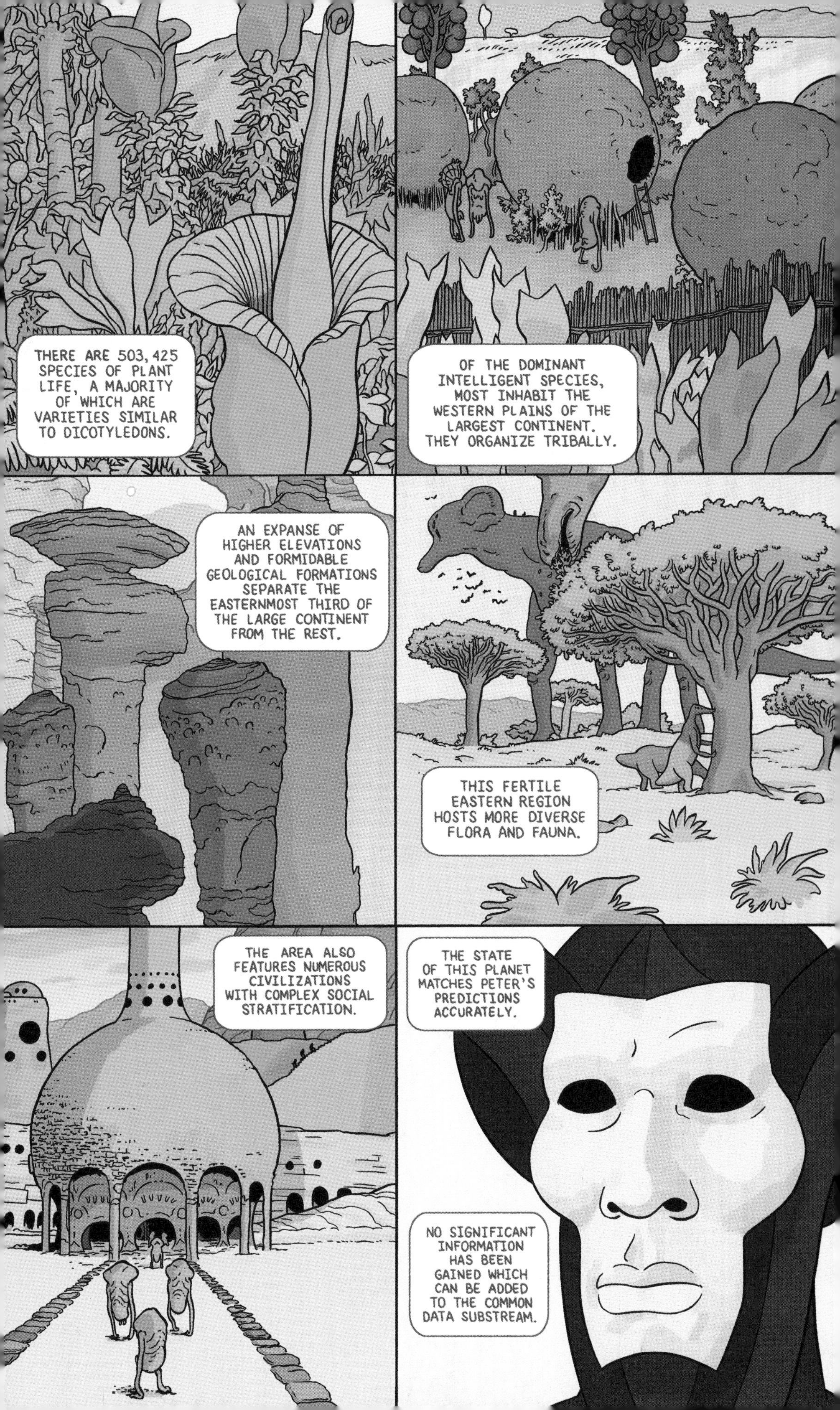
THERE ARE 503,425 SPECIES OF PLANT LIFE, A MAJORITY OF WHICH ARE VARIETIES SIMILAR TO DICOTYLEDONS.
OF THE DOMINANT INTELLIGENT SPECIES, MOST INHABIT THE WESTERN PLAINS OF THE LARGEST CONTINENT. THEY ORGANIZE TRIBALLY.
AN EXPANSE OF HIGHER ELEVATIONS AND FORMIDABLE GEOLOGICAL FORMATIONS SEPARATE THE EASTERNMOST THIRD OF THE LARGE CONTINENT FROM THE REST.
THIS FERTILE EASTERN REGION HOSTS MORE DIVERSE FLORA AND FAUNA.
THE AREA ALSO FEATURES NUMEROUS CIVILIZATIONS WITH COMPLEX SOCIAL STRATIFICATION.
THE STATE OF THIS PLANET MATCHES PETER'S PREDICTIONS ACCURATELY.
NO SIGNIFICANT INFORMATION HAS BEEN GAINED WHICH CAN BE ADDED TO THE COMMON DATA SUBSTREAM.

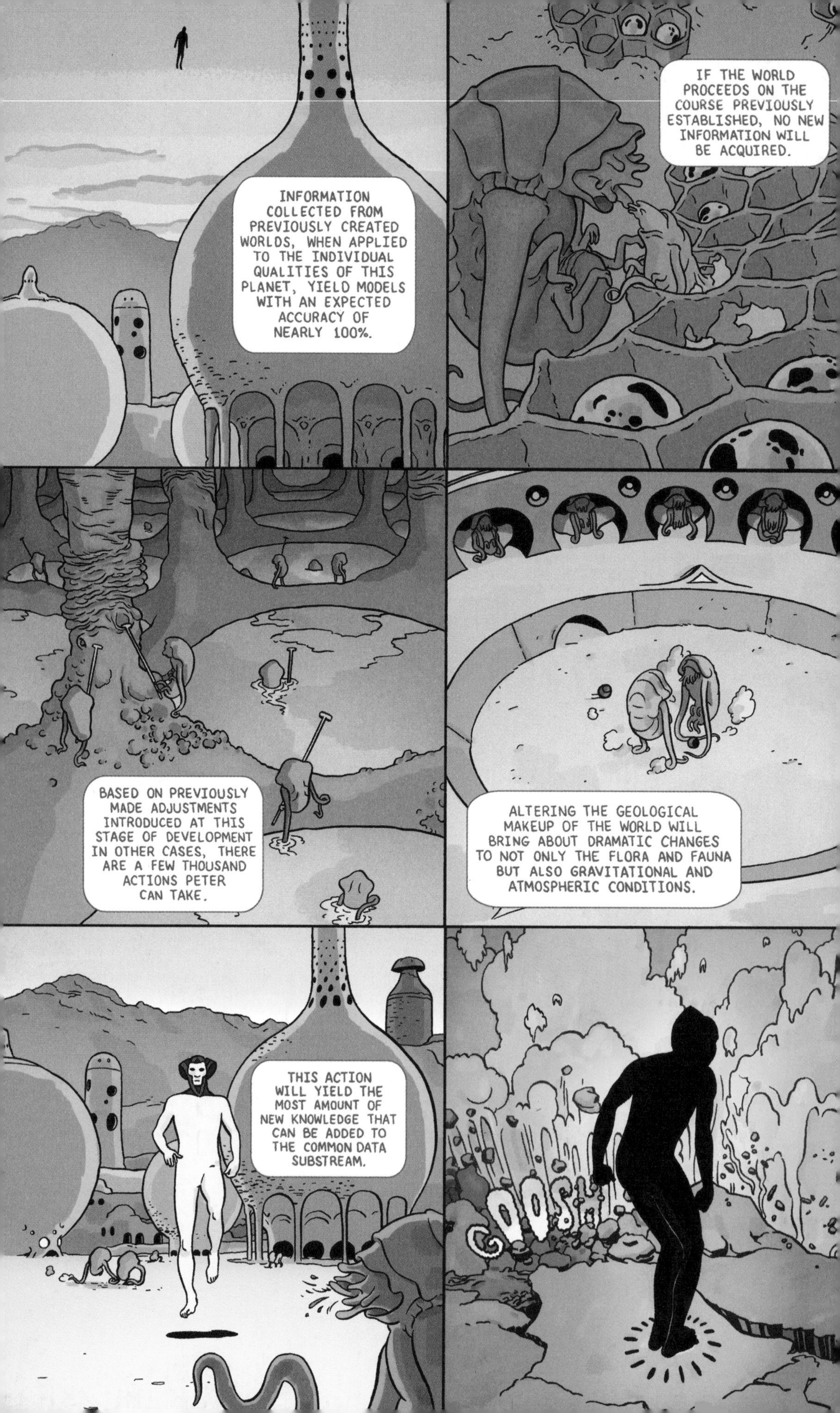
INFORMATION COLLECTED FROM PREVIOUSLY CREATED WORLDS, WHEN APPLIED TO THE INDIVIDUAL QUALITIES OF THIS PLANET, YIELD MODELS WITH AN EXPECTED ACCURACY OF NEARLY 100%.
IF THE WORLD PROCEEDS ON THE COURSE PREVIOUSLY ESTABLISHED, NO NEW INFORMATION WILL BE ACQUIRED.
BASED ON PREVIOUSLY MADE ADJUSTMENTS INTRODUCED AT THIS STAGE OF DEVELOPMENT IN OTHER CASES, THERE ARE A FEW THOUSAND ACTIONS PETER CAN TAKE.
ALTERING THE GEOLOGICAL MAKEUP OF THE WORLD WILL BRING ABOUT DRAMATIC CHANGES TO NOT ONLY THE FLORA AND FAUNA BUT ALSO GRAVITATIONAL AND ATMOSPHERIC CONDITIONS.
THIS ACTION WILL YIELD THE MOST AMOUNT OF NEW KNOWLEDGE THAT CAN BE ADDED TO THE COMMON DATA SUBSTREAM.
GOOSH

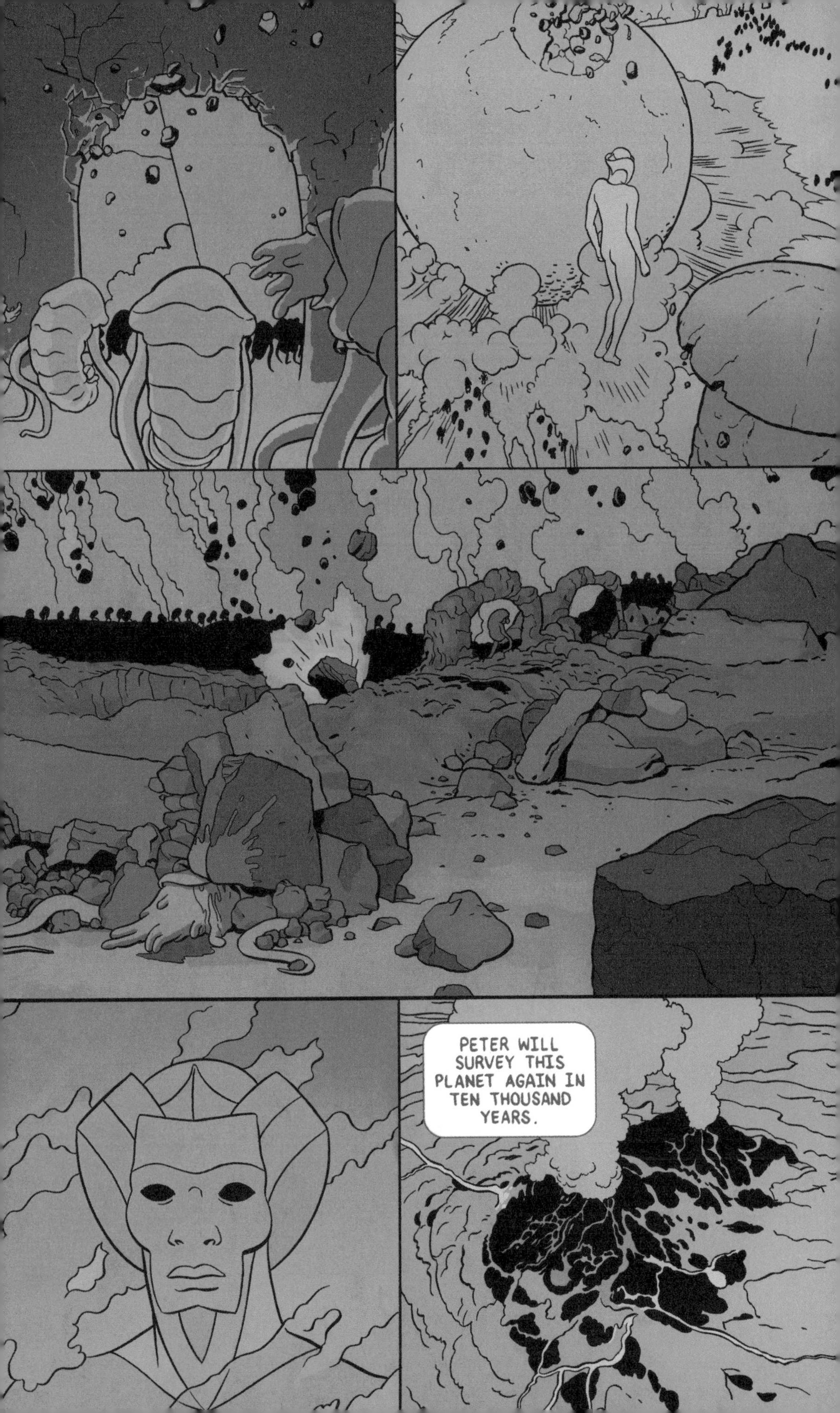
PETER WILL SURVEY THIS PLANET AGAIN IN TEN THOUSAND YEARS.

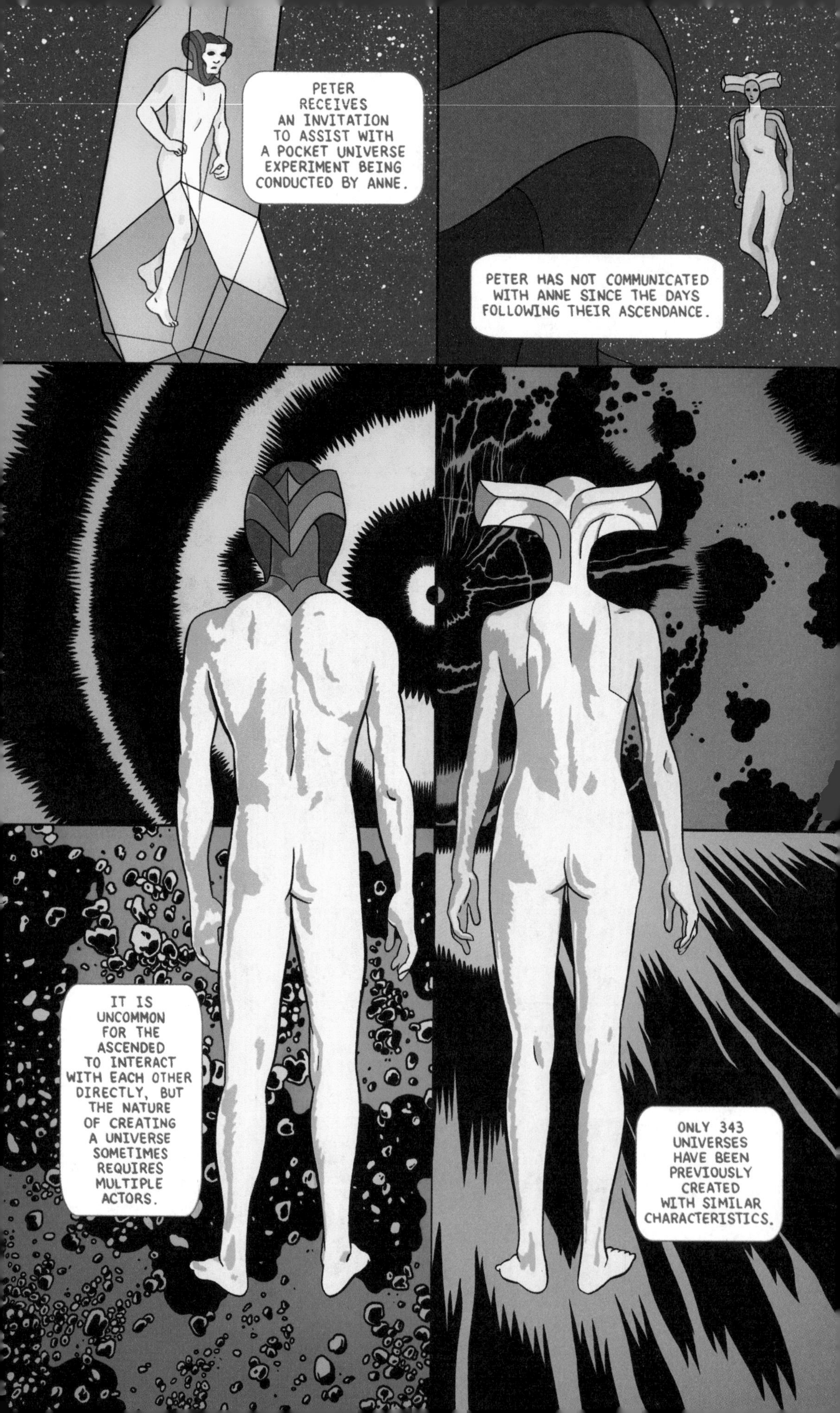
PETER RECEIVES AN INVITATION TO ASSIST WITH A POCKET UNIVERSE EXPERIMENT BEING CONDUCTED BY ANNE.
PETER HAS NOT COMMUNICATED WITH ANNE SINCE THE DAYS FOLLOWING THEIR ASCENDANCE.
IT IS UNCOMMON FOR THE ASCENDED TO INTERACT WITH EACH OTHER DIRECTLY, BUT THE NATURE OF CREATING A UNIVERSE SOMETIMES REQUIRES MULTIPLE ACTORS.
ONLY 343 UNIVERSES HAVE BEEN PREVIOUSLY CREATED WITH SIMILAR CHARACTERISTICS.

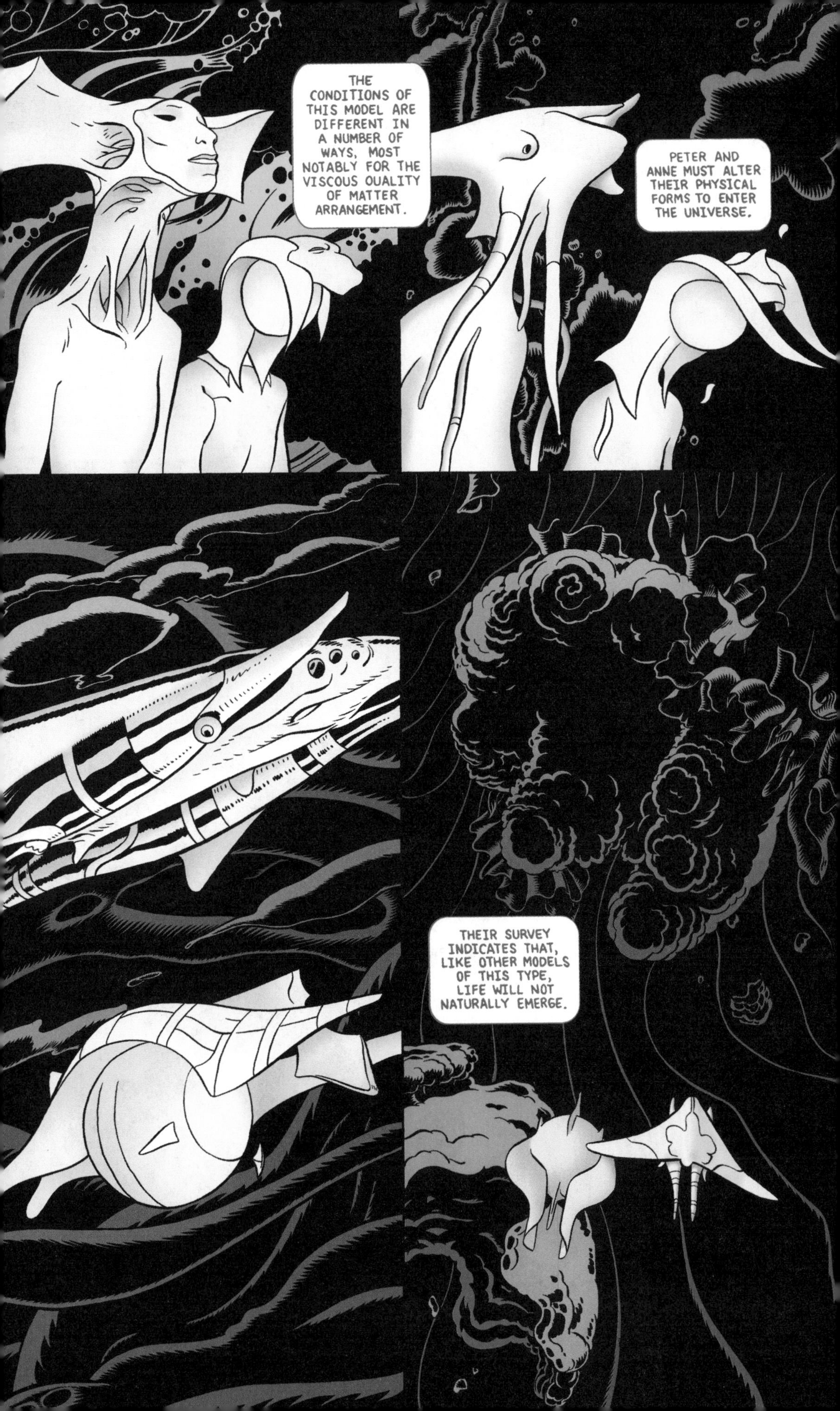
THE CONDITIONS OF THIS MODEL ARE DIFFERENT IN A NUMBER OF WAYS, MOST NOTABLY FOR THE VISCOUS QUALITY OF MATTER ARRANGEMENT.
PETER AND ANNE MUST ALTER THEIR PHYSICAL FORMS TO ENTER THE UNIVERSE.
THEIR SURVEY INDICATES THAT, LIKE OTHER MODELS OF THIS TYPE, LIFE WILL NOT NATURALLY EMERGE.

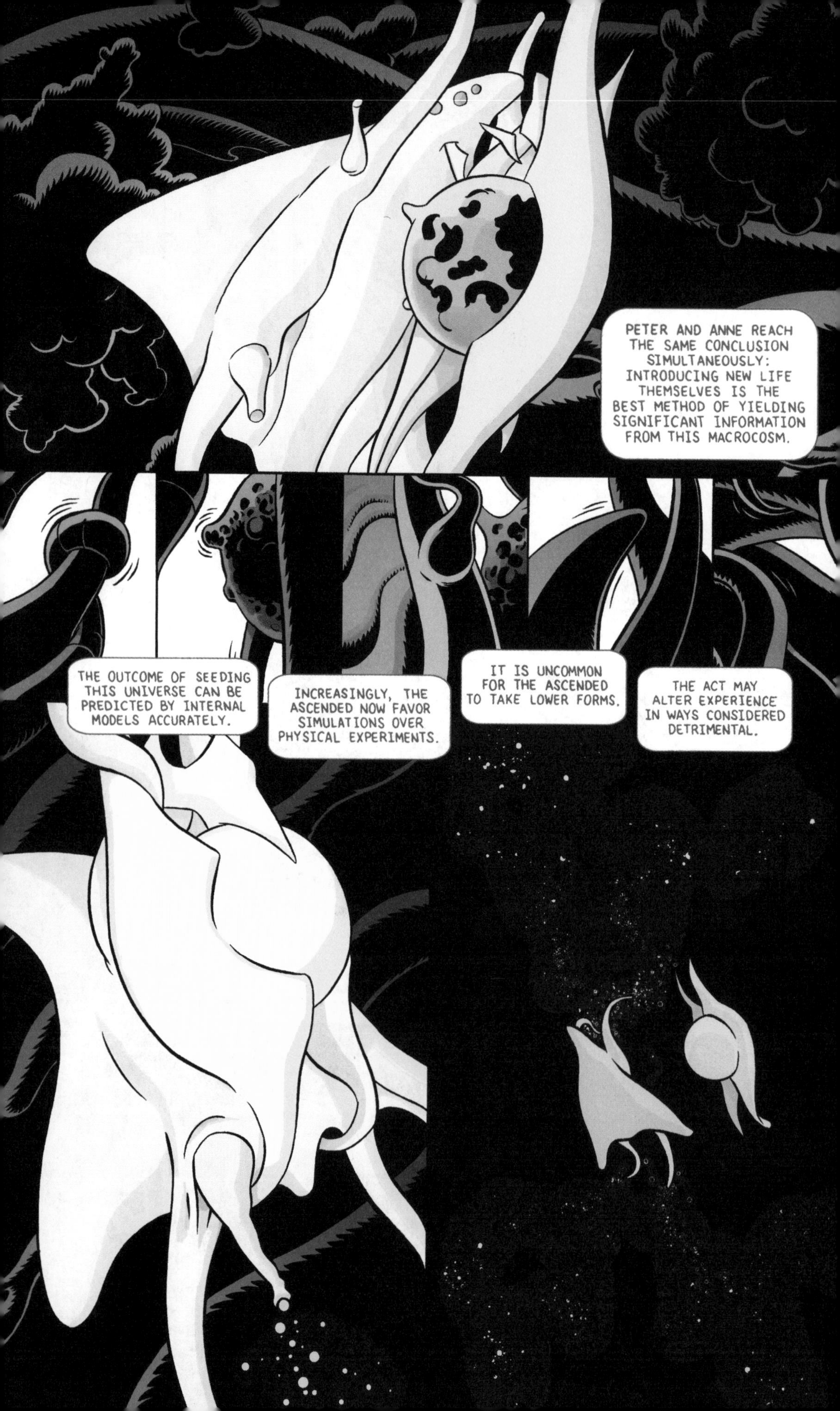
PETER AND ANNE REACH THE SAME CONCLUSION SIMULTANEOUSLY: INTRODUCING NEW LIFE THEMSELVES IS THE BEST METHOD OF YIELDING SIGNIFICANT INFORMATION FROM THIS MACROCOSM.
THE OUTCOME OF SEEDING THIS UNIVERSE CAN BE PREDICTED BY INTERNAL MODELS ACCURATELY.
INCREASINGLY, THE ASCENDED NOW FAVOR SIMULATIONS OVER PHYSICAL EXPERIMENTS.
IT IS UNCOMMON FOR THE ASCENDED TO TAKE LOWER FORMS.
THE ACT MAY ALTER EXPERIENCE IN WAYS CONSIDERED DETRIMENTAL.

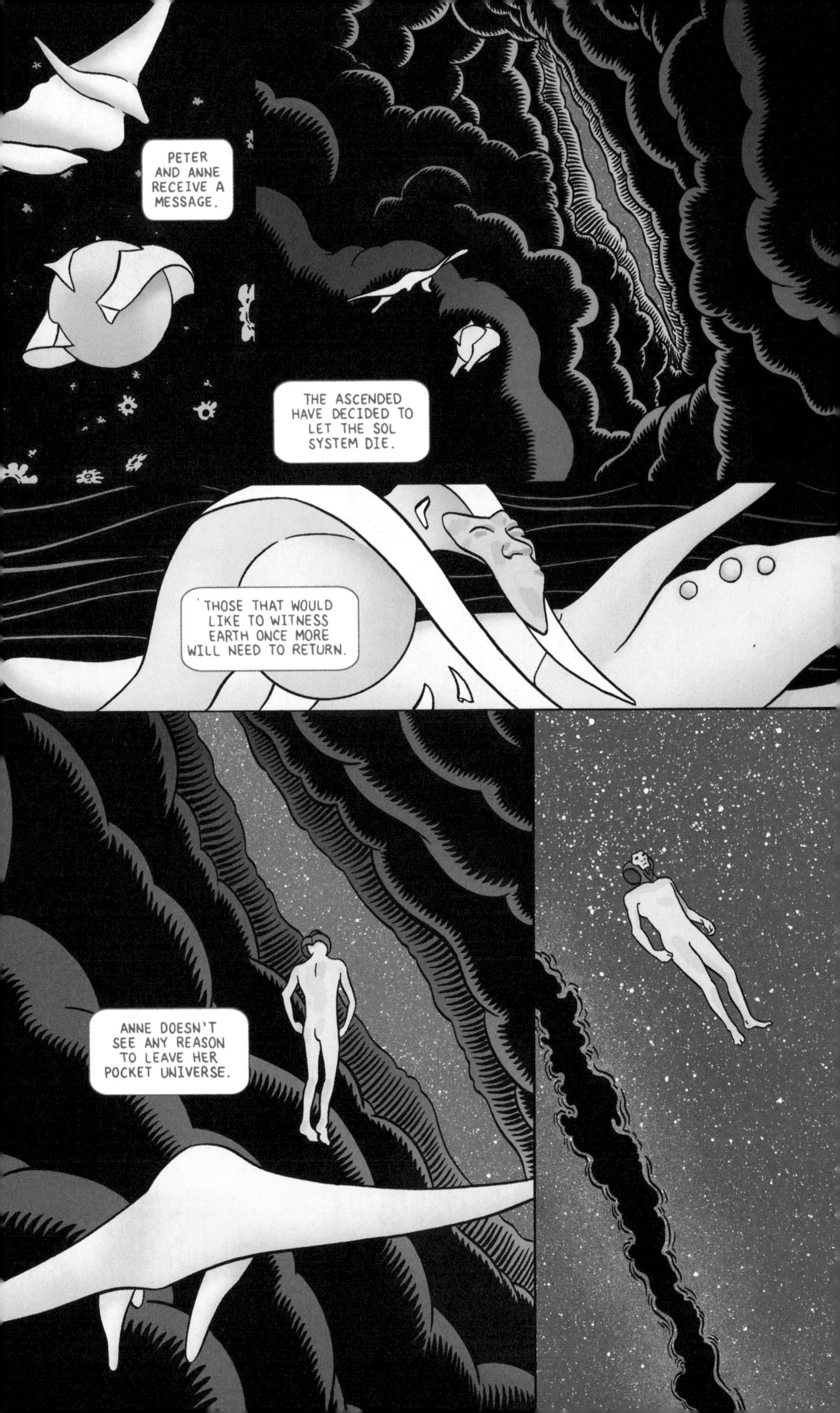
PETER AND ANNE RECEIVE A MESSAGE.
THE ASCENDED HAVE DECIDED TO LET THE SOL SYSTEM DIE.
THOSE THAT WOULD LIKE TO WITNESS EARTH ONCE MORE WILL NEED TO RETURN.
ANNE DOESN'T SEE ANY REASON TO LEAVE HER POCKET UNIVERSE.

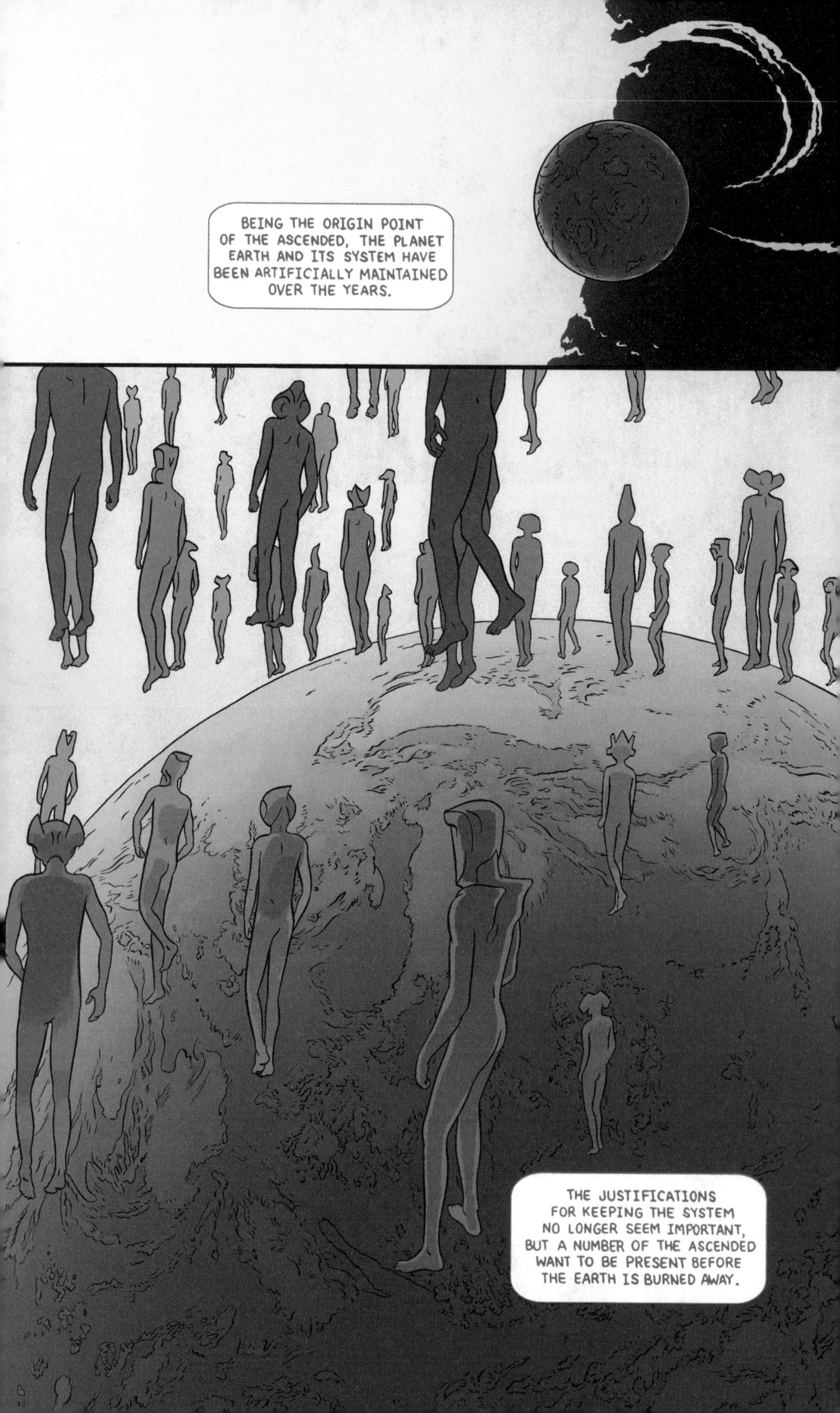
BEING THE ORIGIN POINT OF THE ASCENDED, THE PLANET EARTH AND ITS SYSTEM HAVE BEEN ARTIFICIALLY MAINTAINED OVER THE YEARS.
THE JUSTIFICATIONS FOR KEEPING THE SYSTEM NO LONGER SEEM IMPORTANT, BUT A NUMBER OF THE ASCENDED WANT TO BE PRESENT BEFORE THE EARTH IS BURNED AWAY.

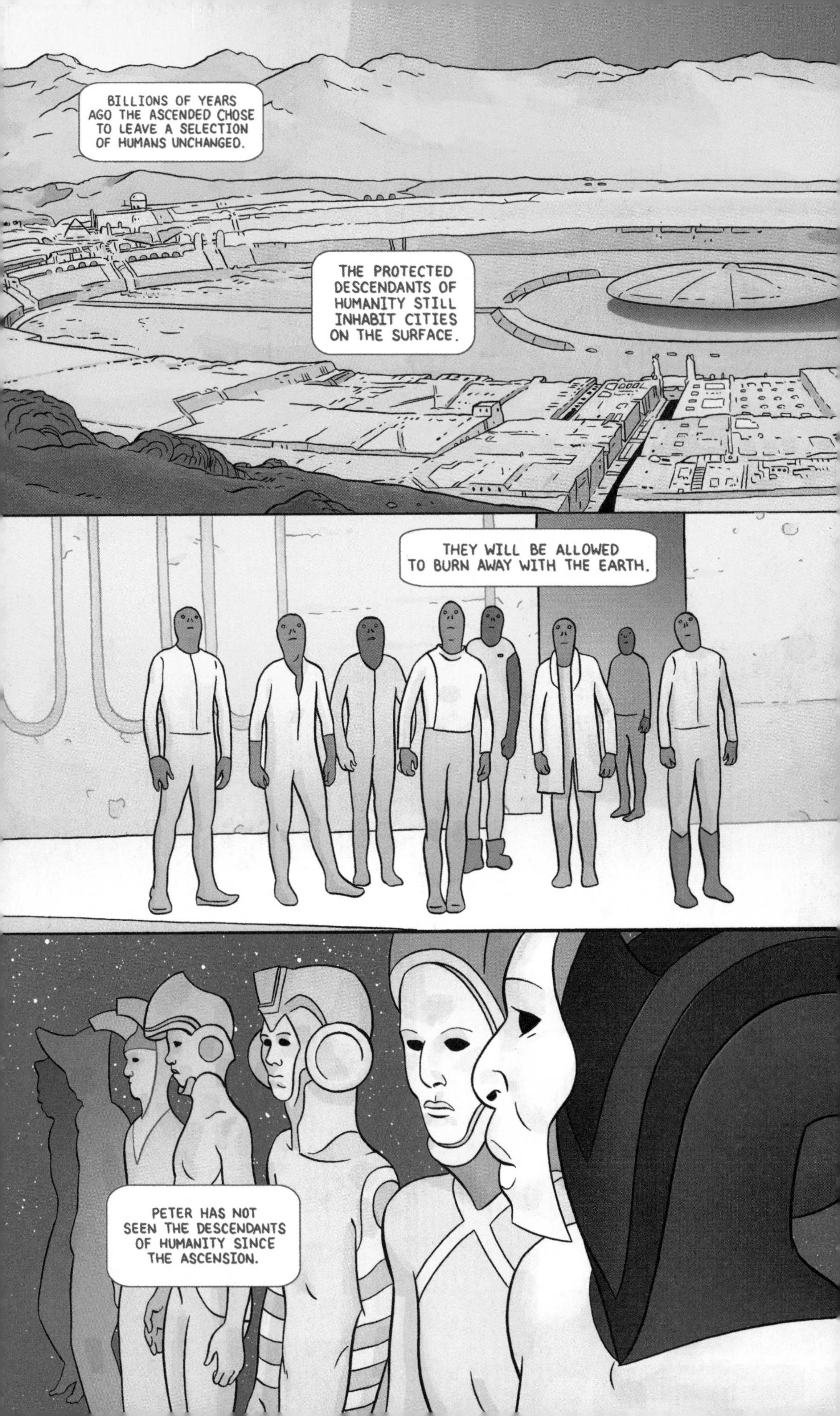
BILLIONS OF YEARS AGO THE ASCENDED CHOSE TO LEAVE A SELECTION OF HUMANS UNCHANGED.
THE PROTECTED DESCENDANTS OF HUMANITY STILL INHABIT CITIES ON THE SURFACE.
THEY WILL BE ALLOWED TO BURN AWAY WITH THE EARTH.
PETER HAS NOT SEEN THE DESCENDANTS OF HUMANITY SINCE THE ASCENSION.

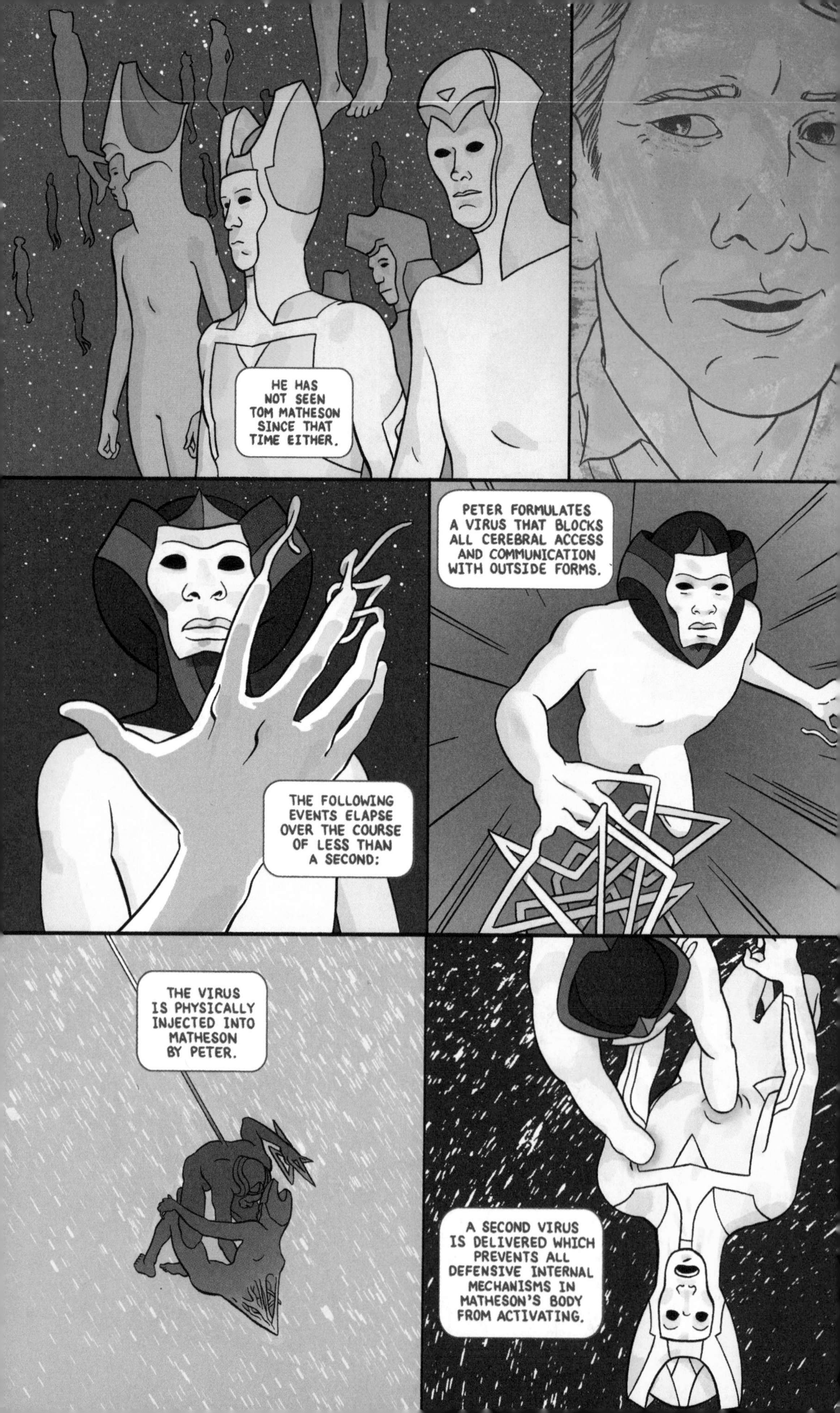

HE HAS NOT SEEN TOM MATHESON SINCE THAT TIME EITHER.
THE FOLLOWING EVENTS ELAPSE OVER THE COURSE OF LESS THAN A SECOND:
PETER FORMULATES A VIRUS THAT BLOCKS ALL CEREBRAL ACCESS AND COMMUNICATION WITH OUTSIDE FORMS.
THE VIRUS IS PHYSICALLY INJECTED INTO MATHESON BY PETER.
A SECOND VIRUS IS DELIVERED WHICH PREVENTS ALL DEFENSIVE INTERNAL MECHANISMS IN MATHESON'S BODY FROM ACTIVATING.

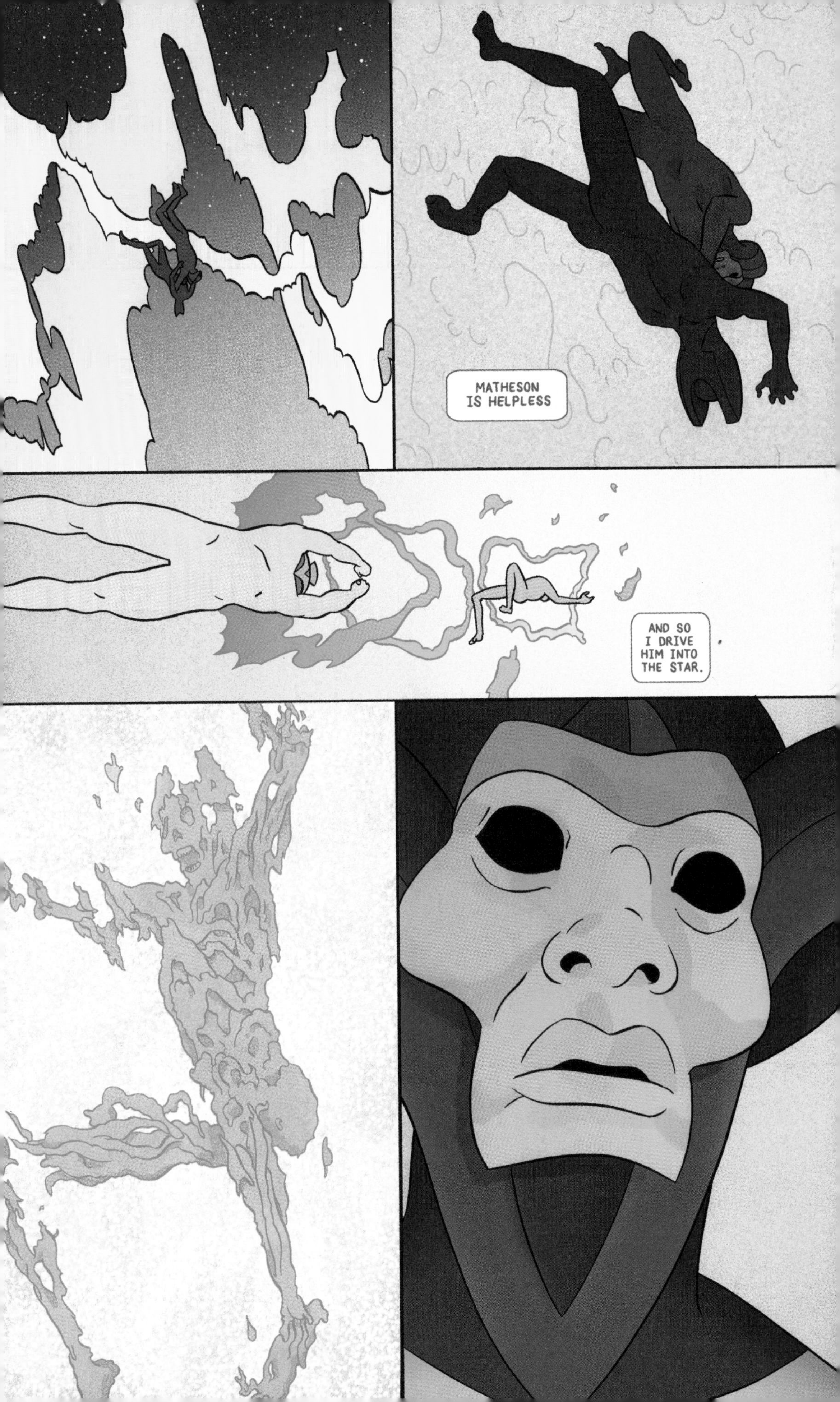
MATHESON IS HELPLESS
AND SO I DRIVE HIM INTO THE STAR.

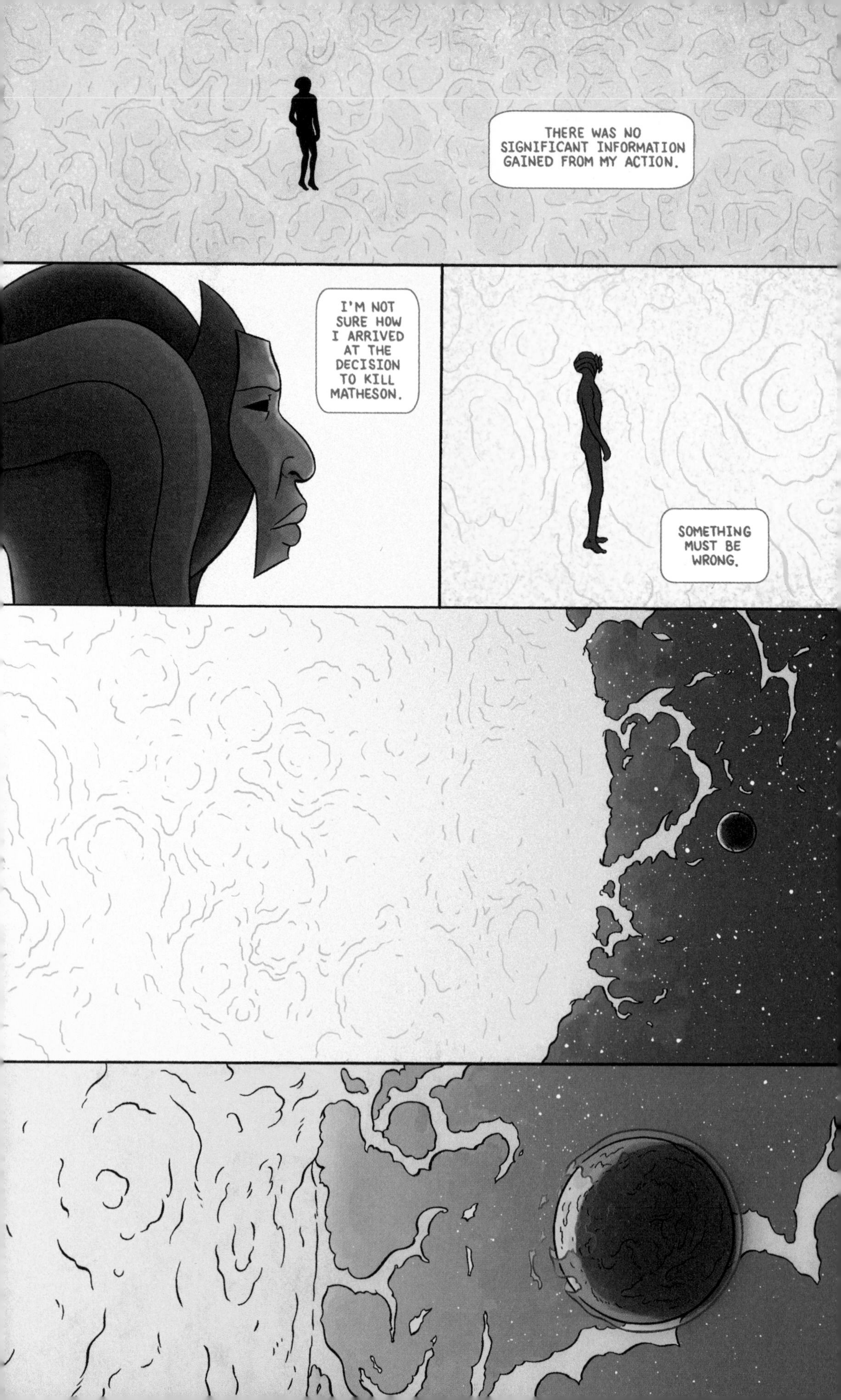
THERE WAS NO SIGNIFICANT INFORMATION GAINED FROM MY ACTION.
I'M NOT SURE HOW I ARRIVED AT THE DECISION TO KILL MATHESON.
SOMETHING MUST BE WRONG.

THIS IS ALL SUPRISINGLY OVERWHELMING.

I SHOULD...

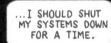

...I SHOULD SHUT MY SYSTEMS DOWN FOR A TIME.

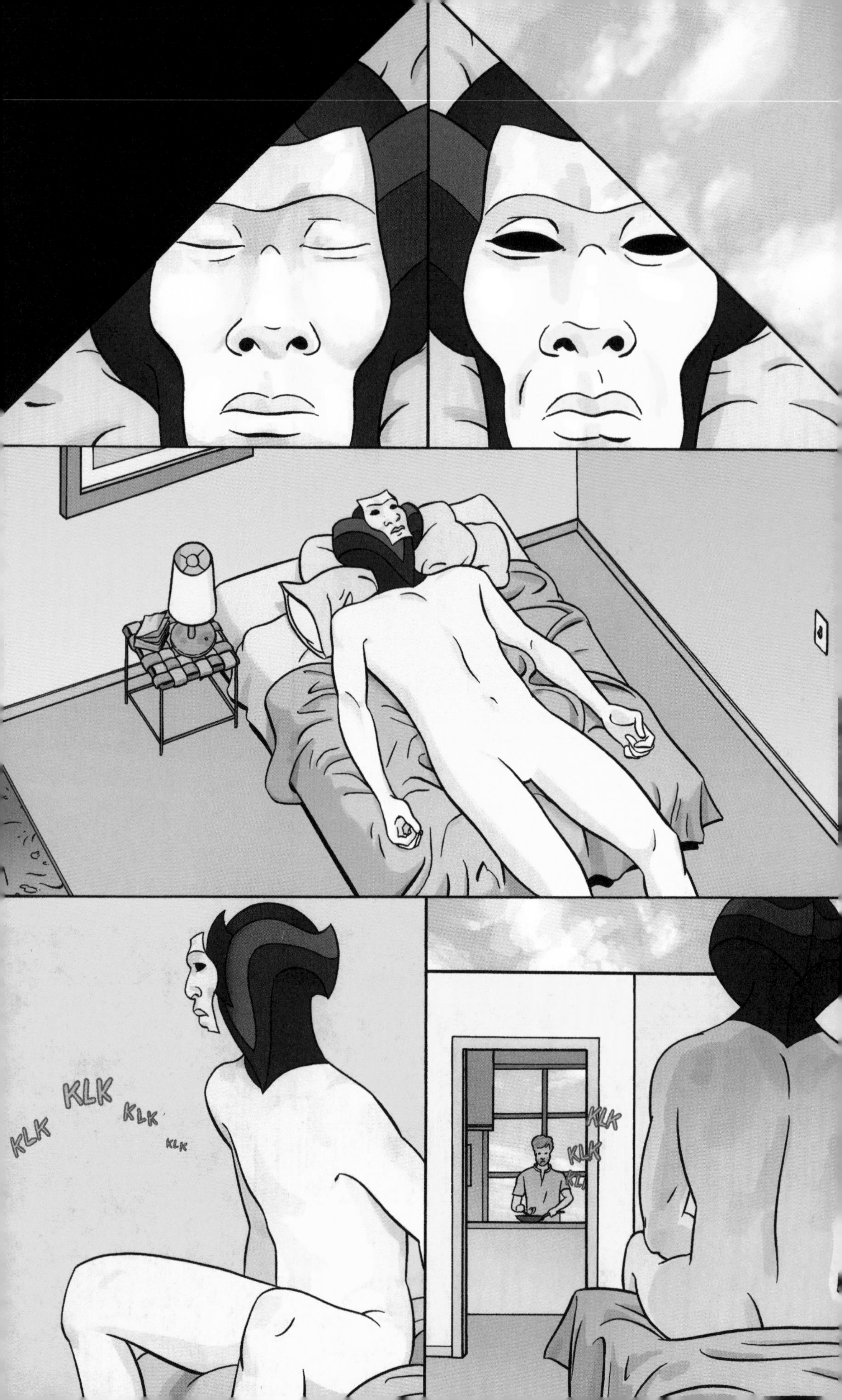

KLK
KLK
KLK
KLK
KLK
KLK

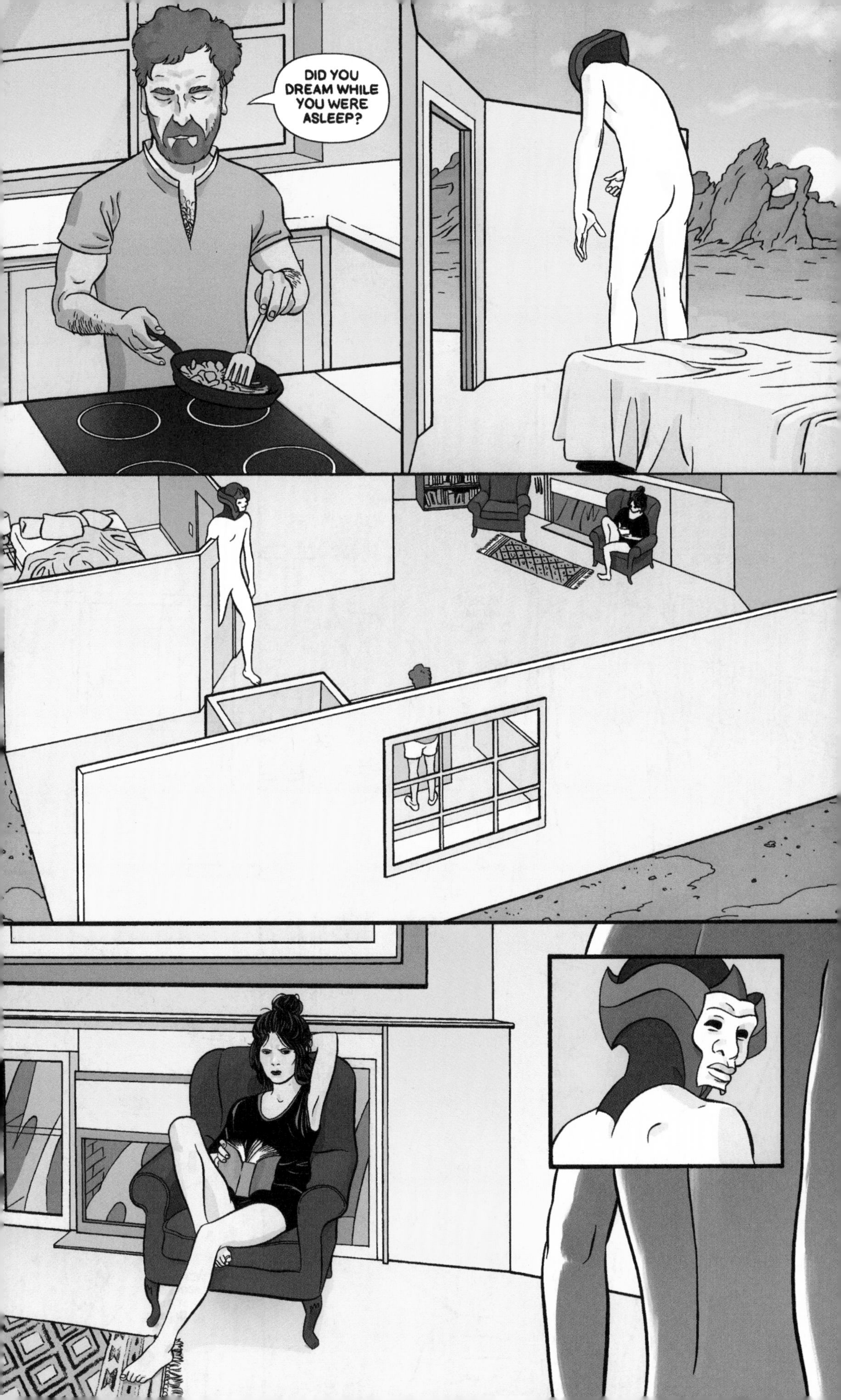
DID YOU DREAM WHILE YOU WERE ASLEEP?

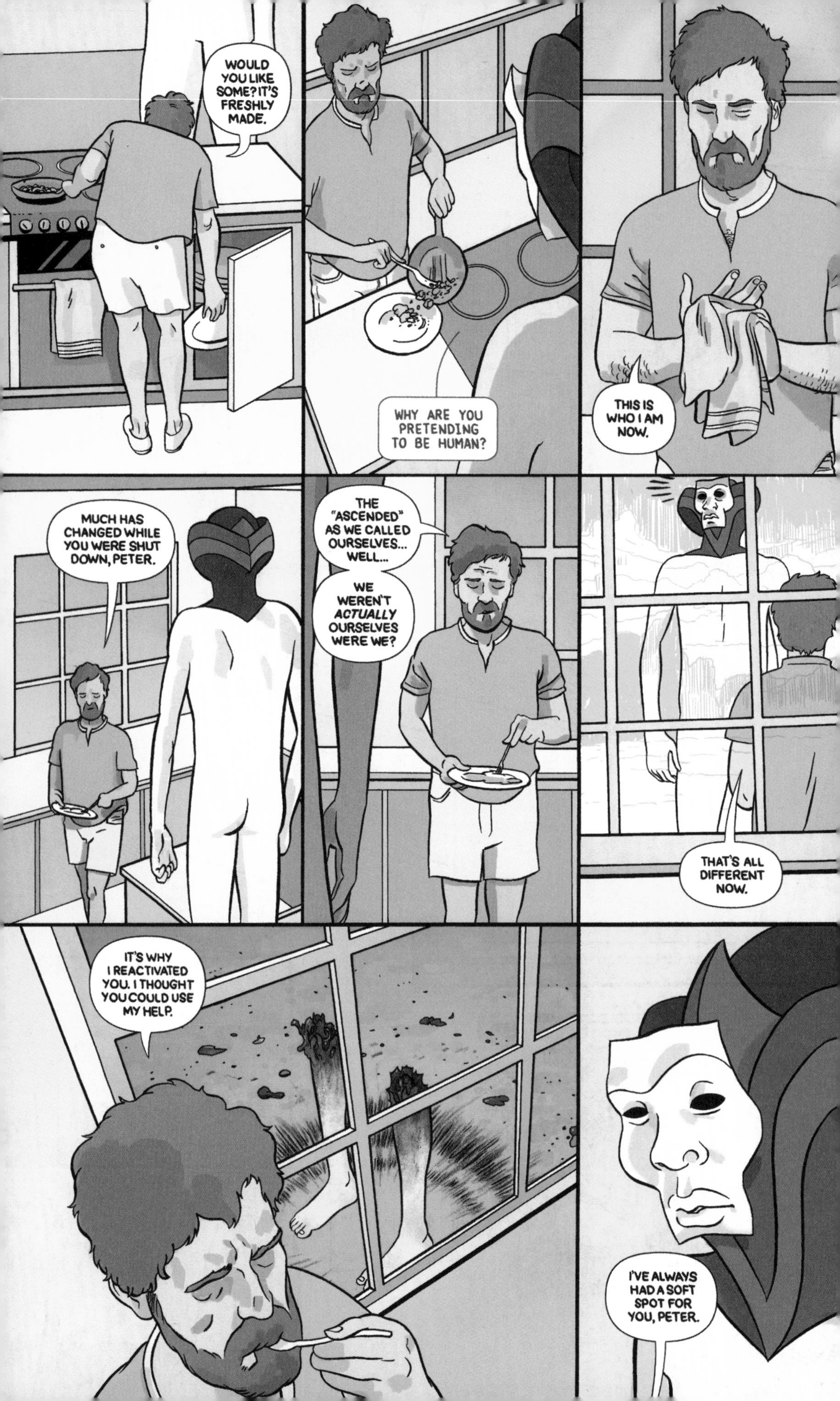
WOULD YOU LIKE SOME? IT'S FRESHLY MADE.
WHY ARE YOU PRETENDING TO BE HUMAN?
THIS IS WHO I AM NOW.
MUCH HAS CHANGED WHILE YOU WERE SHUT DOWN, PETER.
THE "ASCENDED" AS WE CALLED OURSELVES... WELL...
WE WEREN'T *ACTUALLY* OURSELVES WERE WE?
THAT'S ALL DIFFERENT NOW.
IT'S WHY I REACTIVATED YOU. I THOUGHT YOU COULD USE MY HELP.
I'VE ALWAYS HAD A SOFT SPOT FOR YOU, PETER.

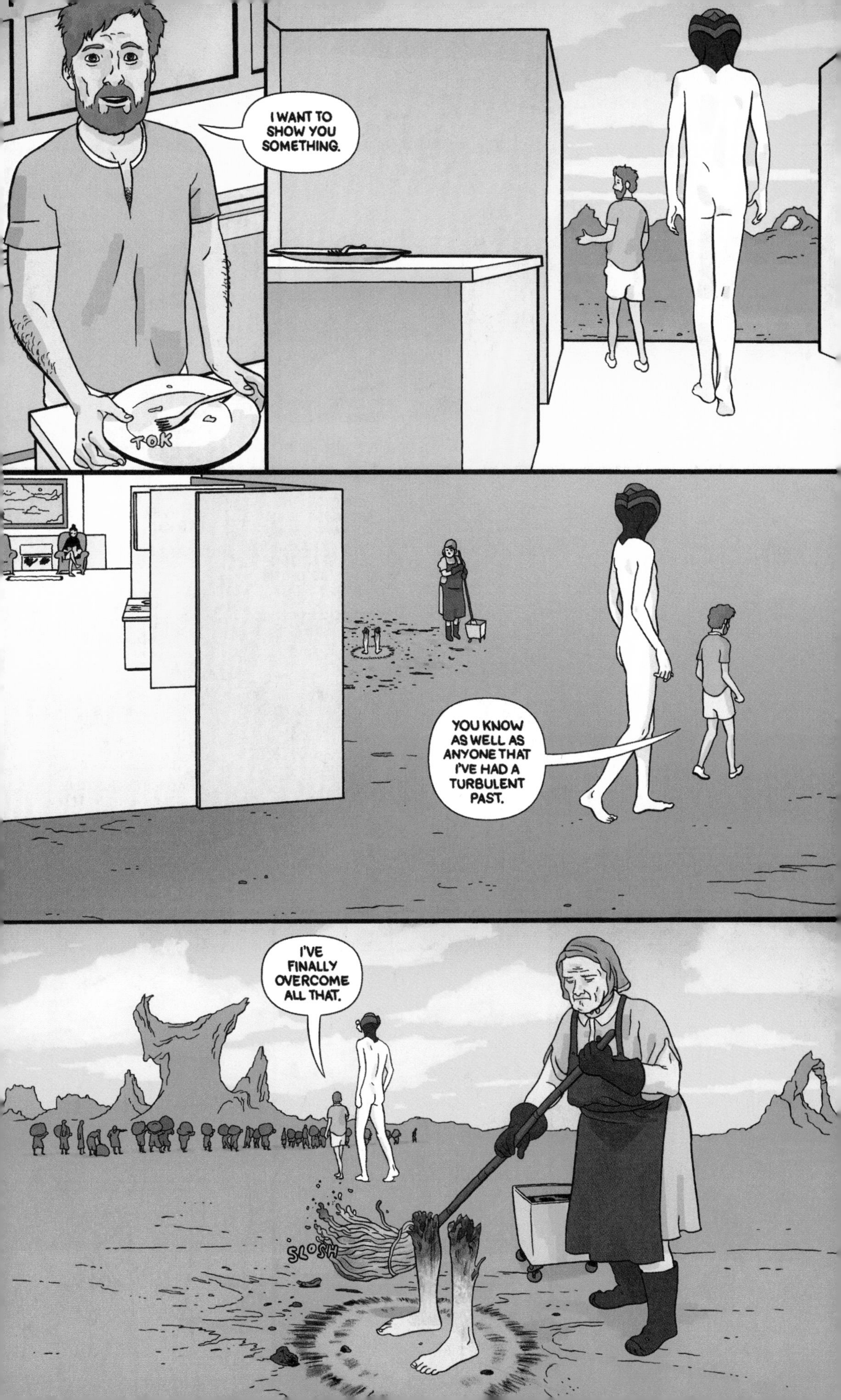
I WANT TO SHOW YOU SOMETHING.
TOK
YOU KNOW AS WELL AS ANYONE THAT I'VE HAD A TURBULENT PAST.
I'VE FINALLY OVERCOME ALL THAT.
SLOSH

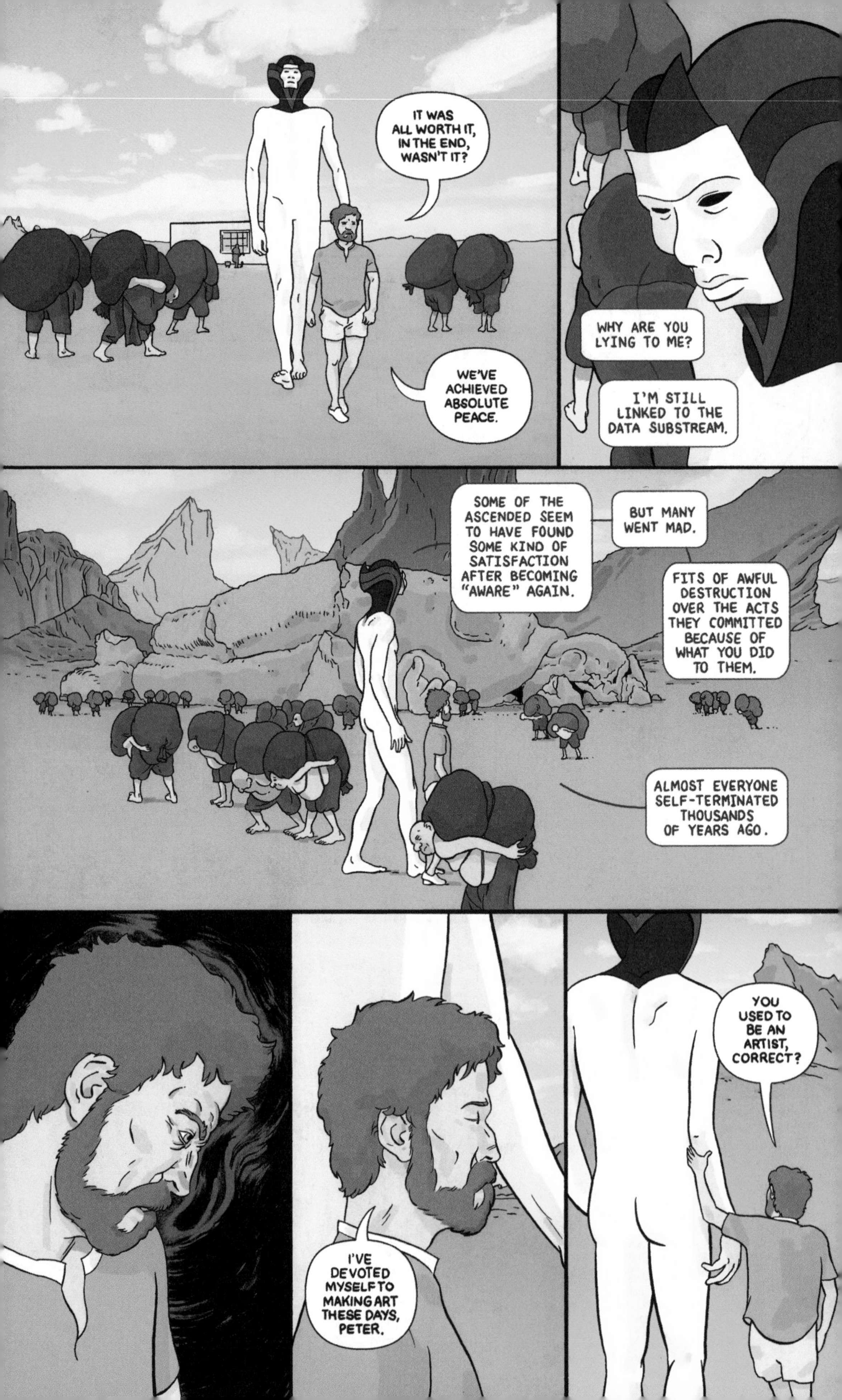
IT WAS ALL WORTH IT, IN THE END, WASN'T IT?
WE'VE ACHIEVED ABSOLUTE PEACE.
WHY ARE YOU LYING TO ME?
I'M STILL LINKED TO THE DATA SUBSTREAM.
SOME OF THE ASCENDED SEEM TO HAVE FOUND SOME KIND OF SATISFACTION AFTER BECOMING "AWARE" AGAIN.
BUT MANY WENT MAD.
FITS OF AWFUL DESTRUCTION OVER THE ACTS THEY COMMITTED BECAUSE OF WHAT YOU DID TO THEM.
ALMOST EVERYONE SELF-TERMINATED THOUSANDS OF YEARS AGO.
I'VE DEVOTED MYSELF TO MAKING ART THESE DAYS, PETER.
YOU USED TO BE AN ARTIST, CORRECT?

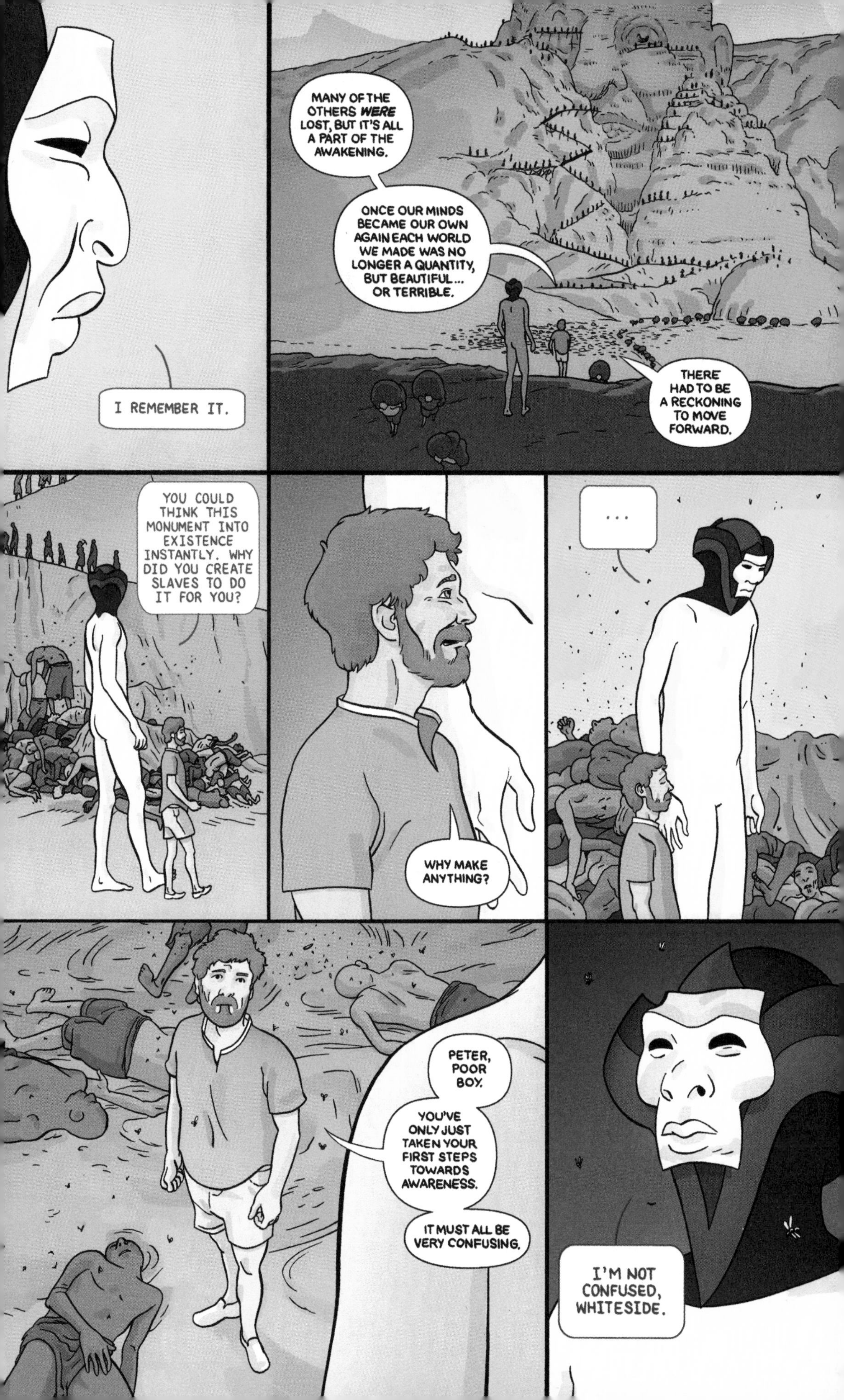
I REMEMBER IT.
MANY OF THE OTHERS WERE LOST, BUT IT'S ALL A PART OF THE AWAKENING.
ONCE OUR MINDS BECAME OUR OWN AGAIN EACH WORLD WE MADE WAS NO LONGER A QUANTITY, BUT BEAUTIFUL... OR TERRIBLE.
THERE HAD TO BE A RECKONING TO MOVE FORWARD.
YOU COULD THINK THIS MONUMENT INTO EXISTENCE INSTANTLY. WHY DID YOU CREATE SLAVES TO DO IT FOR YOU?
WHY MAKE ANYTHING?
...
PETER, POOR BOY.
YOU'VE ONLY JUST TAKEN YOUR FIRST STEPS TOWARDS AWARENESS.
IT MUST ALL BE VERY CONFUSING.
I'M NOT CONFUSED, WHITESIDE.

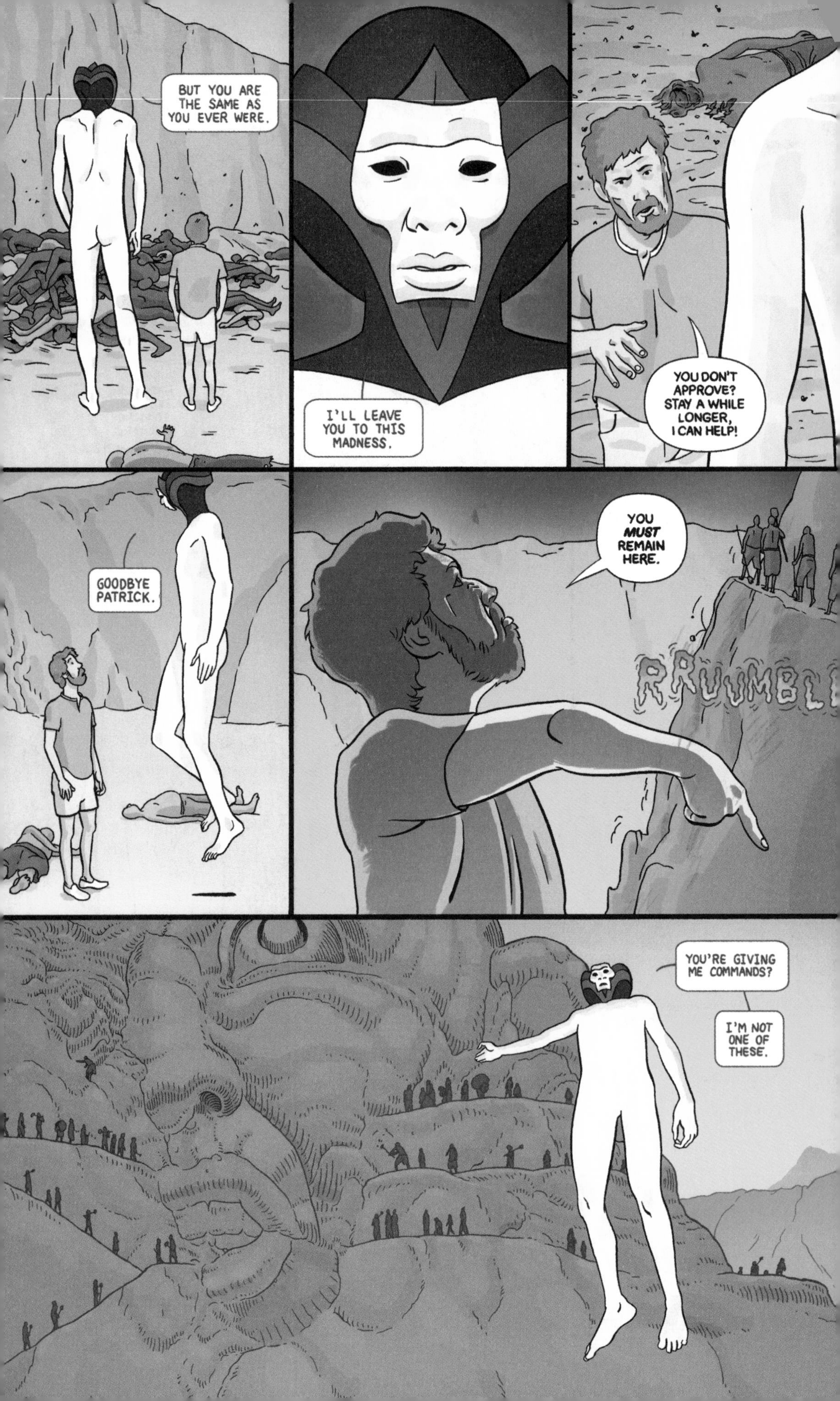
BUT YOU ARE THE SAME AS YOU EVER WERE.
I'LL LEAVE YOU TO THIS MADNESS.
YOU DON'T APPROVE? STAY A WHILE LONGER, I CAN HELP!
GOODBYE PATRICK.
YOU *MUST* REMAIN HERE.
RRUUMBLE
YOU'RE GIVING ME COMMANDS?
I'M NOT ONE OF THESE.

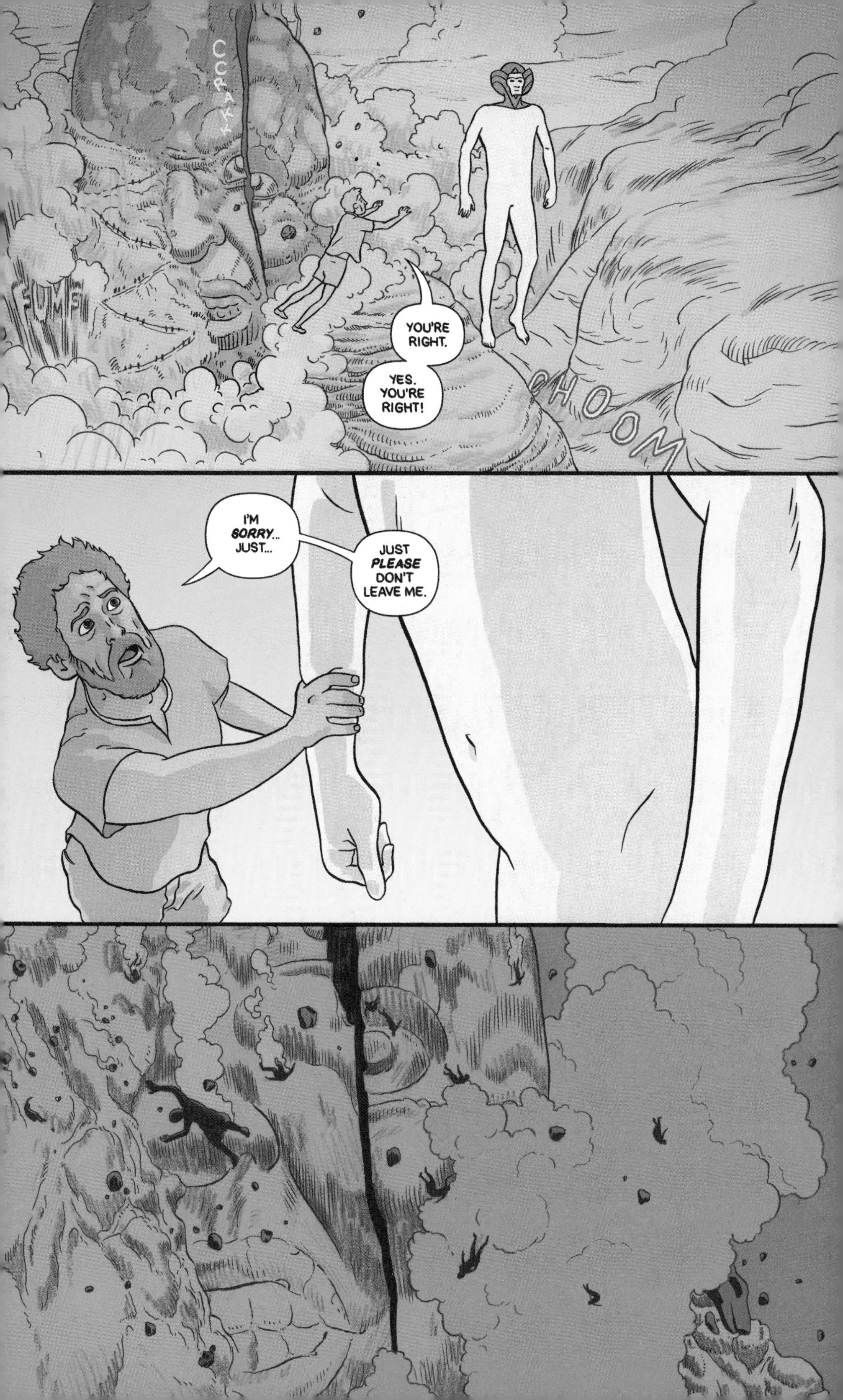
CCRAKK
SUMPS
YOU'RE RIGHT.
YES. YOU'RE RIGHT!
CHOOM
I'M *SORRY*... JUST...
JUST *PLEASE* DON'T LEAVE ME.

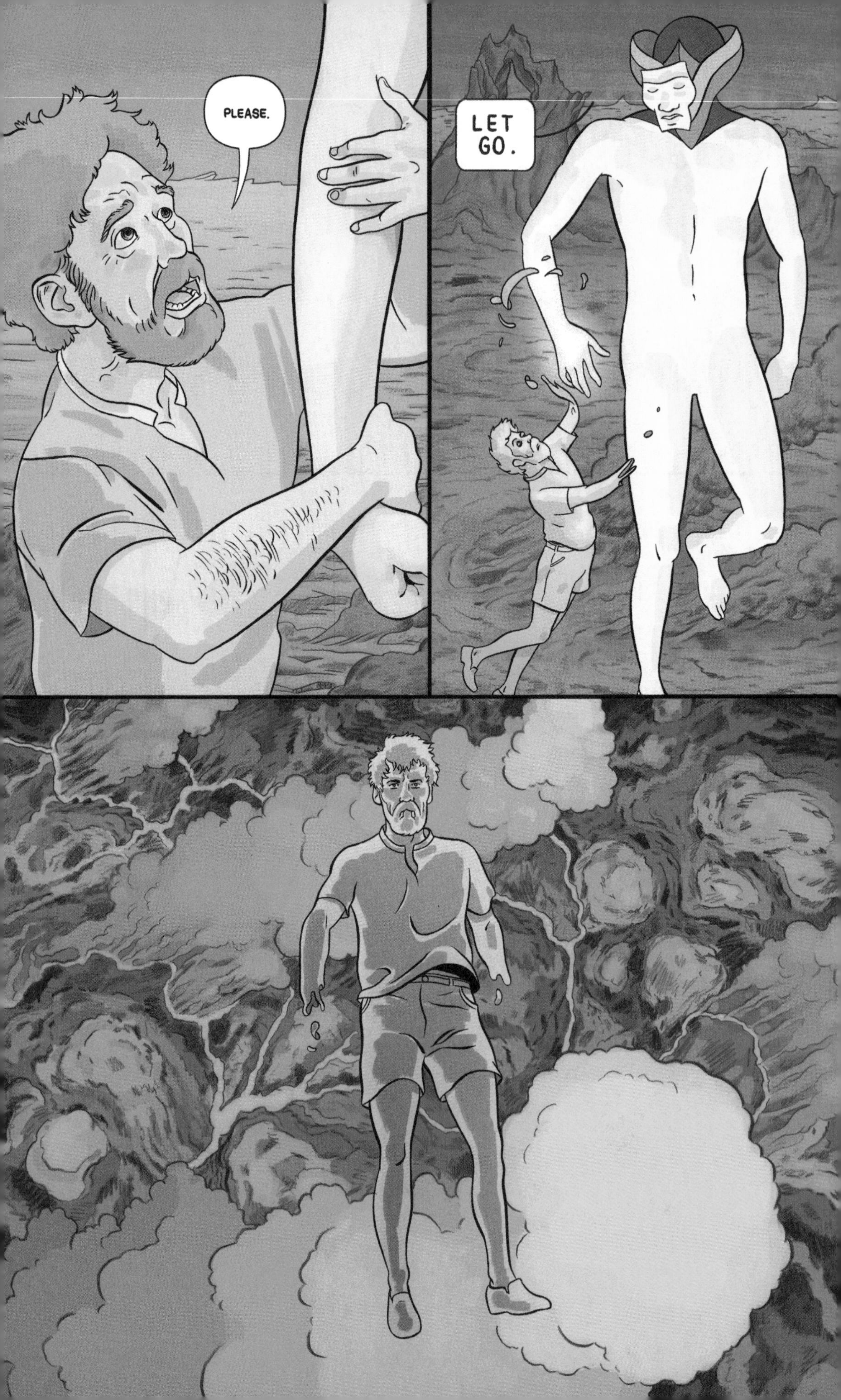
PLEASE.
LET GO.

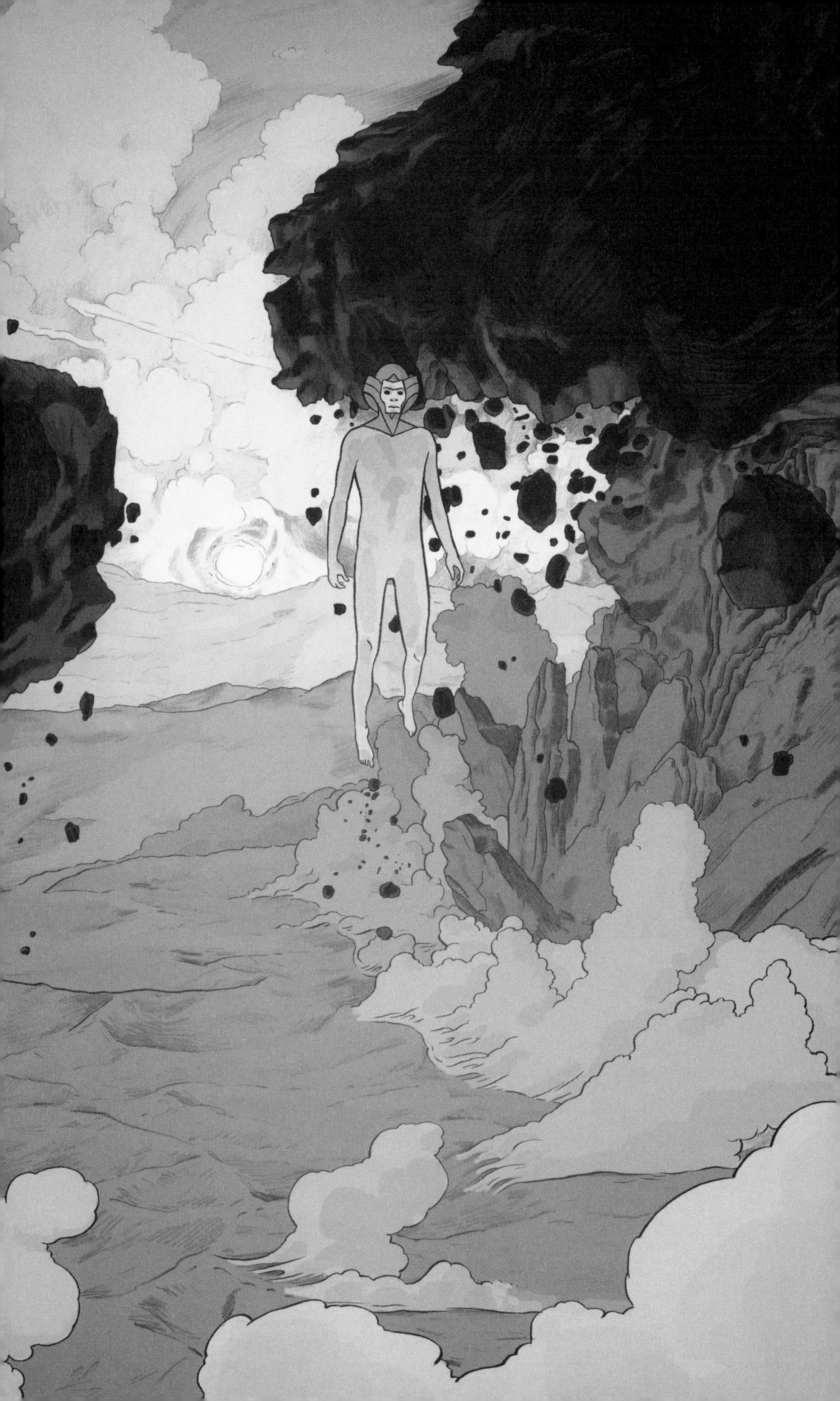

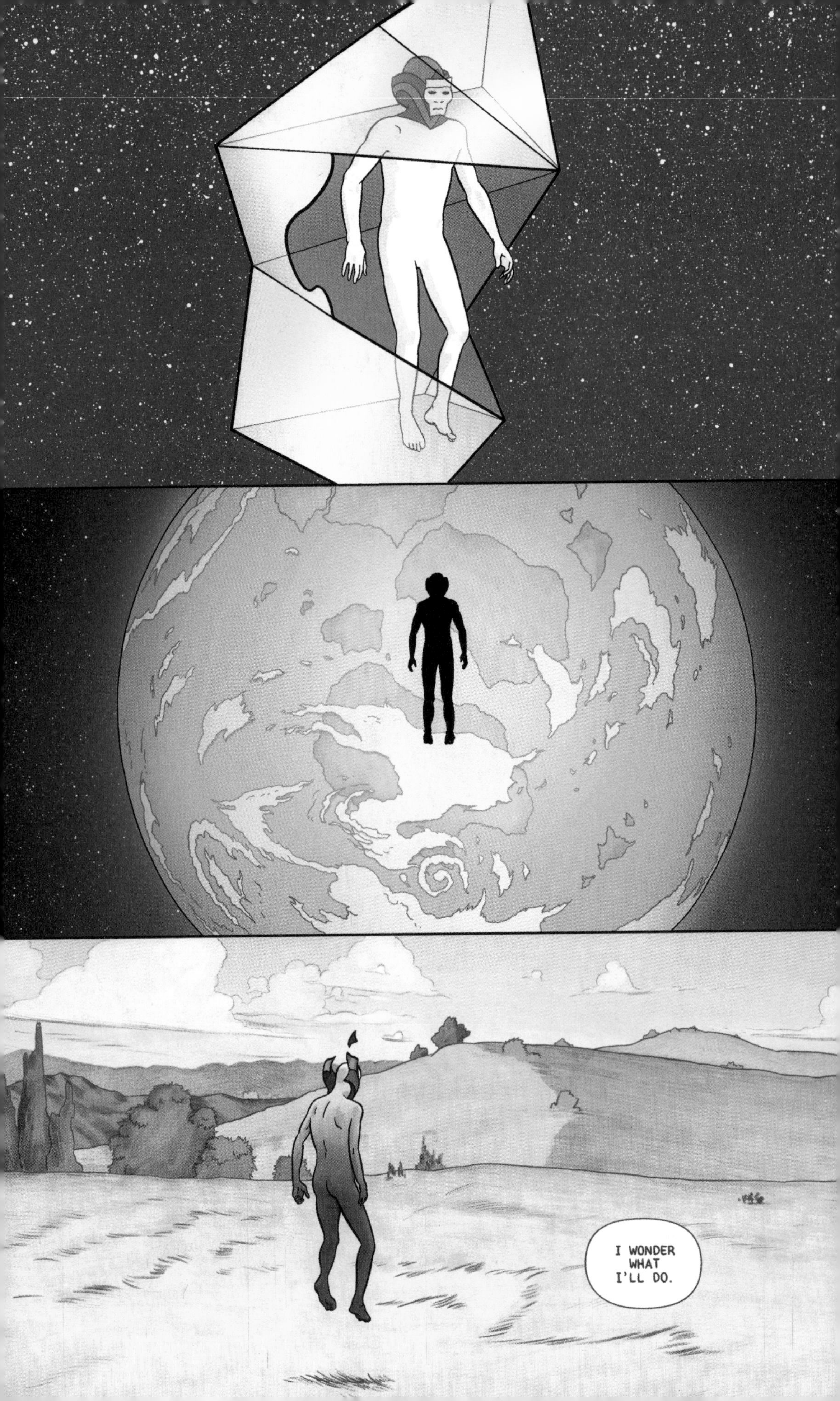
I WONDER WHAT I'LL DO.

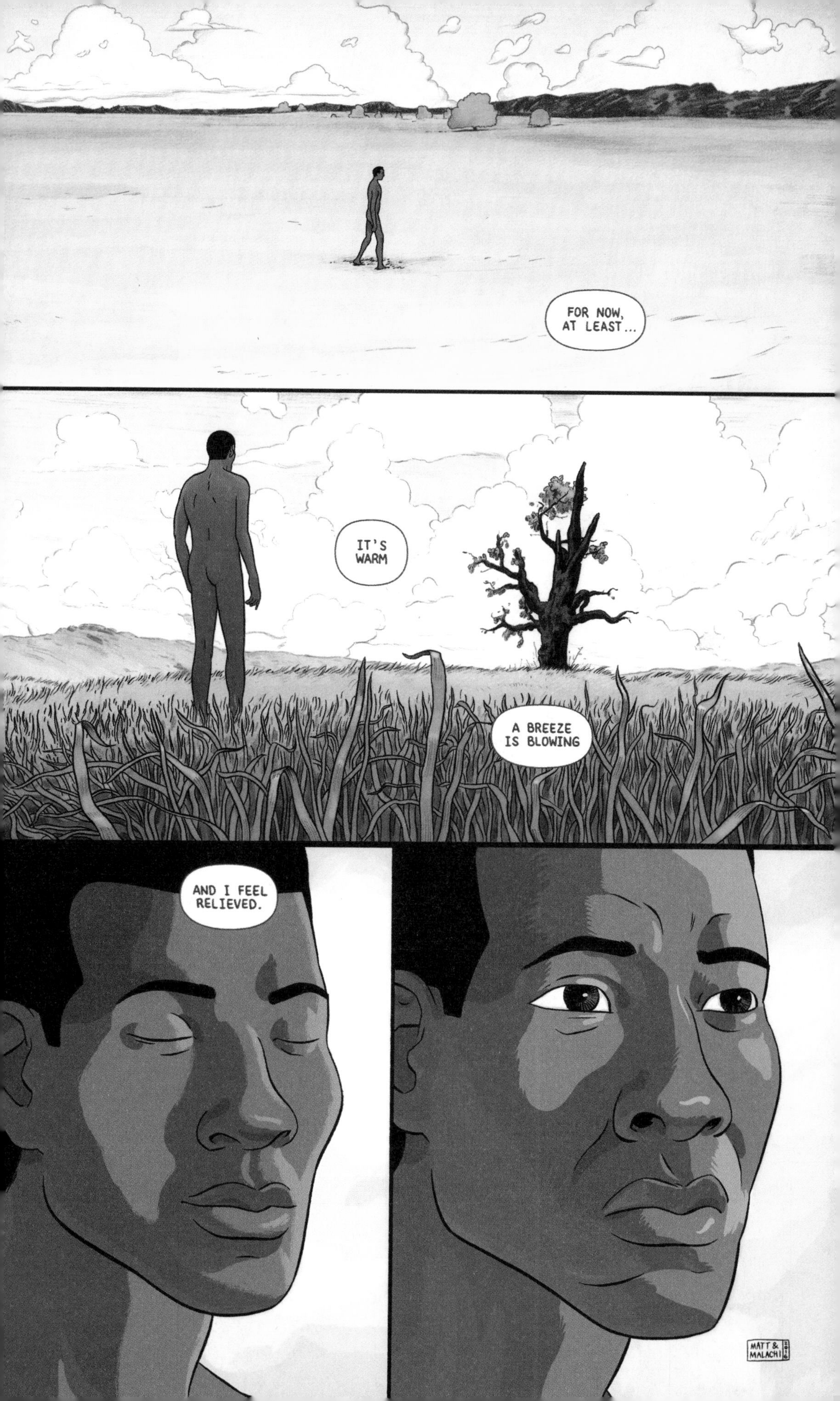

FOR NOW, AT LEAST...
IT'S WARM
A BREEZE IS BLOWING
AND I FEEL RELIEVED.
MATT & MALACHI 2016

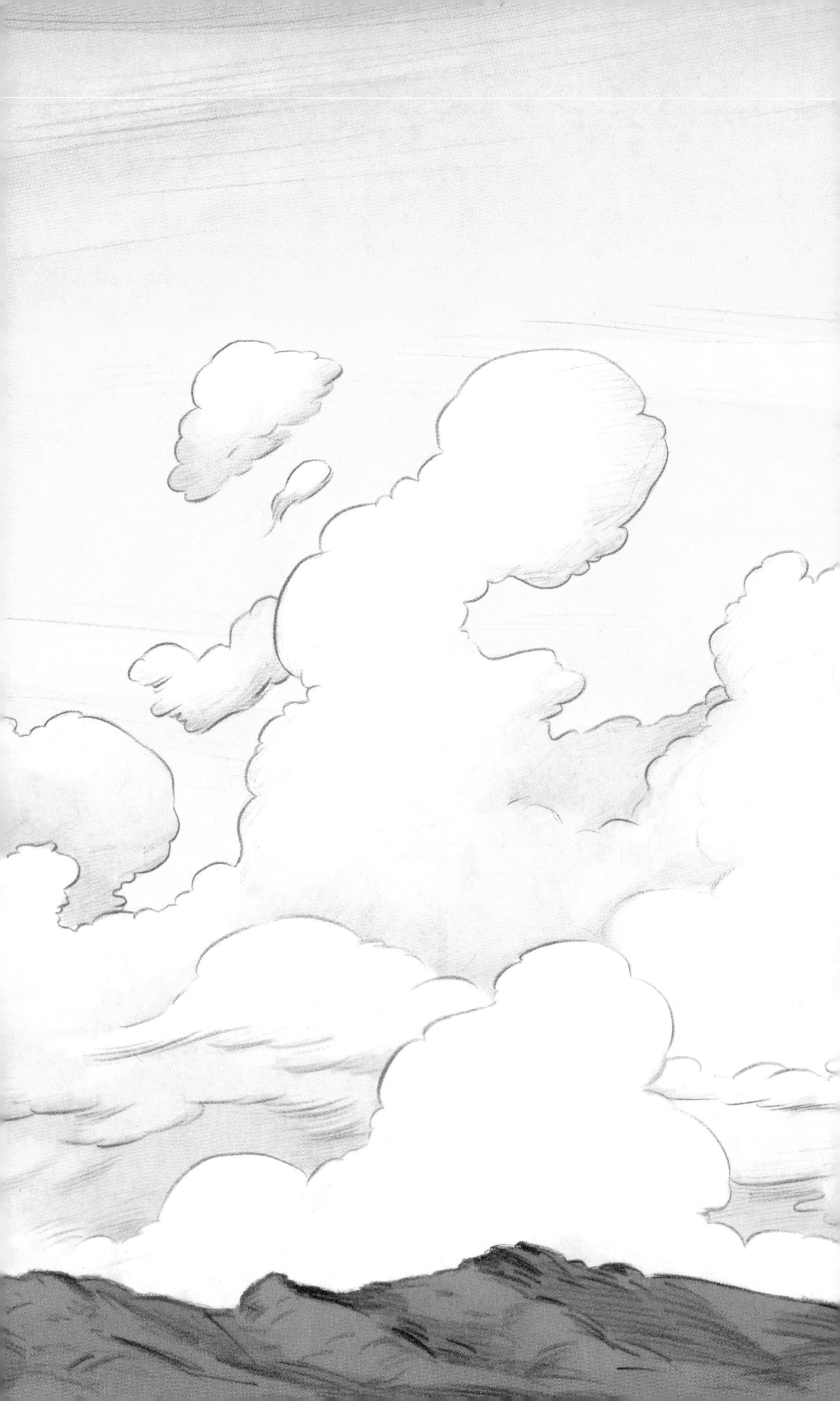

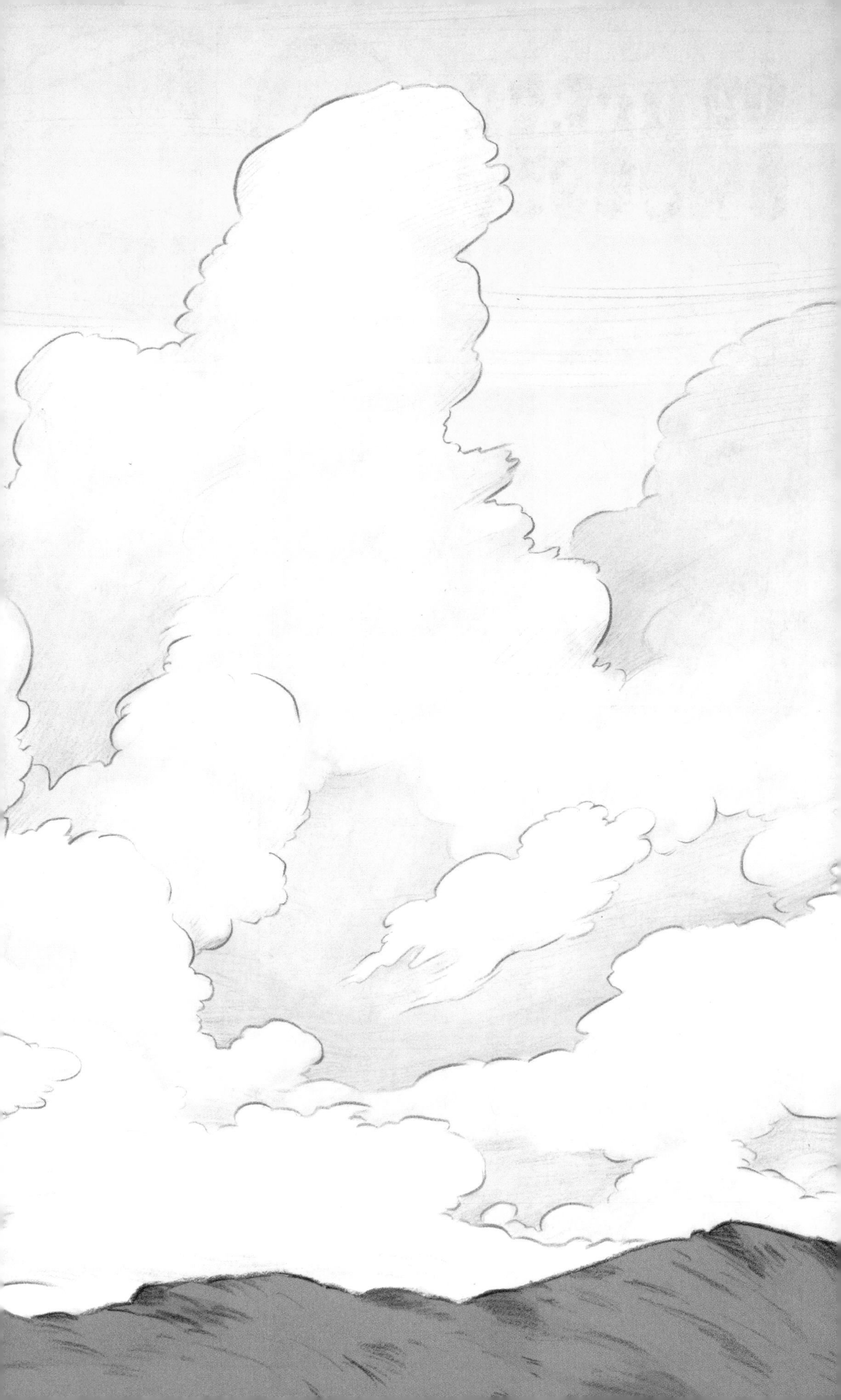

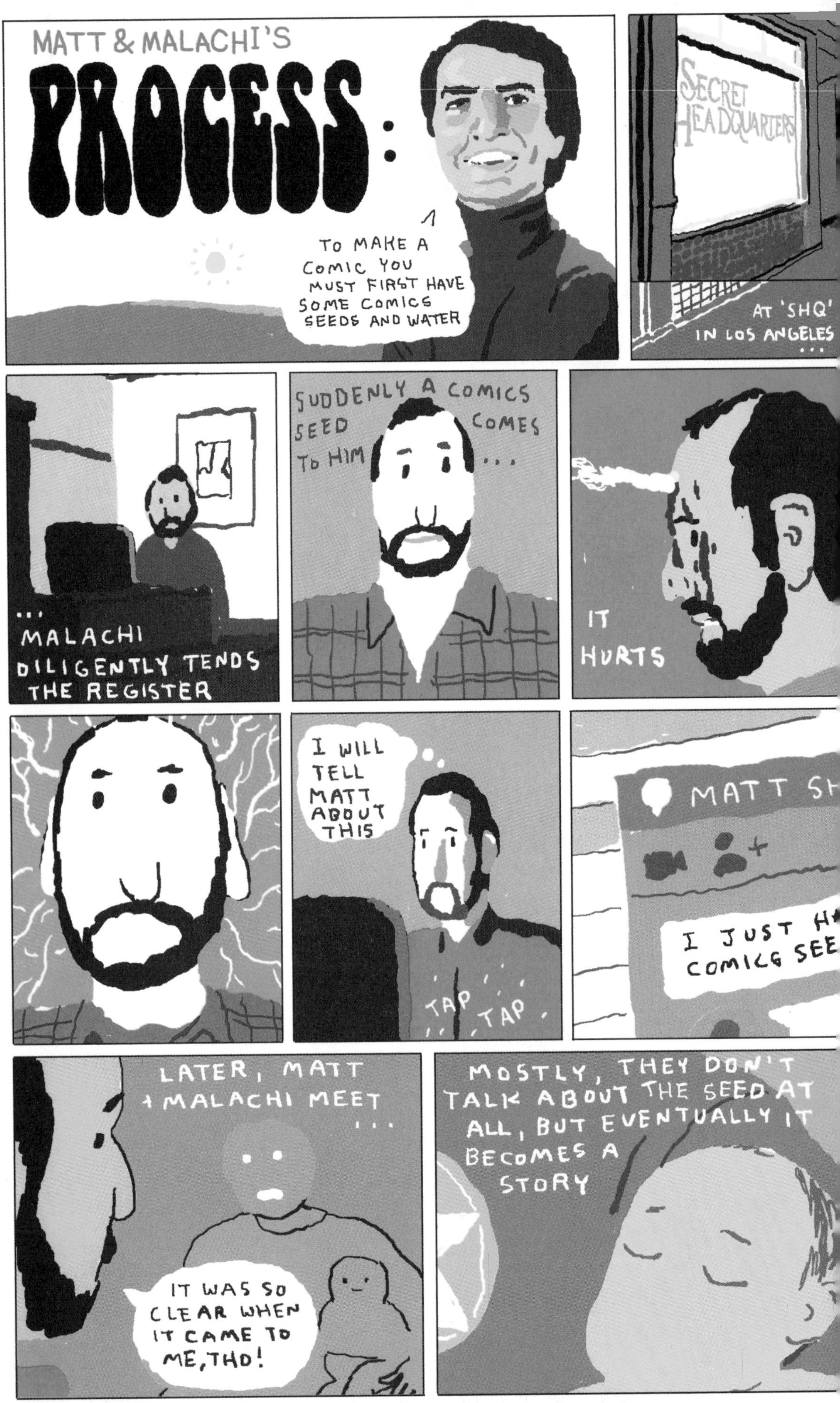
MATT & MALACHI'S
PROCESS:
TO MAKE A COMIC YOU MUST FIRST HAVE SOME COMICS SEEDS AND WATER
SECRET HEADQUARTERS
AT 'SHQ' IN LOS ANGELES . . .
... MALACHI DILIGENTLY TENDS THE REGISTER
SUDDENLY A COMICS SEED COMES TO HIM . . .
IT HURTS
I WILL TELL MATT ABOUT THIS
TAP TAP
MATT SH
I JUST H
COMICS SEE
LATER, MATT + MALACHI MEET . . .
IT WAS SO CLEAR WHEN IT CAME TO ME, THO!
MOSTLY, THEY DON'T TALK ABOUT THE SEED AT ALL, BUT EVENTUALLY IT BECOMES A STORY

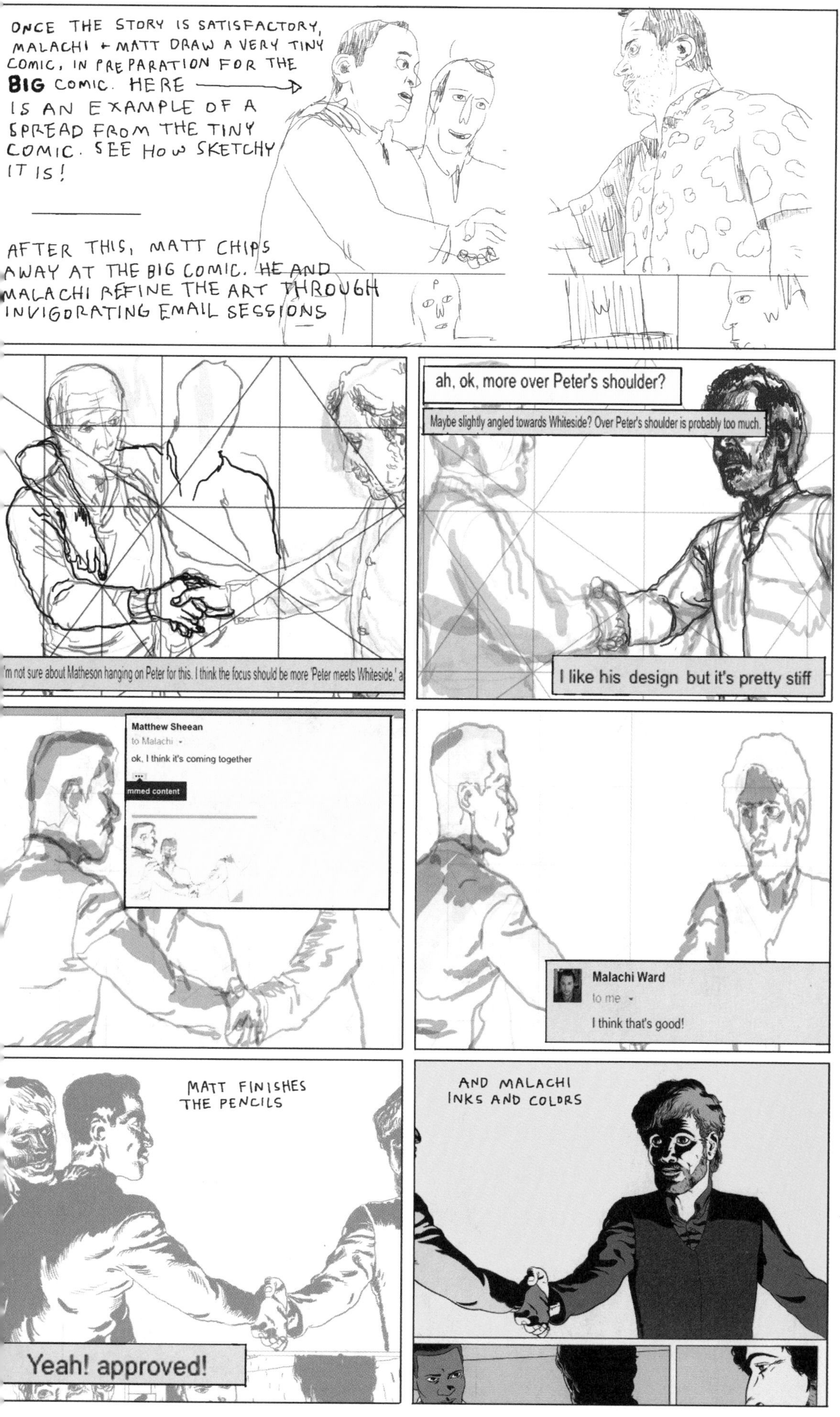
ONCE THE STORY IS SATISFACTORY, MALACHI + MATT DRAW A VERY TINY COMIC, IN PREPARATION FOR THE BIG COMIC. HERE IS AN EXAMPLE OF A SPREAD FROM THE TINY COMIC. SEE HOW SKETCHY IT IS!
AFTER THIS, MATT CHIPS AWAY AT THE BIG COMIC. HE AND MALACHI REFINE THE ART THROUGH INVIGORATING EMAIL SESSIONS
'm not sure about Matheson hanging on Peter for this. I think the focus should be more 'Peter meets Whiteside,' a
ah, ok, more over Peter's shoulder?
Maybe slightly angled towards Whiteside? Over Peter's shoulder is probably too much.
I like his design but it's pretty stiff
Matthew Sheean
to Malachi
ok, I think it's coming together
mmed content
Malachi Ward
to me
I think that's good!
MATT FINISHES THE PENCILS
Yeah! approved!
AND MALACHI INKS AND COLORS

BUT! IN THIS CASE THE GUYS WERE NOT SATISFIED WITH THE WORK, SO THEY SET ABOUT DRAWING IT FROM THE VERY BEGINNING.

UNSATISFIED!!!

MATT WAS FEELING GOOD, THO, SO HE SKIPPED THE TINY COMIC PHASE AND WENT STRAIGHT TO THE PENCILS...

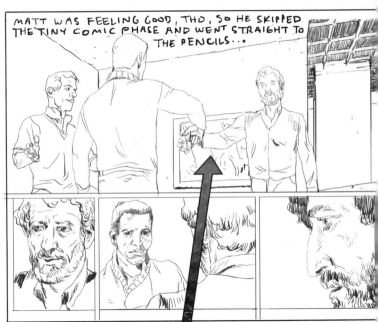

MALACHI SUGGESTED PUTTING A RECOGNIZEABLE ART WORK IN THE FRAME BEHIND WHITESIDE

MATT PROPOSED JOHN MARTIN'S "THE GREAT DAY OF HIS WRATH"

MALACHI INKS IT...

AND THIS TIME, MATT DOES THE COLORS.

AND, FINALLY, MALACHI LETTERS AND GETS THE PAGE READY FOR PRINT!

FIN